Crimson Tassels

By

Bryan Nowak

Table of Contents

Life and Death at the Anderson Farm
May 5th, 1984

Donald Anderson stood in the back of his barn scratching his gray whiskery chin which hid deep wrinkles. Every one of those wrinkles were earned honestly through the life of a man dedicated to living and working on his farm. A hard, but rewarding life. His soda-bottle thick glasses, a few years out of date, framed his big, deep brown, expressive eyes perfectly. Eyes which spent more than their fair share of time lately, framed by a wrinkled brow born of the worry of an uncertain future.

Today his eyes focused on the perennial task at hand, honing a well-worn ax blade to as close to a razor's edge as it could get. With every pass of the metal against the honing stone, experience taught him, microscopic shavings of metal peeled away from the ax head, bringing it closer to the perfect edge.

"Let me know when you're ready, Matthew," Donald said, continuing his labors.

The task of sharpening the blade was boring, in comparison to other tasks at the Anderson farm, but it carried its own therapeutic charms.

"Thanks, Dad, I will. Hopefully she turns over this time."

While Donny Anderson had a talent for farming, Matthew Anderson, his oldest son, had a knack for keeping things running. Since he could turn a wrench, the boy could make just about any mechanical device run as well as possible.

"If anyone can fix that old truck, I'm sure you can." Donald looked out at one of the fields through a small hole in the side of the barn. He thought back to better times, when farming seemed to be the way to go. Even with the advent of new technologies, the annual profits after paying for salaries for seasonal help, insurance, fertilizer, and equipment became less and less. Soon they were forced to take out a mortgage on the property to give themselves some breathing room until the crop prices recovered. After a while, the mortgage payments became unmanageable.

Donald wondered, not for the first time, if putting in the corn this season had even been worth it. But he had farmed this land his whole life, and would farm it till his death ... or maybe until the bank, claimed everything he'd ever loved.

"Ok, Dad, can you try and turn it over?"

"Sure, Son." Donald moved over to the rusty old Chevy. "Now?"

"Yep, give it a shot."

The Chevy turned over a few times, chugging along like a smoker who'd had one too many cigarettes. Matthew motioned for him to stop, waving his hand in frustration. Wiping the sweat from his brow, he shook his head at the uncooperative engine. Then, with a wide-eyed moment of recognition, he picked up a ratchet from the small table next to the truck and leaned into the engine compartment to make a few more adjustments.

Donald went back to his workbench. It was a good ax and he remembered his own father, who worked this land before him,

2

sharpening the same blade every spring. The blade, almost as sharp as it could be, took on a shiny edge. He picked up a piece of sand paper to make a few more passes to get it exactly right. It was a labor of love.

It was the bank's fault. They sent over a man to talk with Donald and his wife, Marylyn, about the farm. She'd made them all coffee and they sat together in the living room. The fancy man from the bank wore a two-piece suit, looking too large for him. He couldn't be much older than Matthew. Donald wondered whether you could really call someone a man if they didn't look like they could even shave yet.

The numbers were all there, and Donald knew it all made sense. He knew, in his heart, there was no way to save the farm that had been in his family for the last hundred and fifty years. The last line of the paperwork became obscured by a large red stamp across the final figures which simply read, 'DEFAULT' in large red letters.

The discussion wasn't lost on his wife either. They'd been married for thirty years and she knew the finances better than anyone. She understood what this man, with a comically large suit and fancy job title, was telling them. Their home wasn't going to be their home much longer. It was only a matter of the final pennies being drained from the accounts and eviction paperwork to be delivered by a sheriff's deputy.

He ran the blade of the ax over the stone. Donald's father used to say the key to a good sharp blade was to make sure the stone stayed wet. If it got dry, you were never going to get a perfect edge. His father was wise; that advice never failed.

Among other life lessons, his father taught him how to fix the old tractor, which still sat in the corner of the barn. It ran like a champ after all these years. Dad always said, "Take care of it, and it will last forever." Donald even had the boys slap on a new coat of John Deere green two seasons ago and it still shone brilliantly. He wondered how many years that thing would last. It would certainly outlast him.

"How about now, Dad?"

"Ok, son, let's give her a shot." He walked back to the truck and turned the keys in the ignition. It turned over a little more evenly this time and sounded like it would catch, but sputtered out again.

"Okay, I think one more adjustment and it will be good to go," Matthew said.

Matthew was the oldest. His wife had a couple of miscarriages until they hit the jackpot with this boy. He was tall, strong, and smart. Always a good head on his shoulders, and a good heart in his chest. Donald wanted nothing more than to hand the farm down to his sons. It was their heritage.

For the last two years, Matthew had been dating Lauren, a local girl. She was a pretty thing. As fond as they were of each other, it would never work over the long haul. Matthew was recently accepted into the pre-engineering program at the university and she was planning to go to college on the west coast.

Donald's preference would have been that Matthew just stay at the farm, working it along side him, but kept these thoughts to himself. The idea of losing his children to the world beyond brought a tear to his eye. A world filled with cities, mortgages, and young non-shaving man-children who wanted nothing more than to destroy the dreams of honest men.

But then again, he'd managed to find a way to keep them all together.

The ax tip took on a brilliant sheen as the fluorescent lights of the barn glinted off the honed steel blade. The flash of light looked vaguely blue in the buzz from the overhead lights in the barn. The evening, now slipping into night, requiring more light than the few fluorescent lights delivered. They'd need to stop work for the day.

"Okay, Dad, this time for sure," Matthew said, wiping grease from his hands.

"Matthew, I want to tell you something," Donald said, looking away from his son. "No matter what happens, I want you to know how proud I am of you. You're a good boy. No matter what happens, this isn't your fault. It's just the way it is." Donald looked approvingly at the ax blade and put it down, leaning the handle up against the side of the truck.

"Dad," Matthew choked back a tear, "look, I know you're worried about the farm. But things are bad for everyone. Tad Johnson said that they were also going to lose their farm. It's just the way things are right now. Something will come through."

Donald wiped away a tear forming in the corner of his eye. "Son, I believe you're right. No matter what."

"Sure Dad, as long as we are together it will be alright. Now let's give this old truck a try."

Donald leaned into the cab's open window and turned the ignition. True to Matthew's words, the truck roared to life. Donald was sure it had never sounded so good. The engine hummed and purred like a kitten. It was a lovely sound.

Matthew was still looking into the engine and making some final adjustments. He was so focused on the carburetor, he failed to see the swing of the ax above him as his father brought it down into his son's skull. Blood hit the fan blade and spun it everywhere. Matthews' arm slid into the working mechanism of the truck's engine, rending flesh and bone from his hands and then arms as the mechanism sucked him into the running engine compartment. Little pieces of singed flesh and spurts of blood painted the walls and floor of the barn.

Donald walked back to the workbench, coated in a fine mist of blood. He took a shop cloth cut from unserviceable clothes and wiped the blood from his hands and the ax. His father was right, there was really no substitute for a good ax.

Before leaving the barn, Donald reached into the cab and shut off the engine. Although it had sputtered when Matthew had gotten caught in the workings, it resumed its perfect-pitch hum. *Boy, that kid has a way with engines.*

Closing the door to the barn, he looked up at the lights burning in the house in the distance. An old home, it was hand built by his grandfather to replace a structure on the same place. It needed a few minor cosmetic repairs, but the house was still solid. Donald wiped away the blood from the ax, admiring its beautiful sheen in the light of the full moon. The blade practically glowed.

The back door of the house led to a small mud room. He remembered having to make Matthew and Robbie take off their clothes in this room one summer day when they both decided to play in the killed when the tractor threw a belt while he was repairing it. Maybe getting out of the business wasn't such a bad thing.

Towel drying himself, he walked back into their bedroom. His wife's blood had soaked through the mattress and bedding. The pages of the book, still in her hand, soaked up the sticky liquid and the paper now turned deep red in color.

Picking up the ax, he took it into the bathroom and used a wet towel to clean it off. Then, drying it carefully, he made his way downstairs. The ax really belonged in the garage, but time grew short and he would have to be content with leaving it in the basement until someone returned it to where it belonged.

Reentering the bedroom, he reached under his side of the bed. It was there that he kept the only loaded firearm in the house. For years, he always had a loaded twelve-gauge at the ready in case they needed it in the middle of the night. Thinking back, he realized he'd only needed it twice, both times for wild dogs.

Laying down in the bed, he reached over and turned his wife's head toward him. Blood had soaked through the bed sheets and wicked up the pillow to surround her head like a halo. He wiped a smudge of blood away from her cheek. Her blank eyes stared back at him, he gently closed her eyelids. She was beautiful, an angel who had chosen to stop at his house to rest one evening and stayed with him for the rest of her life.

"I love you so much," Donald said.

He placed the end of the shotgun against the fleshy part of his chin and looked at his wife one last time. With a sigh he uttered, "And now, we'll all be together. Blessed be the tie that binds. What God has put together, let no one tear asunder."

Outside the house, the springtime song of insects hummed along with the slight breeze in the air. Somewhere in the distance frogs croaked out a melody to prospective mates. The tranquil night scene was interrupted with a sudden thunderous boom, which shook the house, and then there was only silence.

A New Home for a New Beginning
Monday, June 27th, 2017

A small hatchback made its way along a flat, straight, corn-lined highway. It was a beautiful summer day. June had been kind to central Illinois. Stopping at a gas station, the newly conferred, Dr. Jack Milburn talked to an old farmer and found himself engulfed in a local discussion about corn.

"Knee-high by the Fourth of July is the rule here in corn country," the old farmer advised Jack. "Going to be well past that this year." The whole region held a good corn growing weather pattern of occasional soaking rain, buffered by three or four days of sunshine.

The old farmers gave him a crash course on life in the Midwest, weather he wanted it or not. He'd excused himself, as he got the impression they'd gladly continue talking about corn well into the afternoon. His wife, waiting in the car, wanted nothing more than to get to their new house.

After paying for a full tank of gas, two colas, and a bag of pretzels, he climbed back into their hatchback.

Elizabeth Milburn, glared at her husband as he walked out of the store. Twenty-two years old, blond hair and blue eyes, she sat as the picture of a Norwegian princess. Another foot and a half taller and she would make a most convincing Valkyrie, the legendary female warriors of the Norse gods.

"Well, that certainly took a long time," she said.

"I think they were trying to initiate me into the life of a

Midwesterner. I now know how important it is to get your crops in early, the importance of having the corn grow up to a certain level by the Fourth of July, and the all-important issue of dunking versus rubbing the butter on an ear of corn."

"Oh really," she said, opening the cola he handed her. "And the verdict?"

"Put out a big ole pound of butter on the table and rub the corn over it. Then salt, eat and repeat. Apparently, overeating corn on the cob is a thing here."

"Oh geez, I think I already miss crab-cakes," she shook her head. "Will it take us long to get to the house?"

"No, it shouldn't. We're only going another twenty or thirty miles. Not too long at all, are you excited?"

With a shrug, she said, "Let me think about this. Am I excited? I'm going to a house which has been boarded up since the 80s, to start a new life with my new husband, a million miles from any of our nearest relatives. Am I excited ... about cleaning the house for the next five years just to get all the dust out?"

"Okay, okay, fair enough. How about this then, are you happy? I think that's the better question."

"Yes, Dr. Milburn, I'm happy. I'm deliriously, unequivocally happy. And tonight, I'm going to make you happy too."

"Careful there Mrs. Milburn, you don't want me getting us into an accident. Think of how disappointed the realtor would be."

They drove on for another fifteen miles, negotiating the exit off the highway to their new town. The realtor said the home sat vacant since the middle of the Reagan Presidency, but the house was structurally sound. They wanted nothing more than to find a fixer-upper Elizabeth could tear into, making it their own. Once a farmhouse of a four-hundred-acre farm, the farmer, so the story went, had gone bankrupt during the corn crisis.

Jack was introduced to his future wife by his sister at school. Although he was nineteen and she was only seventeen at the time, they hit it off right away. When she turned eighteen they could officially start their courtship and they became inseparable. When she turned twenty-two, they were married. The two were madly in love with each other. Moreover, they respected each other.

As they drove through the town, he could see all the basics he would need to make a life here. There was a small grocery store, a gas station, and most importantly, a hardware store. Jack pulled the car into a space in front of the hardware store.

"Don't you want to see the house first?" Elizabeth asked.

"Well, there are some things we are going to always need. Drop cloths, brooms, bleach, and lots and lots of dust rags!"

"Bleach! Oh stop, you made me weak in the knees at bleach. I'll come in with you." Elizabeth Milburn could never resist the temptation to clean something, a habit she picked up from her mother.

The pair walked into the store arm-in-arm. Although the store was small, it had most of what they'd need. An older man stood behind the register and greeted them with a smile. "Afternoon kids, can I help you find something?"

"Thank you, yes. We need to pick up a few things before we head to our new house."

"New house, you say? No new houses around here in the last forty years."

"Ah, new to us I should say. We're moving into town."

"Oh, that's fine, very nice. Glad to have some fresh faces. My name is Adelbert Gulliver, yes like 'Gulliver's Travels' and no, I've never read it. Most people just call me Mr. Guilliver on account of the weird first name, and I taught the science class at the high school for more than a few years." He smiled at his own unfortunate name. Then, sweeping his hand across the store, said, "This here's Gullivers Hardware. Mrs. Gulliver is around here somewhere. She makes a mean apple pie."

"My apple pie is not mean, you old coot." An elderly, bespectacled woman came up behind them. "How are you doing? I'm Sandra, don't let this old goat scare you away. I'll keep him in line. And who might you two be?"

Jack instantly liked them. There was something about them that clicked. They were warm, friendly, real people. "I'm Jack, and this vision of beauty is my wife, Elizabeth."

"It's an honor to meet you both," Sandra said. Extending her hand, Jack could feel her tight grip. This was a woman who worked hard and had the calluses to show it. It was like meeting the inverse of the people he knew at the university. His friends and fellow academics had soft hands and wore polo shirts on casual Friday. These people wore overalls and worked hard for a living.

"So, Jack, where you moving here from?" Mr. Gulliver asked.

"From northern Virginia." Jack found that Midwesterners tended to react with less scorn if you told them you were from Northern Virginia than if you told them you were from Washington D.C. "I took a job at the University."

"That's about all we got up here, the university and farming," Mr. Gulliver said. "How about you, little lady, are you working or you gonna stay at home and raise a litter of young'uns?"

"Well, as I live and breathe, don't be so rude," Sandra said. "Don't pay that old fool any mind. He spent one too many days sniffing turpentine. Why don't you come with me while the men-folk talk about whatever it is men-folk jabber on about."

Jack and Elizabeth exchanged smirks as Sandra escorted her to another part of the store. Mr. Gulliver walked with Jack as he picked up a few tarpaulins, a push broom, two garbage cans, and a box of rags. He also picked up some oil soap, on Mr. Gulliver's recommendation.

"I can't recall any houses for sale around here. Where did you say you were moving into?"

"It's the old, abandoned one just northeast of town. Been boarded up, in caretaker status, since the eighties. We bought the whole kit and caboodle for real cheap, but it's going to need a ton of work. I have the feeling you'll be seeing a lot more of us."

"Northeast of town," Mr. Gulliver said, scratching his whiskery chin. "Don't recall any place out that way."

"It's an old farmhouse. I think someone called it the 'Anderson place'." Jack was looking at a box of bungee straps. The bag said it had multiple sizes and widths, but they all looked the same to him. Turning back toward Mr. Gulliver, the man looked white as a sheet.

"Do you mean ... Donald Anderson's farmhouse?" Mr. Gulliver Stammered.

Jack suddenly felt bad about bringing it up. "Yeah, I suppose so. Why? Are you feeling okay? You don't look so good."

"I'm alright," he said, waving a hand. "At least, I think I am. Just tired maybe. The Anderson home ... I never thought I would ever see anyone live in that place again."

Jack felt like he was in the middle of a crime drama where the perpetrator was about to be revealed or maybe a gunshot might ring out in the back of the store. Suddenly, what had been a warm store, felt cold and foreboding.

Mr. Gulliver silently rang up his sale and took Jack's money. "Let's sit down for a moment, while the ladies get acquainted. He gestured to two plastic lawn chairs sitting near the register. "What did they tell you about the Anderson farm?"

"Not much, really. They said the family died in some sort of accident, and the house sat empty since then. The house is still full of their stuff. We have a dumpster coming the day after tomorrow. I imagine I'll throw a lot of it out."

"I see."

"Did you know the Andersons?" Jack asked.

"I did," Mr. Gulliver said. He stared off into a dark corner of the store. The old man's eyes suddenly looked worn out. He reminded Jack of his grandfather when he talked about the soldiers with whom he fought in the Korean War. There was definitely pain behind whatever memory he was replaying in his head. "Donald Anderson was a good friend. Great family. Shame about them. Did they tell you how they died?"

"No, I didn't think it was important to ask."

"Maybe you should have," he said. Mr. Gulliver knitted his eyebrows together. He regarded Jack the same way someone looks at a child who had just asked an inappropriate question. "Lots of things you really should know before buying a place like Donald's farm."

"Like what?" Jack sensed the old man wanted to tell him something, but was unsure how. Mr. Gulliver just sat there, rubbing the armrests of the chair and rocking back and forth slightly.

"Donald Anderson murdered his family, Jack. He murdered them in that house."

"What?" Jack's eyes opened wide as he processed the idea. "I'm sorry Mr. Gulliver, but I find that really hard to swallow. You'll forgive me if I ask for a little more information."

Mr. Gulliver let out an elongated sigh and braced himself on the arms of the plastic chair. "His oldest boy was found in the barn alongside the house. The other boy was found in the living room, and the wife in their bedroom. She still had a novel from the library clutched in her hand. Donald was next to her, his brains splattered all over the bedroom wall."

Jack saw the old man's hands shaking slightly. Upon noticing Jack looking at him, Mr. Gulliver held one with the other and took a deep breath to steady himself. He continued, "That old barn burned down about three years ago. I am pretty sure it was nothing more than some old faulty wiring. But, other people, more superstitious people, say they saw Donald's ghost out by the barn, dancing around it as it burned."

"Why wouldn't anyone tell us this?" Jack's mind raced. They might have been the victims of an elaborate deception. People generally wouldn't buy a house where something like that happened. Not that it would have necessarily stopped them from purchasing the home, but it would have been a factor in negotiating the price. Jack wasn't a religious man and didn't believe in ghosts, so that didn't bother him. But he knew Elizabeth would find it creepy.

"After the murders, the farmland got carved up to the highest bidders and sold off to pay remaining debts. Ironically, back then, it was worth more at auction than as a single piece of viable farmland. The house, as well as the remaining ten acres, which were no good for farming stayed with the family. They kept it up, but no one's lived there in years. They used the barn to store things. I think a cousin was the last person to live in the house. The family trust maintains the property and it's sat on the market for many years. They tried to just bulldoze the thing once, but family feuds ensured no one could ever come to a consensus."

"What were they afraid of?" Jack asked.

"Donald." Mr. Gulliver said, in a matter-of-fact way. "They figured his spirit still roamed the house, blaming everyone for the death of his family except for the one person who was responsible."

"Which was?"

Mr. Gulliver took a deep breath. "Himself. To be fair, he had to have lost his mind. That has to be the only reason a man would do somethin' like that. The day before it happened, I talked to him and he seemed as rational as you or I. And then, it happened." He looked lost in thought for a moment, obviously reliving an old conversation.

Just then, Sandra and Elizabeth made their way around a display of glue. They were laughing about something unclear to Mr. Gulliver and Jack.

"Do me a favor," Jack said to Mr. Gulliver in hushed tones. "Don't tell Elizabeth. She's weird about that kind of stuff."

Mr. Gulliver gave Jack an uncomfortable look. "Alright, but promise me you'll be careful in that place. Somethin' off about it, that's all."

Elizabeth carried a shopping basket full of extra items. Jack took it from Elizabeth and said, "Wow, honey, it looks like you found a whole other store hidden in here somewhere." She laughed at the feeble attempt at humor.

He wondered if keeping the new found information about the house was the best idea. For the moment, she seemed really happy and this news might bring her down a bit. She and Sandra obviously hit it off. Maybe keeping the murder/suicide a secret for now was really best for all of them.

"Looks like Elizabeth is going to sing in our choir!" Sandra laughed.

Jack let out a little groan, realizing this likely meant Elizabeth insisted on making good on his promise to attend church with her. She didn't share his agnostic sentiments. Jack often wondered if it were really necessary to demonstrate how good a person you were by prostrating yourself weekly to an omnipotent God. He figured an omnipotent being should already know if you believed in him or not.

As he got older, Jack found himself thinking more and more about God. If they had a child, how would they raise it? Would he agree with her insistence to raise it in a church community? Finding out their new home was the site of a triple homicide and suicide was perhaps just one more reason to attend church. They could use all the help they could get.

"Oh yeah?" Mr. Gulliver said. "You gonna join us for services this Sunday?"

"I guess so." Jack suddenly felt impatient to get to the house. He looked at his watch and saw it was nearly one o'clock, when they were supposed to meet the realtor and get the keys. He stood up and looked over at Elizabeth. "C'mon sweetie, we need to go meet Rita."

Sandra handed them a piece of paper with their phone number on it. "You two kids have fun, and good luck. If you need anything, please call us anytime."

Elizabeth took the piece of paper and gave Sandra a hug. Jack thought to himself, *these are nice people. This is why we moved out here.*

Jack loaded the paper bags and other items into the back of the car. It seemed like too peaceful of a town to have something like that happen. By his nature, he was skeptical of stories like the one he heard Mr. Gulliver tell. Rumors and urban legends have a way of morphing from bad to worse. He opened the driver's side door and stared out at the skyline over the roofs of the buildings across the street. In the distance, he saw a dark line of clouds. *May not be much of a skyline, but at least you can always tell when the storms are coming.* Turning out onto the main street, the GPS, which he affectionately called Sarah, told them they still had eight minutes until they reached the house.

The two-lane road, leading out of the center of town, rose slightly. It passed over an old covered bridge which carried a sign that read, 'Refurbished by the Covered Bridge Society, 1994'. On either side, a meandering stream, identified as Swallow's Creek, stretched out to the horizon. With the bridge, the corn, and the darkening skyline in the distance, he thought it looked like a greeting card.

Jack became lost in his own thoughts. He was happy. Obviously a little taken aback by the news that his new home had such a grisly past. Even with the new information, he felt a sudden urge to steel himself against it and provide a nice home for his wife. He'd been fortunate in life and now had to grab his life by the horns and bring it under his control. It was now or never. He had it all: a great new job, a drop-dead gorgeous wife, and a fixer-upper that needed some TLC but was otherwise structurally sound. He looked forward to the challenge.

Behind him, somewhere in the distance, lightning struck the ground. It was going to be a wicked storm. He briefly mused about taking his new wife out back of their new house and making love to her in the rain.

Nice to Meet You Rita

Pulling out of the parking space in front of their new local hardware store, Elizabeth's phone buzzed. The caller id indicated it was Tanya, an old roommate from college. After catching up, Tanya asked her how married life was treating her. She smiled at Jack and said, "He still has that new husband smell."

Elizabeth Merryweather was born to an urban family. They lived in an apartment on the upscale side of Philidelphia. The Merryweather's were wealthy by most people's standards and she spent most of her teenage years partying and doing everything she could to make her nanny's life miserable. One night her parents dropped a bombshell on her that would change her entire life.

Boarding school.

She was to pack her bags and head for boarding school for the rest of her high school life. It was, as they said, for her own good. She needed to be somewhere she could stay out of trouble and learn how to be a responsible adult. She hated her parents for it, but she did as she was told.

There, she befriended a shy girl named Angelina. Angelina introduced Elizabeth to her older brother, Jack. Jack was a college student who had a penchant for seeing life through the eyes of a pure academic. She felt bad for him since when he visited his sister he always kept his nose buried in a book or working on homework. Elizabeth finally convinced him to go outside and see the beautiful campus and they became close friends.

Jack, tutored Elizabeth on the more difficult subjects and she kept him from being, what she called, too bookish. It didn't take long for Elizabeth to feel herself falling deeply in love with the handsome college student.

As he drove the car down the road, Elizabeth leaned over a little and said, "I love you so much, you know that?"

"Well, I sure hope so," Jack said. "You married me, after all."

"Tonight, I have something special in mind for you."

"Really? Do tell." He let out an exaggerated gulp.

She reached her hand into his inner thigh and caressed the crotch of his jeans. "I'd rather show you."

His breath became shallow as her fingers found their mark. "Seriously honey, you are going to make me run this car off the road and kill us both. Or I'm going to have to pull into some poor guy's yard and fuck you on the hood. It's hot out here and the metal would likely burn your ass."

Elizabeth threw her head back on the seat's headrest and laughed. "Are you happy?" she asked. "Is this what you really want?"

"Yes honey, it's what I really want."

"Good." She knew they were only about a minute from the house, so she started picking up her magazines and empty soda bottles from the floor of the car. It would need a good cleaning before the day was through. The first night of their marriage had been spent in an upscale hotel, but the drive took a total of three days. They were both exhausted from the open road.

Sarah said in her monotone voice, "Three hundred feet, and you have reached your destination."

"Thanks, Sarah," Elizabeth said, shutting the GPS off. Jack maneuvered the car into the river rock driveway of the house looming in front of them.

It was real. She had to admit, it was even more beautiful than the pictures Rita sent them. The house was two stories tall. The lower level had a wraparound porch which started with a large bay window. They were home. At the time they were supposed to go on a house hunting trip, Elizabeth came down with a severe flu and had to stay home. Elizabeth trusted Jacks instincts.

She could tell the window treatments would need to be replaced. The paint looked like it had seen far better days. Scanning the lower level windows, she saw shadows of chairs and a table inside. The sunlight, quickly diminishing in the building clouds, hit the front porch. She could imagine herself sitting in the gently swaying porch swing on the deck, nursing a newborn.

This could be an ideal home.

Scanning the top of the house, a movement caught her eye. In the far left window, she thought she saw someone looking out at her. But as quickly as she saw the apparition, it was gone. She felt a sudden chill run up her spine. It abated just as quickly.

A plump but fit woman with reddish-silver hair walked around the house. She was wearing a burgundy dress shirt, jeans, and a pair of Charles Taylor lace-ups. Elizabeth regarded the woman for a moment, and then smiled. Rita was the perfect realtor for them. A touch of class with a fun streak.

"Hi, Rita!" Elizabeth yelled.

Rita Stimson was a hard-working country realtor in an area no one wanted to move to. It was a difficult living, but she liked doing it. This was her home town, and she loved it.

"Jack and Elizabeth, welcome home! I have a bottle of Chardonnay and a case of beer in the fridge for you. I also picked you up a few things from the store for the first night: pasta, bread, and some sauce. I figured you two would be busy enough the first few days, am I right?"

"Thank you so much, Rita," Elizabeth said. "We stopped by the hardware store and picked up a few things too. The dumpster arrives soon and we can start throwing things out."

"Well, don't go hog wild. I've got people that might be willing to buy some of it. Mostly just the big furniture." Jack moved in for a hug, but Rita waved him off and immediately wrapped her arms around Elizabeth. "Ladies first, Jack!"

Elizabeth gave into Jack's wishes to buying a home in the middle of nowhere. It wasn't her first choice, but it would do for now. She made it clear the house would have to be gutted and updated. In her own words, she'd decorate the hell out of her new home. She wasn't planning on taking a job right away, so she would have nothing but time to make it their home. At their wedding reception, the cards overflowed with cash, and she could buy till her heart was content. Based on the photos and the condition of the outside of the house, Gullivers Hardware would be getting a huge influx of money.

"Ah, the Gullivers are great couple. You get to know them, and they'll take good care of you."

"Yes," Elizabeth said. "I think we're sitting next to them in church on Sunday. Is Adelbert really his first name?"

"You know, I'm not sure," Rita said. "He's always just been Mr. Gulliver. Let me show you the house. Jack, do you mind if I take your bride for the grand tour?"

"Oh no, you don't!" Jack said. "Husbands first, Rita!"

Jack lifted Elizabeth effortlessly into the air and carried her toward the door of their new home. Drunk with a delicious joy, she was overcome by the smell of the corn growing in the fields, the dirt of their driveway, and the smell of her husband's sweat. She giggled in ecstasy.

Rita, having clued in on what was happening, ran ahead of them with the speed of a woman half her age. She pushed open the door and moved to the side to let Jack in, doing her best impression of a doorman.

Elizabeth looked into his eyes. Jack was handsome when they first met, but as they got a little older Jack became distinguished looking. The boyish immaturity he had when they first met seemed to give way to a sophisticated countenance.

Jack set her down and gave her one of those deep kisses only people truly in love can give. It was passionate, it was hot, and it made Elizabeth's heartbeat in a way that nothing else could.

"Mmmm ... hmmm," Rita said, clearing her throat.

"Oh, Rita, sorry. Forgot you were there," Elizabeth said. "Jack honey, why don't you start bringing our stuff in, and I'll try to figure out what we have to do to make this place livable for tonight."

Elizabeth watched Jack walk out the door, back toward the open trunk of their car. Over his head, she could see the darkening sky. The clouds, no longer distant, threatened to make the task of unloading the car more difficult if they waited too long.

"Don't worry, this time of year, we get lots of those storms," Rita said, seeing her concern. "They roll through every few days. Once it passes, everything will be fine. But that does remind me; I need to show you where your cellar is."

Elizabeth gave Rita a quizzical look. "Cellar? What's that for?"

Rita chortled, "Let's put it this way: if you hear a long siren that doesn't seem to be stopping, you grab Jack and your baby and get into that cellar as quick as you can."

"Rita, I don't have any children."

"I know, just seeing if I could trip you up. You know, maybe a bun in the oven?"

"Oh gosh no!" Elizabeth turned beet red at the insinuation. They hadn't been trying to get pregnant, choosing to learn how to be a couple first before adding a child to the equation.

"Okay, okay, a girl has to ask, doesn't she?"

"I suppose so," Elizabeth smiled. "Well, let's see what we have to work with." Jack had seen the house in person, but she'd only seen pictures up till now. The photos really didn't do it much justice. Although dated, the house still had a regal presence. In front of her, a dark wooden staircase stretched upward like a luxurious mahogany tongue, the rails must have been handmade. A simple runner ascended to the second story which had definitely seen better days. She pulled

30

out a notebook and made a notation about replacing the carpet.

To her right was the formal living room. Although major structural repairs had all been addressed, the furniture hadn't been replaced. Most of the furniture was in the Victorian style. Depression era glass decorated a few of the shelves. Although it had a certain charm, it was definitely not her thing. But, it would suffice until the new furniture showed up.

As she suspected, the window treatments would all have to go. Finding a place to buy new ones, however, would require a little work.

Seemingly reading her mind, Rita offered, "Joliet ... if you want to shop for window treatments, you have to drive into Joliet. Maybe next week you and I can run out there. I need some things anyway. About a forty-five-minute drive."

The living room led immediately into a formal dining room. A huge walnut dinner table took up most of the space. It looked like the deck of an old ship. An extravagant piece and stood in sharp contrast to the rest of the furniture in the house. In the corner of the room sat a large china hutch with an abandoned card table sitting behind it, seemingly forgotten.

Elizabeth looked over at Rita. "Maybe we should hang onto this dinner table, what do you think?"

"Well, I have a buyer who is willing to pay top dollar for it. Plus, you won't even have to ship it; he'll come get it himself."

"How much?" Elizabeth hadn't given much thought about the fact that she could sell any of these items that only a few hours ago she didn't even know existed.

"Two thousand for the table and chairs. Minus my twenty percent commission, of course."

"Rita darling, you're a born saleswoman," Elizabeth said. "That's a good amount of money. I guess we'll take it."

As they made their way toward the kitchen, Elizabeth felt an uncontrollable urge to look at the folding table. She resisted the temptation, choosing to run her finger through the dust along the top of the thing. Suddenly she was gripped with a feeling of sadness and loss, feeling cold inside.

An image gripped her. An arm lay across the table's nylon top. Blood covered it and the hand lay outstretched, trying to grasp at something unseen.

"Elizabeth!" Rita grabbed her by the arm. "Sorry, you were off in space somewhere for a moment."

"Oh yeah." Her face turned red, and felt hot with embarrassment. "It's all the excitement. I'm better now. Shall we continue?"

Off the dining room a door led to the kitchen and another which led to a mud room. The kitchen was huge. The appliances, though newer than the rest of the house, had few redeeming qualities. Elizabeth decided all of them would hit the dumpster as soon as suitable replacements could be ordered.

The counter tops were Formica, which was popular with re-modelers in the 80s. Elizabeth made another notation in her notebook to order new counter tops, or more precisely, order them as soon as she could convince Jack to let her order them.

Jack came from a poor family. In college he sought scholarships and student loans. Although he was a hard worker, he always seemed to work twice as hard for everything. Once to earn the money, and the second time to earn the grades.

Elizabeth's family dined with governors and presidents. Her grandfather was a self-made millionaire at a time when people weren't likely to become millionaires. He insisted every one of his kids go into the military or the Peace Corps. Out of all of the values preached in their family, service was one of the most important. They didn't tolerate slackers.

The night her parents met his for the first time was especially tense. However, Jack's father presented Elizabeth's parents with a bottle of wine. He was deeply worried about offending Elizabeth's parents. It was a wine from Virginia's Hannah-Dog Vineyards, the owner of which Jack's father was good friends with. At the moment of presentation, Elizabeth's father took the wine, read the label, and immediately laughed out loud at the, as of yet, unspoken irony. Elizabeth's father had been an early investor in the vineyard and knew the family very well. It was a coincidence, but one which immediately cemented a friendship.

The mud room was a simple affair: clay tile floor and dingy walls covered in a hideous wallpaper which had once been vibrant oranges and yellows. It looked like a scene out of a 70's commercial. Rita hadn't been joking when she said the previous owner had left everything. Lined up like soldiers on a small runner set against the wall sat a collection of shoes. At the end nearest the door, two boots had been hastily left on the small throw rug. One boot laid lazily on its side, while the other sat upright.

Elizabeth couldn't help but feel a momentary sense of loss for the people that lived here. She wondered what happened to them. What became of their hopes and dreams? Based on the furniture, she had to guess the couple who lived there were older. Were they still alive? Do they miss their old house? Was it just too big for them?

Were they murdered?

Elizabeth immediately dismissed the idea. What made her think that? It seemed like an oddly random thought to go through her head.

Rita and Elizabeth made their way upstairs. On the walls, there were drawings and photos of places neither of them could recognize.

"Rita?" Elizabeth felt a twinge of apprehension asking this question. "What happened to the people who lived here?"

Rita stopped for a moment at the top of the stairs. Elizabeth thought she saw a moment of panic flash across the normally optimistic face of her realtor, but it was gone just as quickly as the person she swore she saw in the window. "I'm not really sure. I'll see if I can find out."

Elizabeth had no reason to believe Rita would lie to her, but she got the sense that Rita *did* know something, and was hesitant to tell her.

"And here is your main bathroom, there is a half-butt bathroom on the bottom floor."

"Half butt?"

"Yeah, just a toilet. You literally have to back into it."

The upstairs bathroom made up for the small stature of the one on the first floor. It had a big, beautiful, claw-foot bathtub that could easily fit three people and have room to spare. For a moment, Elizabeth saw herself and Jack making passionate love in it, immediately shaking off the idea as she saw herself having to sop up all the water afterward.

It had two large wash basins with brass appliances. It was by far the fanciest room in the house. "Why is this room so much more ... I don't know how to put it."

"Less like a funeral home?" Rita offered.

"Oh, Rita! How grim, but accurate. So why?"

Rita thought about it for a moment. "I believe there was a brother in the family that wanted to refurbish the house in the 90's to sell it, but he only got as far as this room. I think his name was Paul. He went a little crazy. Things finally got so bad, they had to have him committed. It's too bad, he was a good carpenter before he lost his marbles. This room is astounding. By the way, I do have someone who would love to buy that tub."

"Over my naked, wet, and drunk-on-Chardonnay ass you'll sell my tub." To illustrate her point, she climbed into the tub and sat down, crossing her arms over herself. Both women laughed.

"I kind of figured. But to be fair, I would rather see Jack's naked, wet ass. He's a keeper! Where did you find that gorgeous hunk? I'll trade Hal for him any day."

Elizabeth smiled at Rita. She'd quickly grown on her. "Oh stop. Besides, you trade in your husband and then you have to train a new one. Who'd want to do that?"

"That's true, Hal is like an old dog or a worn-out sweater. Comfortable and reliable. I can leave him on the couch in the morning and be damn sure he'll be there in the afternoon. But, I've had thirty-three years to break him in. You kids are just getting started. Shall we move on to the bedrooms?"

Elizabeth rose from the tub to a cloud of dust. She'd decided she would clean the bathroom, kitchen, and bedroom today. After that, she could work on the rest of the house at her leisure.

Jack suddenly appeared at the top of the stairs. "What are you girls talking about?"

"You know, girl things," Elizabeth said, putting her hand on Jack's chest. "Comparing husbands, what kind of new curtains to buy, how much work I'm going to need to do before I can break your spirit and you become like an old dog or a worn-out sweater."

He shook his head. "I really need to rebuild that barn out back. It'll give me a place to hide."

"See," Rita said. "He's already looking for a place to retreat to. Jack's coming along nicely. A couple nights of great sex and he'll be almost housebroken."

Jack panted and put up his hands like a dog begging for a treat. He kissed Elizabeth on the cheek. "Where do you want the cleaning stuff, babe?"

"Probably the kitchen for now. Let us finish the tour and I'll come help."

"You got it," Jack said. He turned away, but stopped for a second. "Hey Rita, did you happen to bring us any coffee?"

She gave him the thumbs up sign. "Yep, cabinet next to the fridge. I got you a loaner coffee pot from my house. You're gonna want to rinse the dust off first. There's a bottle of dish soap on the counter too."

"Seriously. Rita, I have no idea what we would do without you," Jack said. He ran downstairs to the kitchen.

"He's good, Elizabeth. You're lucky. I see lots of people come out here with the wrong attitude. The wind, corn, and quiet drive em' crazy in short order. You two will do fine."

The bedroom was a sprawling affair. It had a door into the bathroom on one side and a walk-in closet on the other. The sleigh-style bed looked like something out of a 1920's deluxe suite from an upscale hotel. It was massive. A new king-size mattress, delivered that morning before they arrived, lay on the bed encased in plastic.

Elizabeth was momentarily speechless. It was at once so enormously beautiful, also completely out of style with their tastes. "And, how much were they going to give us for the bed frame?"

"Fifteen hundred."

"Minus twenty percent commission, right?"

"You catch on quick." Rita clapped her hands together. "You know, once you get settled here, I could use some help with my small liquidation business. I'll split the commissions with you."

"That's tempting, I might just take you up on that offer."

"There are two other bedrooms, but they are typical boy bedrooms. If I were you, I'd leave those for last, but you might want to hurry so you can have a baby's room ready." Rita said, her voice trailing off.

Elizabeth shook her head. "Oh for Pete's sake, Rita. I'm not pregnant. Give it a rest."

"Okay, okay. Tell you what, I know Jack has to report to work tomorrow. I'll come by in the morning and run you around town. By the way, are you going to buy another car?"

Elizabeth looked over her shoulder into the hallway, checking to see if Jack was still downstairs. She could hear him whistling as he moved things around in the kitchen. "Day after next, Jack gets a big surprise. I bought him a truck. Four-wheel drive, the whole shebang. He doesn't know it's coming."

"Wow, Hal would kill me if I did that. He'd still drive it, but would kill me."

"Well, it's a belated wedding present. Besides, I'm not going to be stuck here without a car."

Rita smiled at Elizabeth. "Good thinking girl. Okay, shall we go downstairs?"

"Actually, Rita, I think I'm going to stay up here for a few minutes. I want to look around a bit."

"Well, sweetie," Rita said, giving her a big hug, "it's your house. Make it your home. I'll see you tomorrow. I have to go feed Hal. Remember to feed and water your husband regularly."

Rita left the room, and Elizabeth could hear her new friend descend the stairs. With a few words to Jack, the front door opened and closed. Watching her out the window, the tail lights of Rita's car blazed red against the darkening world outside.

Just then, a few drops of rain hit the window of the bedroom. It was the same window she was sure she'd seen the figure in earlier. The raindrops made the world blur like a life-size watercolor painting.

As Rita's car turned left onto the highway in front of the house and disappeared toward town, the sky opened up into a torrential rainstorm. The driveway became a minefield of mud puddles.

Elizabeth could've sworn she heard something behind her. Turning, she expected to see Jack standing there, but instead saw nothing. A cold draft suddenly overtook her. Shivering against the sudden chill, she wrote in her notebook, *Find sources of drafts.*

The Itsy Bitsy Spider

Jack tried to remember a time when he was happier, but he couldn't. On top of it all, he managed to get everything inside the house before the rain started. In the distance, he could see the lightning strike something on the ground over the horizon. He wondered how often things were struck around here and how good the lightning rod on top of the house was.

The house looked different than when he was there before. But, to be fair, it was early spring at the time. The farm fields surrounding the house had been freshly plowed, and planting was in progress. It rained a little, but the farmers said it was dry enough to get the corn in the ground. Watching the tractors pulling the planters behind them was surprisingly therapeutic.

He left their bags sitting at the bottom of the stairs while he brought in the things from the hardware store. After consulting with Elizabeth, he put the cleaning supplies in the kitchen. Then he found the coffee that Rita had brought and started making some. It was going to be a long day. He knew Elizabeth would have him cleaning soon enough. Maybe he would get extra husband points if he started cleaning the kitchen right away.

He was never one for hay fever, but the dust was really starting to bother him. With every step he took, thirty years of dust accumulation followed him like Pigpen from the *Peanuts* cartoon.

Leaving the front door open, he propped opened the back door to try to get a nice cross breeze going, perhaps use the warm summer wind to suck the dust out of the house. To him, it seemed like the house hadn't been cleaned in years. As he started wiping down the counters, he thought about what Mr. Gulliver said.

While it was a grim story the old man had told, he wondered how much of it was just a fairy tale locals made up to justify the inability to sell an old farmhouse with no acreage attached to it. Maybe someone did actually die in the house. Who knows, maybe they were even murdered. But a triple murder-suicide seemed far-fetched. He'd have to go to the library and see if he could find any news clippings about the Anderson farm.

After wiping the counter, the cloth was already in desperate need of a good rinsing. But he was pleased that, underneath the years of dust, the counter tops looked largely intact. The dirt of the kitchen mocked him, and Jack wondered how much cleaning would be required before Elizabeth would declare the house suitable for habitation.

Just then, he heard Rita coming down the stairs. "Hey Rita, did you lose my wife upstairs?"

"Oh no, she wanted a moment to herself." She pointed to the cup in his hand. "Found the coffee, I see. It's already looking more like a home instead of an empty old house." She stopped at the edge of the living room as she made her way toward the door. You kids know how to reach me." She looked down at the counter tops and then met Jack's eyes. "Cleaning? You really are a good guy. You need to spend some time with Hal."

"I'll see what I can do with him. Thanks for everything, Rita. I really appreciate it."

"You're welcome. I'm going to check on your wife tomorrow, while you're at work, and show her around our booming metropolis."

"Sounds good, I know she'll appreciate it."

"Good luck tomorrow," Rita said. He watched her walk out the door and toward her car. It was just starting to rain outside, and her closing the car door seemed to be the weather's signal to open up and drench the world outside. He stood by and watched as her tail lights disappeared down the road.

A sudden weight descended upon him. The reality sunk in that they were alone out here. He stood there, leaning against the door frame, looking out at the puddles of water on the driveway. It all seemed a little surreal; new house, new job, new marriage. It was a lot of change to take on all at once.

His parents were overjoyed when he and Elizabeth told them they were engaged to be married. In spite of everyone's reassurances, starting their new lives was overwhelming. He didn't want to disappoint anyone, least of all Elizabeth.

Wiping away the last bit of grime from the counter, he moved to sweeping the floor of the cobwebs and the dead flies that had accumulated below the rear window. As he swept, he noticed a door which had remained so concealed, he almost missed it completely. He was pretty sure he didn't go down there when he did the inspection.

The gust of air behind the door reeked of the acrid smell of dust and disuse. The ambient light of the kitchen just barely illuminated the outline of a switch on the wall and the landing atop a set of stairs descending into the blackness below. His mind raced through all the discussions he'd had about the house, and he thought he remembered someone mentioning a cellar of some sort. Perhaps a root cellar or a tornado shelter. He reached for the switch to illuminate the depths when an intense feeling of dread stayed his hand.

Come on, Jack, pull yourself together. You're not a child.

Shaking his head against an adolescent fear of the dark, Jack felt an old-style switch plate. On it were two push-button switches. His thumb grazed something under the switch, which had an unexpected texture making him pull his hand back momentarily. Marshalling his resolve, he boldly reached forward.

A flash of light sprang up at him from the bottom of the stairs. The light back-lit a huge object, only inches from his nose. As his eyes struggled to bring the object into focus, it moved, sending chills up his spine. He jumped back from the unidentified thing and stumbled into the kitchen, scrambling away with a yelp.

Something grabbed hold of his arms. In his moment of startled terror, he tried to bat it away.

"What on earth are you doing?" a very confused Elizabeth asked.

"Ummm ... well, I ..." Jack stammered.

"What's the matter, tough guy? Did the dark scare little Jackie?"

"No, something in the stairwell."

Elizabeth stepped over her husband and looked into the lit space. "Oh, this must be the cellar Rita told me about. She said she'd show it to us, but she forgot. Well, sweetie, it looks like we have a spider in the cellar. That's your department. It was in our vows, remember?"

Jack got to his feet. "Oh, right. After that part about back rubs and mani-pedis. I remember now." He looked over her shoulder back into the space he had so lubberly exited. In front of them, trying desperately to get to safety, was a common house spider. "Indeed, Domus Araneus."

"Sure, he can domus somewhere else. Kill that thing. You know how much I hate them." Elizabeth shivered and scratched her arms reflexively, mentally brushing away phantom spiders crawling all over her.

Jack went to the counter and grabbed a paper towel. Moving back into the stairwell, he squished the spider between his fingers. It made a satisfying pop, indicating the spider's reign of terror was over. He used the rest of the paper towel to remove the spider web from the entry way.

"There you are, M'lady, free of all spiders."

She patted him on the behind. "My hero! Wonder what the heck is down there?"

"Not sure. But I do know it's ours. Let's take a look."

Jack could tell the lights were an afterthought by the way the electrical wiring had been strung. It was a little scary, but it looked basically intact. "Hey, if you want to buy me an expensive present, you can have the house rewired."

As the two descended the stairs into the cellar she said, "I can't tell if you're kidding or not."

"Totally not kidding. The wiring is a little terrifying. I don't mind fixing plumbing, but electricity is out of my lane."

The cellar wasn't finished, and the floor was composed mainly of rock and dirt. The cellar was accessible by a door to the outside of the house as well. In one corner were three empty plastic garbage cans and a shelf with tarps and old paint cans. Pointing to the garbage cans and tarps, he said, "Well, these should come in handy."

Jack turned from the plastic garbage cans to see his wife, staring at something on the table. Her hands hung at her sides, her mouth was slightly open, and her eyes glassed over. She seemed to be having a conversation in her head, all to herself.

Elizabeth was prone to short fits where she sat encapsulated in her own thoughts. This, however, was different. His wife wasn't simply talking to herself, she was engaged in a deeper conversation with something or someone unseen. It scared him.

Jack touched Elizabeth's elbow, seemingly bringing her out of her internal dialog. Looking over at him, she smiled, indicating the old Elizabeth had returned. "Sorry, I was spacing out there for a minute. Look at all of this. Amazing that the family would just leave this all hanging here."

Facing them, a collection of tools hung from the pegboard. The old work bench was curiously devoid of tools with the exception of the old ax that looked like it had once been a formidable tool. Now, covered with rust, it had seen far better days. A small tag on it had the word 'Evidence' across the top of, but most of the tag was torn off at some point. Jack pulled off the tag and threw it into the trash can sitting at the end of the work bench.

Elizabeth ran her finger over the time worn handle, leaving a trail of dust in the wake of her finger. She pulled back suddenly and violently, almost smacking Jack in the face. Holding her finger, a tiny bead of blood formed where a sliver embedded itself into her flesh. "Ouch, dammit."

Jack quickly grabbed her hand. "Are you okay?"

"Yeah," she put her finger in her mouth and licked the blood away. "Just a little sliver. This thing is pretty creepy."

"But useful. It'll take some steel wool and maybe some oil, but I bet that old ax will still hold a nice sharp edge. Looks like it's been sitting here for a long time."

Elizabeth turned and put her hands around her husband's waist. "Let's get out of the cellar, okay?"

The chill from her hands seeped through his clothing as if she'd held two ice cubes on him. Which was strange considering the temperature and humidity in the cellar were almost at tropical levels. "Hey, sweetie, are you okay?"

"I'm alright. This cellar gives me the creeps. I just want to get upstairs and back to cleaning."

"Alright, tell you what? You only have to come down here when spiders need killing," he said with a wry smirk. They started up the stairs.

She glared at him. "Not funny, Jack."

Stepping back in the kitchen, she practically shut the door on him as he cleared the threshold of the stairwell. They looked at each other for a moment. Dusty from the day so far, and they had a long way to go. Something in the cellar had scared his wife, so he'd have to keep her out of there. He felt her hands again. Although they were still cold, they were warming up.

"Are you sure you are okay? Something down there seemed to put the fear of God into you and nothing ever scares my wife."

Jack reflexively pulled Elizabeth in close and for a brief moment he thought he felt her pull away. She stared up at him, looking like a scared child who was just asked an embarrassing question. "No, it's just a ton of stuff to take in all at once."

She was so beautiful. Even with her hair covered in spider webs, she could probably walk into a beauty pageant and win first place. He leaned in close, opening his mouth in delicious anticipation, his body suddenly stiffening with lustful desire.

"Not so fast there, Mr. Milburn. You need to keep it under control or we're not going to have anywhere to sleep … or do other things … tonight. By the way," she said, licking his bottom lip. "Cleaning the kitchen is so incredibly sexy."

She quickly backed up from him, retracting her hands. "You finish the kitchen; I'm working on that bedroom upstairs. I only came down to take a short break, the dust was threatening to overtake me. Whoever's done first can start on the bathroom."

Jack felt a little hurt by his machismo being shut down, but she'd noticed the kitchen, and that was a small victory.

I sure do love that woman. I wonder if I'll ever stop worrying about her. He watched her walk up the stairs and disappear into the bedroom.

Jack Milburn, philosophy professor, spider killer, sex machine, and devoted husband, turned back to the task of wiping down the inside of the kitchen cabinets. It would be good to get them cleaned before he put the rest of the food away that Rita had wisely left inside the bags. Judging by the dust and spider webs, they hadn't been cleaned in quite some time.

For the next few hours, they worked in their separate rooms. Jack thought about his wife's reaction to the cellar. It was like she was terrified of what might be down there, or maybe something in the house. But, her excuse made sense. It was easy to see how too many new experiences could overwhelm them.

One of the things he loved was her insistence that he know everything about her and her family before they got married. When she first brought the idea up, he figured she was going to tell him something awful, like they were a mafia family or something. The truth was more benign: they were just good people who worked hard and whose ship had come in. She brought quite a bit of money into the marriage, enough that they could live comfortably off her trust fund for the rest of their lives, but neither one of them wanted that kind of lifestyle. He wanted to teach and have a professional life. She wanted to be a housewife, to enjoy the normal things in life, if only for a while. And that suited them just fine.

Behind him, the sound of feet bounding down the stairs interrupted Jack's scrubbing of the remaining spot of dirt in the kitchen, stubbornly refusing to give in. Elizabeth called from halfway up the stairs. "You should see the bedroom." Jack playfully raced through the living room and grabbed Elizabeth's hand as she pulled him up the stairs.

She threw open the door and motioned inside as if she was

presenting the grand ballroom at the Waldorf-Astoria and Jack got a whiff of oil soap and the vague factory smell from their new mattress.

Her efforts certainly paid off. In place of the dust ridden, broken down bedroom he remembered from the tour, it looked like a completely different room. She'd removed the cobwebs, pulled down the beat up shades, and evicted the dust bunnies. Elizabeth even enlisted an old bed sheet to cover the window, which did a better job of shading the room than the old shades. The old wooden wardrobe, dresser, and mirrored desk looked almost youthful with their new coat of polish. A pile of old clothes which had been dug out from inside the dresser drawers now lay in the hallway.

"Wow, you certainly got farther in here than I got downstairs."

"Well, sweetie, I'm a woman."

He feigned incredulity. "Hey, what's that supposed to mean?"

"Well, you know, husbands try. Wives do."

Jack laughed. "Besides, the kitchen is far dirtier. That stove is ancient, and it looked like the last thing they cooked in it was a space alien."

"Will it work for tonight?" she asked.

"Oh yeah, nothing is going to stop this husband. I got it all cleaned up. I'm just glad we grabbed the oven cleaner from Gullivers."

She pulled him close by the shoulders of his shirt. "Look at you. Already talking like a local. I'm impressed. It's sorta hot." She leaned in close to him. "So hot, you know what I want to do right now?"

"Throw a wild sex party?"

"No, better. I want to go through the closet."

"Wow, you sure do know how to turn a guy on."

She laughed. "Seriously, though, back to work, Dr. Milburn. We have tons more to do before we can call it a night."

"Yes Ma`am," he said. To Elizabeth, the house was her project, and she'd tolerate no slacking on anyone's part. He loved that about her.

Broken Pieces

Jack Milburn fell in love with a wild girl. Elizabeth made some pretty poor choices in her younger days. One of those poor choices, name Craig, physically abused and raped her. In retrospect, she admitted, she should have seen how negative an influence he was in her life. Boarding school was, in a very real sense, a wakeup call that she needed to do something different with her life. Jack was the 'different' she needed.

Jack showed her ways of thinking she'd never thought possible. To her, he was like a habit she knew would be hard to break. Most importantly, she never wanted to. From the moment she realized she loved him, and he reciprocated, their lives became solely for one another. She fell in love with his mind and he was one of the most brilliant men she'd ever met.

Elizabeth's thoughts wandered to the ax in the basement. There was something about it that was hard to comprehend. What set of circumstances led it to be left on the bench all by itself? Every other tool in the basement had a hook or a place. It would be easy to imagine the other tools purposely staying away from it. Like the ax had done something wrong, and been excommunicated by the other tools.

The ax head, now dull with rust and age, could be imagined easily in the prime of its life. The handle had some spots where a small animal chewed on the wood. She could almost imagine the person who took such great care of the blade, taking equally good care of the handle.

In her daydream-like state, she saw someone sharpening the blade.

The image in her head morphed and the person sharpening the blade became her. She could hear the sound of the metal running over the top of the honing stone. Each pass bringing the head closer to being as sharp as the steel would allow.

Take care of it and it will take care of you, that bastard said.

The thought ran through her head like a train pulling through a station without stopping. There one moment and then gone the next. The quickness of the thought scared her, words entering her head not from a person, but the house or maybe the ax itself. Stepping back from the closet, she grabbed the wall for support. That was it, the ax beckoned her to join it downstairs.

Remembering her trip into the basement, the ax frightened her. Turning her back on it wasn't enough to quell the unease. No, Elizabeth felt it behind her, glaring into her soul. She didn't tell Jack how she felt. It had to be nothing more than a mixture of exhaustion, excitement, cleaning solvent fumes, and the heavy cloud of dust hanging in the air. At least she hoped it was.

Now, standing alone in the bedroom, holding the wall, she felt the urge to be close to Jack. She wanted his touch, to feel him inside of her. She wanted to lay next to him, naked and warm, combating the cold isolation the ax silently offered her. And yet, the ax had its own allure.

Pushing through her feelings, Elizabeth focused on the work at hand. A lot needed to be done before they could take a break. Pushing herself away from the closet, she felt a little better as a breeze of fresh air displaced the dust in the air.

There you go Elizabeth, that's all you need girl; just some fresh air.

Not to be deterred, she refocused on the closet, which was still filled with the previous owner's things. Rita advised her to go through everything with a fine-tooth comb. They bought the entire house and its contents, so anything she found was legally theirs. So far her search only resulted in some junk jewelry, and a collection of silver dollars.

Elizabeth quickly understood Mrs. Anderson's passion from the items they'd left behind. She'd obviously loved to make clothes, particularly dresses and knew what she was doing. Pulling each dress off the hanger, she searched the pockets. In a few of them, she found some cash stashed away. She remembered her mother storing away small piles of cash the same way.

Elizabeth's eye was caught by a flash of red behind a stained old house-coat. Moving the time-worn garment out of the way, color spilled out from the closet. Off the rod, to which it clung, she pulled a luxurious velvet dress. It had a bow on the top and straps which crisscrossed in the back. It too was handmade, but of a far superior quality. The rest of the dresses were plain and had been worn repeatedly. They hung solemnly from wire hangers. This dress had a special padded hanger and was wrapped in plastic from a dry-cleaner. Not an ordinary article of clothing, it was made for special occasions and was highly treasured.

Elizabeth carried it out and laid it reverently on the bed. It looked like it was just the right size for her. She even liked the length. She ordinarily wore her dresses a little shorter, but this would be perfect for an official college function and would guarantee dirty looks from some of the faculty members and side-ward glances of jealousy from others.

Slipping it out of the plastic, Elizabeth hung it from a hook on the back of the bedroom door. Stepping out of her tee-shirt and jeans. She slipped the dress over her head and quickly glanced up toward the mirror.

Elizabeth only had a moment to process the image and the movement. The woman in the mirror not only didn't look like her, but was covered in blood from head to toe. In her hands she held an ax, slung over her shoulder at the ready. The semblance stared back at her, face frozen in an evil scowl for a brief moment and then took a long stride toward her. Elizabeth fell backwards, trying to escape the visage, tripping over the hemmed edge of the carpet under the bed, sending her crashing to the floor.

For a brief moment, Elizabeth sat frozen in fear. Her heart beating like it was trying to escape from her chest. Eyes slammed shut, she dared not open them for fear something, or someone would be waiting for her.

Oh, sweet Jesus, this is utter nonsense.

Elizabeth opened one eye to see her own face staring back at her in the worn mirror. Convinced it was truly nothing more than the dust and hard work getting to her, she pulled herself up from the floor. Examining the dress in the mirror. Chastising herself for her reaction to what was certainly nothing more than an image born out of exhaustion and looking at the mirror out of the corner of her eye, she laughed at herself.

No harm was done to the dress and she smoothed out the fabric. It was of the finest quality, like butter under her fingers. Adjusting the bodice so her breasts settled into the appropriate places, she looked again at her image in the mirror. It was stunning, certainly rivaling dresses in stores selling for hundreds of dollars, and yet, here was one hanging in the closet of a home that had been abandoned for the last thirty years.

Keep it. It's my gift to you. In fact, I made it just for you, Elizabeth.

The seemingly intrusive thought, pushing its way into her mind should have given her more pause than it did. Elizabeth knew it was right. She looked like a supermodel in it and no dress looking this good could possibly be wrong. She just couldn't wait until she had a chance to show it off.

She took off her new favorite dress and put back on her t-shirt and jeans. Continuing her cleaning, occasionally she threw things into a small box which she'd designated as the 'keep' pile. She found a collection of old bobby pins, a measuring tape, and a few small paintings of a little boy by a wishing well.

Standing at the door to the bedroom, surveying her work, it painted a far more hospitable picture than when she first walked in. The bed was made, most of the dust bunnies were evicted, and the floor was vacuumed. The window treatments would still have to go, but she'd found something to block the light for now. Judging by the number of cars she'd seen drive by the house, she really didn't think it would matter. They could walk around their front yard in the nude and likely never attract attention.

She walked over to the window and looked out at the expanse of cornfield on the other side of the road. The green leaves shimmered like waves in an obnoxiously green sea.

Again, a sudden chill hit her. It reminded her of the sudden rush of air which hits you when you walk from the hot outdoors into an air-conditioned house. The feeling made her turn around to see if the window or a door had suddenly been thrown open, but it wasn't.

Leaving the bedroom, she saw the legs of her husband on the floor, poking into the hallway from the bathroom. At first glance, the carpeting looked like blood had soaked into it from the bathroom floor. Jack might have been the victim of some grisly murder.

"Jack, are you alright?" Elizabeth shook her head against the gruesome image.

"I'm wiping the dust out from under the bathtub. I don't think anyone has ever cleaned under here. But I think I was able to get most of it."

"You're done with the kitchen?"

Jack stretched as he stood up, his hair covered in spider webs. "Done for tonight. We can finish it up over the rest of the week. No big hurry."

"As long as I can cook in there. Besides, I'm exhausted. What do you say we take five and sit on the porch for a little while?"

"Sounds good to me."

She grabbed his hand, and they walked down the stairs and out onto the porch. The strongest portion of the earlier storm had been brief, leaving them with a steady rain the weatherman predicted.

They sat down carefully on the porch swing, unsure if it would hold their weight. The metal chains creaked slightly in protest but held. From this angle, they had a commanding view of the driveway which led to the road, its black surface contrasting with the green of the corn fields.

"You know, that old bedroom of ours is pretty drafty," she said. "Particularly near that window."

"Drafty, huh? We'll have to look into resealing the windows. Should be an easy fix. A little caulk here and there. Maybe repaint the window sills while I'm on the ladder."

Elizabeth stared out at the cornfields. "You know, it's actually pretty warm out here. The draft I felt in the bedroom, almost like an air conditioner kicking on."

"Definitely not the AC, that old thing hasn't worked in years, I suspect. We'd need a new one, which makes the draft you felt in the bedroom even stranger. I opened the doors to get the house aired out, and it felt like the air didn't budge an inch."

"It was a cold draft, too."

He put his hand on her leg. "Are you feeling alright?"

"Yeah, fine. I'm just tired. We did a lot today, you know."

"Well, you can keep on it tomorrow, I have to go to the office. I'm guessing it's maybe a thirty-minute drive from here. Should be great fun during the winter."

Elizabeth couldn't help herself, "Do you think we need to look at putting winter tires on the car?" She smiled inwardly, picturing his face when the new truck showed up.

"Probably. Maybe I can find a used pick-up, something with four-wheel drive."

She almost burst into laughter, but managed to keep herself in check. "Do you really have to go to work tomorrow? Kids aren't even in school now."

"Afraid so. I have to work on my curriculum and put the finishing touches on the textbook. It's going to take a few weeks to get the edits done. The publisher has set a firm date."

"You can't do that at home?"

"Not until I have my log-in and password for the university website. It does bring up a good point. Which room do you want to use for an office?"

Elizabeth raised her finger as she remembered something important. "Rita thinks we need to clean one out to use as a nursery. She tried to get me to slip up and tell her we were having a baby. She seemed disappointed when I told her we weren't in the market, as of yet. I suppose the two extra bedrooms can be converted into an office and, one day, a nursery."

A loud crash came from inside the house, startling the pair. Jack stood up, pulling Elizabeth with him. Both ran upstairs to the hallway. In front of one of the bedroom doors, the ones they were just talking about, a vase lay on its side, shattered to pieces.

Elizabeth looked at Jack and then back at the vase. "That's odd, I don't remember a vase even being there. Wonder how that happened?"

Jack shook his head in disbelief. "The wind maybe knocked it down."

"The wind couldn't be *that* strong, and I'm pretty sure there was no vase in front of this door. Where did it come from?"

Jack shrugged. "No idea. At least it wasn't a particularly good looking vase. I'll go get a broom. You start picking up the bigger pieces."

Elizabeth carefully knelt on the floor. Thankfully, the majority of the vase broke into three large pieces, with only a few small splinters left for the broom. As she picked up the largest of the pieces, the bedroom door to her right opened, bouncing lightly against something interrupting its swing. The hinges made a high-pitched creaking sound, like a single violin string having a bow slowly pulled across it. She felt like an intruder in her new home. A little like she just opened the door at a friend's house to find them in the middle of changing their clothes.

The door stopped against the side of the bed which occupied the right side of the room. She could see that the bed was still perfectly made, perhaps by the people who lived here last. To the left was a small desk with an old electric lamp. The window shades were the old nylon kind that had to be pulled down.

This was the first time she'd seen any of the bedrooms, other than their own. It struck her as odd that she hadn't bothered looking in every room until now. It was her home, and she should at least get an idea of what the rooms looked like.

A sudden cold breeze hit her from inside the room, similar to the draft she'd felt earlier. The door slammed shut.

Jack's footfalls overtook her senses as she stared, dumbstruck, at the door. "Honey, are you alright? I thought I heard the door slam."

"You did, and I got a draft again. Stupid drafty house."

"Which door slammed? I was up here a while ago, and they were all closed."

"This one." She pointed to the door in front of her. The feeling she'd glimpsed something only she was meant to see closed tightly around her.

Elizabeth picked up the rest of the large ceramic pieces while he swept up the remaining shards. As soon as they were done, they returned to the porch swing with the Chardonnay in two cups. Neither one of them said anything as they looked up at the gray sky.

The rain had stopped, but the clouds remained firmly entrenched. Jack brought out a small transistor radio he found and put fresh batteries in. They spent a few minutes listening to the local radio station, with the smooth-talking announcer promising a beautiful day tomorrow.

Even though the temperature had hovered around seventy-two degrees, Elizabeth couldn't help but feel cold. She even put on a sweatshirt over the tee-shirt she was wearing. Something unsettling took place in that hallway, and she was at a loss to make any useful sense of it.

Elizabeth looked at her husband, dressed in a pair of comical boxer shorts and a tee-shirt. The chill she was feeling didn't seem to bother him. "I'm worried maybe this country life is a little too agreeable to you. You seem to be letting it all hang out there." They sat on the porch swing, drinking the Chardonnay Rita had brought to celebrate their first night in the house. Elizabeth drained and refilled her cup to calm her suddenly frazzled nerves.

They stared out at the fields, watching the darkness descend with surprising quickness, fusing dark green leaves of the corn plants into deep hues of blue and purple. Unseen grasshoppers had taken up their nightly orchestral. Off in the distance, a pond played host to the deep-throated calls of amphibians.

She felt like the corn was watching her from the darkness, like a legion of quiet soldiers waiting for the night to come to begin their assault. She knew these feelings were crazy. Just her mind responding to a combination of exhaustion and stress.

Soon they would be standing under a warm shower, with Jack insisting he wash her hair. She thought about his firm sex against her back. The thought of their impending carnal meeting was comforting to her. They were both physical lovers, and his touch was reassuring. She felt safe with him. And safety was suddenly something she desperately longed for.

Down on the Farm

Elizabeth made an offhand comment about his present choice of clothing, a tee-shirt and boxer shorts. In reality, they had no one to dress up for and it had been hours since they saw anyone drive by on their little secluded highway.

"I had to get out of those clothes, it felt like I'd been working on a construction site all day."

"Well, that's convenient, you smell like you did." Elizabeth snuggled up close to Jack as they sat in the swing. "I'm sorry I got a little freaked out earlier. This was a lot to take on in one day and I am pretty well exhausted."

Neither one of them spoke for about ten minutes. Jack considered the world around them. There was something therapeutic about watching the corn swaying in the breeze. The orderly rows of plants suggested something good and pure. Life in this part of the world had its own charm and he could see himself becoming enveloped in it.

Elizabeth stood up. "You hungry?"

"Actually, I am. Do you want me to make dinner?"

"No, I got it. You just hang out here in your boxers. You need to air out anyway. Whoof!" She waved her hand at her nose in an exaggerated manner.

The night before, they had slept in a hotel outside South Bend, Indiana. They had a suite reserved with extra feather pillows and a bottle of wine ordered for the room. Something had gone wrong with their reservation, though, and the hotel didn't have a room for them.

They ended up sleeping in a hotel reminiscent of a slasher movie. It was so dirty that neither one of them undressed. They avoided the shower after the water came out cold and brown. But they did get enough sleep, and it gave them the perfect reason to get an early start the next morning.

Behind him, in the house, he heard Elizabeth clattering pots and pans around the kitchen. They would need to make a grocery run tomorrow, but Rita had gotten them enough to suffer the rest of the day in relative comfort.

The broken vase in the hallway was puzzling. There was no logical reason the vase should have been in front of that door. Even more puzzling was how any gust of wind could have knocked it over. Based on the size of the pieces he swept up it was a substantial vase. A hurricane would have been needed to knock it down. There had to be an explanation, but it eluded him for now.

Draining the cup, he let the last few drops of the wine drum the bottom of the plastic cup. He wasn't a big drinker, but he liked a beer on the weekend, or after mowing the lawn. The wine felt good. It had an air of civility against his grimy body. His fingers felt worn down by the chemicals he used to clean the kitchen.

Walking into the living room of the house, he stopped to watch Elizabeth in the kitchen. She was frying some ground beef which was allegedly fresh from a local cow. She was unaware of Jack's surreptitious observations.

Jack smiled at his wife, content to just watch her. She moved around the kitchen in rhythm to the big band tune coming out of the old radio. Dumping the sauce into the pan with the meat, she turned down the burner. She was poetry in motion. There was something so unspeakably sexy about watching her do even the simplest of things.

He watched Elizabeth fish a noodle out of the boiling pot, tasting it to see how close it was to being done. His mind flashed back to their first real date. They decided on an Italian restaurant that had a reputation for being less than terrific. They agreed to try it and compare notes on how bad they thought it really was. It was there they realized neither one of them liked the term 'al-dente', but both hated overcooked pasta worse. As promised, the pasta was bad, and the sauce was acrid tasting. But they cemented their love that day.

She turned her head slightly, comparing the doneness against noodles of the past. As she did, she noticed Jack watching her.

She stood there with her hand on her hip, the sexy way women do without meaning to. With a smirk, she said, "Almost ready."

"Oh my kitten, I can assure you I'm more than ready." He came over to her and wrapped his arms around her while staring into the pots cooking on the stove.

"Ah-ahh, Mr. Milburn, you need to put that prick of yours away. Don't want to overcook dinner. Can you grab a couple of plates, please?"

He gave her a sly grin. "Yes, my queen."

Soon they were sitting back on the porch, eating pasta, garlic bread, and drinking water, having finished the wine. The wind died down, and the humidity was now the star of the show. The temperature seemed to have increased slightly as well.

He looked at Elizabeth as he chewed a piece of garlic bread. "So, Mrs. Milburn …"

"Yes, Mr. Milburn?"

"We have our castle, but it would seem it needs some repairs on the parapets, maybe a new drawbridge, and the tapestries need to be replaced. So the question we have on the floor now is what do we do first?"

"I would add that we need new painting, as well."

"If you mean all the walls, and not Rembrandt or Picasso, I agree. Continue."

Elizabeth shook her head. "First off, let's just agree now that I never … ever … go down into that cellar ever again. As in, don't you dare die down there, because I'll leave your dead or dying body until someone comes along."

He winced at the idea. "Grim, but okay. Only in an absolute emergency, like tornadic activity, will you be required to go into the cellar."

"Extra style points for using 'tornadic' in a sentence," she said with a wry grin. "I think we should start with the walls in the bedroom. I want to peel that hideous wallpaper and maybe look at refinishing the floors. But in the meantime, I want to go into the city and find some window treatments. I'm going to grow tired of putting on a show for our neighbors."

"Sweetie, our neighbors have ears but no eyes."

Elizabeth rolled her eyes at Jack. "Oh funny, we're making corn jokes now?"

"New blinds sound fair enough to me. I know you and Rita are going to paint our bustling city a fair shade of maroon tomorrow. Maybe you can stop by Gullivers and pick up some paint samples."

"Oh yes, and tomorrow, I'm going to stock our gourmet kitchen with all the best the city has to offer." She frowned a little.

Jack looked out at the yard and smiled. "Oh, come on, it isn't that bad. At least we'll always have fresh veggies to eat around here. And think, soon it will be corn-eating season. Fresh corn whenever we want it." He stopped talking for a moment. "Honey, are you really happy out here? I mean, this is really a huge change for us. We didn't grow up out here, and this is different from anything we're used to. If you're ever unhappy and want to leave, just say the word. I'll give up my job and we can move back East."

He regretted saying it the moment it left his mouth. She looked a little hurt for a moment, but then she grabbed his hand. "No, this is not exactly where I'd choose to live. But, Jack, this move is for you. I'm only going to be happy with you by my side, and that's all that matters to me. I can live anywhere on planet Earth as long as I have you here with me. Is this my favorite place? No, of course not. But, can we make it my favorite place? You bet we can. I don't know what the future holds for us, but I do know this is true. I have a house to redecorate, I have a couple of new friends, and who knows, maybe I can even go work for Rita. It sounds like it'd be a good time."

"I know," he began. "You did this move for me. This is my dream, and you are following me on it. I just want you to know that no matter how this little excursion turns out, if we hate it here, love it here, or the

69

corn rises up and takes over the house, just say the word and we'll go wherever you want to. But, thank you for taking this journey with me. It means more than I can ever say."

"Well," she said, "I suppose there is one thing you can do for me. You can caulk those damn leaky windows in our bedroom. As much as I'd do anything to be with my husband, it would do you no good if I freeze to death."

"You got it."

She took his plate and cup and went back inside. A few moments later, he heard the water in the sink running as she washed the dishes.

Teaching was his passion and writing his own textbook was more of a side project. It could provide good money, but he never set out to be an author. He only wanted to write an updated textbook as a teaching platform for his students. That's why the invitation to become an associate professor was so timely: it gave him plenty of time to research while teaching.

Jack's innate curiosity about the history of this house was nagging at him. He wanted nothing more than to drive down to the library and see what information he could find out about the murders which supposedly took place here. A big part of him suspected all, or at least part of the story, was bull.

The story Mr. Gulliver told him was plausible, but it seemed highly unlikely. Even if there had been a murder in this house, the odds that someone would just close the door on the farmhouse as well as all the acreage seemed far-fetched. Even back in the 80's, the property should have been worth a fair amount, and the contents of the house were top quality for the time. At auction they could have made out alright.

So far, Jack hadn't seen anything in the house that looked like it once was a murder scene. If it was, someone had done a fantastic job cleaning it up. Maybe he could find more evidence if he knew the exact details of these crimes. But, then again, he wasn't a detective.

During an earlier break from cleaning, he walked around the side of the house and looked at the barn. According to Mr. Gulliver, that was where one of the boys was murdered. However, all that remained of any crime scene were now charred pieces of wood, overgrown with weeds. A few pieces of the original wood beams had fallen down on a piece of rusted steel. He couldn't tell without closer inspection, but the object could have been an old farm tractor. Maybe, in the morning, he'd put on a pair of work gloves and get a better look at it. The old barn presented an interesting archaeological dig that was too tempting to pass up.

He was better off not saying anything to Elizabeth about the murders until he knew more. She would just let her brain go crazy jumping to conclusions. Her imagination was prone to go into overdrive and jump from one item to the next without real facts to reach any conclusions.

Jack was caught off guard by how hard the bedroom door slammed shut. He didn't see it close as he climbed the stairs with the broom and dustpan. There was no way Elizabeth could have slammed the door that hard from a sitting position. It could've been something as simple as a draft or a sudden gust of wind. Maybe she was right, perhaps the windows needed caulking sooner rather than later.

When he found Elizabeth in the hallway, a moment of panic gripped Jack. She was staring off into space and didn't seem to be aware of his presence. Just like in the basement, something held her attention captive. It reminded him too much of the odd events in the basement.

He reasoned she was thinking about the possibility of having children. While she never said so, she wanted kids. She made the argument about not waiting too long. As she put it, she wanted to be young enough that when the kids went off to college they'd still have some life left in them. It was definitely a fair request. Maybe it would be good to clean those extra bedrooms out as soon as possible.

Tomorrow, after his meetings and getting his office set up at the campus, he would come back and start on the cellar. He wondered if the university had an arachnid specialist who could tell him how to kill the little bastards. Maybe he needed to let a snake loose down there to eat them.

Yeah, letting loose a snake in the house would NOT go over very well. Do they make spider bombs?

Elizabeth walked back onto the porch. Half of the water from the dish washing looked like it had found its way onto her sweatshirt. She took it off to reveal his worn tee-shirt. It too was soaked.

He quipped, "Best wet-tee-shirt contest in town. Well, maybe the only one in town, but still the best. Did you leave any water in the sink, or are you wearing it all?"

She glared at him. "Okay, smart ass, next time you get to do the dishes." She sat down on his lap and wrapped her arms around him. "One thing we don't have to worry about is any lack of hot water. It practically comes out as steam. You may have to turn the temperature on water heater down a bit, or we could all die a horrible boiling death when we take a shower."

"Speaking of shower, maybe this would be a good time to hit the showers and get some sleep." He yawned, his exhaustion waiting until that precise moment to back up his plea for bedtime.

She looked deep into his eyes. "Oh no, no one is going to bed. I need my horny knight in shining armor to wash my hair." Taking his hands, she led him back into the house. She let out a giggle as he grabbed her hips from behind. The two made their way up the stairs.

The Doctor is In

Elizabeth woke up confused and disoriented for a moment. The improvised window shades blowing in the summer breeze made sounds and shapes unfamiliar to her. Various unfamiliar shadows danced along the walls of the bedroom in their own secret rhythm. Temperatures had already hit what most would consider the warm range for such and early hour. The clock on the dresser read 7:45.

In the early morning light, she could swear she heard two voices in the kitchen. One she knew was Jack's deep baritone. Suddenly a laugh erupted which she knew could only have come from Rita.

Sitting up, she stretched and yawned. The summer breeze wafted through the window, blowing against her bare skin. She hunted around for her bathrobe, which she almost wished she didn't have to put on, before heading downstairs.

Moving down the stairs, the smell of coffee and cinnamon rolls was intoxicating. "Good morning, sunshine!" Rita said.

"You're here early," Elizabeth said. On the table was a white box filled with cinnamon rolls. "But you brought breakfast, and you'd be amazed what I'd forgive for baked goods in white boxes."

Rita picked up her spoon and stirred her coffee. "You're a farm girl now, honey; you need to get used to these early mornings. When harvest comes, they'll be making noises out in that field that will wake the dead. But by that time, you'll be getting up just as early as them."

Jack came in from the kitchen, carrying a cup of coffee for Elizabeth.

"While Professor Jack is off at school today, we have a ton of things to do." Rita picked at a roll on her plate. "By the way, Jack makes the best coffee around here."

Jack smiled in response to the compliment.

"Really, Rita, if you have something else you need to do today, it can wait," Elizabeth said. "I don't want you to feel like you have to take care of me."

"Oh, no worries. I have no showings, no sales, nothing. I'm all yours."

"What about Hal?"

"Well, he left me this morning."

Elizabeth choked on a bit of her cinnamon roll. She was awash in disbelief, like someone just told her a favorite grandparent had died.

"What? Are you kidding me? He left you?"

"Yep, he left me this morning. For the golf course."

Elizabeth winced at Rita's attempt at humor. "Oh geez, you're a real comedian. There's a golf course around here?"

"Why sure. What do you think these old farmers do when they have their crops in and nothing else to do but wait for the corn to grow? With auto-irrigation, crop-monitoring software, and automatic fertilizers, they keep an eye on everything from their smart-phones. I remember a time when you actually had to walk the fields almost every day to make sure things were moving along as planned. Now they just drive the truck around and download data. And some of them are using UAVs to do it all so they don't even have to drive a truck around. It's definitely not your grandpa's farming."

Jack stood up from the table and stretched. "Well, ladies, I have a few chores to do, and then I am outta here. You have fun today. Rita, try to bring my wife back in one piece." Jack grabbed a pair of work gloves off the counter and made his way out to the yard.

Elizabeth watched him stop in front of the pile of rubble, taking a few pictures.

"Well, last night must've been interesting," Rita said. She lifted her coffee cup up to her lips while cracking a bit of a smile.

"And what, exactly, is that supposed to mean?"

"Well, you have that fresh, 'I was just ravaged to within inches of being a porn star', look about you this morning."

Elizabeth put her hand up against her mouth and looked furtively around. She hoped Jack was well out of earshot. "Oh my God, Rita!"

"What? Hey look, Hal's great and all, but we're getting up there in years, and I have to live vicariously through my younger girlfriends. I'm not saying Hal doesn't have his ... talents—"

"Oh wow, Rita ... stop! I don't kiss and tell." A slight smirk played across her lips. "But, if I did, I'd have to say we set some sort of record. I wonder if I can return the box spring. I think we may have broken it."

They both laughed for a few minutes, and soon the conversation descended into the mundane aspects of home ownership. Rita gave Elizabeth the lay of the land. There was only one grocery store nearby, and it was pretty limited. For everything else, it was a twenty-minute drive to the next town over. It had the big grocery store which had everything she would need and more. Rita also advised that ordering things on-line was usually a pretty good option.

Opening the door to Rita's car, Elizabeth looked back at her husband. Jack was picking through the pieces of the burnt out barn. She stood there for a few moments, watching him. He looked like he was dissecting the remains like it was a crime scene he'd been tasked with investigating. Just for a brief moment, she feared for him. Like the world itself was set to crash down upon him.

At once she wanted nothing more than to be with Jack. To protect him from some undefined evil lurking somewhere, waiting to pounce. She calmed herself, reasoning that it was nothing more than an irrational fear to being away from him. They had spent a week together, and a wonderful week at that. They were learning how to function as husband and wife. A task they both relished.

He'll die here.

What made her think that? It was an unusual thought. Likely just born out of her overactive imagination. Still, she wanted to go hug him.

"You be careful, honey," she yelled, mostly to calm her fears.

"I will. You have fun today. See you later."

She forced herself to get into Rita's car. Pulling out of the driveway, she felt a magnetic impulse to remain at the house. Like it was pulling at her insides, compelling her to stay. She looked behind them as they reached the road, only a brief glance, but an image appeared in the living room window. A figure, someone who was not supposed to be there. She looked back again and saw nothing but those dingy blinds.

Their farmhouse was only about ten minutes outside of town. It was not much of a town, Rita explained, but most of the townspeople loved it. What it lacked in size and utility, it made up in charm. "You have almost everything you need right here. You already know the Gullivers. They're the linchpin of the town. Anything you need, they can normally get."

They parked the car in one of the slanted parking spaces before exiting. Elizabeth was amazed at how clean the streets were. Half of the buildings looked abandoned, but the stores that were open looked to still be doing good business. There was a small grocery store, a laundromat, a clothing store, and a large grain and feed store at the end. The busiest of the businesses seemed to be the tack shop which sold an array of equestrian gear.

"Times are hard in this little town, but this is really the most stores we have had open at any time in years. The library moved into town when their old building was condemned a few years ago."

She pointed across the street to a building with a cheaply painted 'Library' sign over the top of it. There was a repurposed mailbox in front, painted yellow, with the words 'knight drop' on it, with the figure of a knight holding a lance with books skewered onto it.

"They have all the town's newspapers for the last hundred years or so," Rita said. "All scanned onto a computer database. They thankfully got the project done before a small fire destroyed the physical papers. So, if there is anything you want to know, that's where to look."

"I'd really like to know more about my house," Elizabeth said. "Something that old should have an interesting history to it."

"Yeah, I'd be careful if I were you."

"Why's that?"

"Sometimes, houses have a history better left alone. You know, let sleeping dogs lie."

"You're being weird, Rita," Elizabeth said. "What are you not telling me?"

Rita shook her head. "Look, something bad happened in that house many years ago, and no one really told me the whole story. It was before Hal and I moved out this way. Someone died there, I think. Under mysterious circumstances."

"Well, ghosts don't scare me. I'll look it up and see what I can find."

"All I'm saying is, be careful. Sometimes it's better not to know."

The little town also had a fairly good sized drugstore, called Bacon Drug, which made the majority of its money on selling medicines to the town's aged residents. It also had a lunch counter which, Rita claimed, made the best hamburgers in the county. It also sold a selection of greeting cards, wrapping paper, and a small kiosk for buying mail supplies. The town's post office closed years before in an effort to save the Postal Service money.

"This town looks like it was built for tons more people than live here now. Seems a little odd. Did something happen to it?"

"Yeah, sad story really. Back in the 70s, this place was a big deal. We had an elementary, middle, and high school. Half the town is deserted today, but it was bursting at the seams back then. That's what the old duffers will tell you."

"Must have been impressive. So what happened?" Elizabeth

wondered as they climbed back into Rita's car.

"A couple of things hit all the farms hard. I remember it well, because I grew up in Indiana and it hit there pretty hard too. You were probably too young to really remember the whole Farm Aid movement. But farmers had a problem with falling corn prices and foreclosures on their properties. It was suddenly impossible to make a living selling corn. We lost a lot of good families in the business back then."

"What happened to them?"

Pulling out of town and onto an intersecting country road with no traffic control signs, and little need for any, a few buildings appeared on the distant horizon.

"A lot of them gave up farming. The banks foreclosed on the land and sold it to big farm companies. Some farmers were working two or three jobs to scrape by. A few of them did, but not many. I don't mean to sound offensive, but most people your age don't want to farm for a living. It's a lot of work, and you have to use pesticides and fertilizers if you want to make it in this business."

After ten minutes of driving, a few large buildings poked up in place of the farms. Then a large department store and a massive grocery store dominated the landscape. To Elizabeth, it seemed very much out of place.

Rita pulled into the grocery store parking lot. "Okay lady, let's get some food to feed that man of yours. You're not a vegetarian, are you?"

Elizabeth was shocked at Rita's suggestion they were vegetarians. "Oh gosh no! I want my dinner to have either mooed, clucked, or swam at some point."

"Well then, you'll get along fine out here."

For the next three hours, they shopped their hearts out. Rita's small car was overflowing with bags of groceries and other things Elizabeth knew they'd need to make their house a home. She even found a local coffee shop that roasted their own coffee. Being out of the house had a therapeutic effect on her; although, the exact reason alluded her. She hated to complain, Jack was trying his best, but being out in middle America's grain belt could be a little unnerving if you weren't used to it.

The shopping made her new life feel more normal. Elizabeth promised to take Rita with her into Joliet in a week or two. Maybe they would even make that appointment to get mani-pedis as a thank-you for being so helpful.

Rita pulled the car back into the driveway, as the sun was beginning its final descent toward the horizon and still had a few hours of daylight left to provide.

To Elizabeth, the house painted a different picture than this morning. The windows and door frame sagged a little, as if the house felt slighted that everyone had left it alone for the day. She wasn't sure if a house could possibly have feelings, but this one just felt sad. Likely a product of her overactive imagination, in the bedroom window, for the briefest of moments, she thought a figure stood there watching them, much like when they first arrived at the house.

I really need to find out more about the history of this house.

Rita and Elizabeth spent the rest of the afternoon putting away groceries, cleaning supplies, and the other items they bought. It had been a good day, something she needed after the long drive from the East Coast. A day of normalcy.

As Elizabeth chopped vegetables in the kitchen, Rita went upstairs to use the bathroom. The blissful quiet of the moment was rudely interrupted by a loud noise. It was metallic, but not mechanical. A grating sound, coming from the cellar.

For a moment the world seemed to fall away from her, like an old-time movie reel was being played before her. She saw something metallic and heavy being dragged through gravel. The vision scared her, although she couldn't say why.

Rita put her hand on her shoulder. "Hey, Earth to Lizzy! Oh Elizabeth?"

Elizabeth shook her head to clear her momentary day-dream. "Oh my gosh, Rita, I'm sorry. I spaced out there for a minute. I could have sworn I heard something."

"Like what?"

"Something in the cellar. Maybe a pipe or something. It was an odd sound, and can't really place it. Maybe a piece of metal being drug along the ground."

"Oh sweetie, these old houses make all kinds of noises. Hmmm … sort of like Hal."

Elizabeth gave Rita a smile at attempt at levity.

"Look, if it bothers you that much, we should go down and have a look. I'm being serious when I say that old houses do need constant monitoring. The last thing you want is for a busted water pipe to be laying on the floor dumping thousands of gallons of water into the basement."

"I don't know Rita, I really would rather wait until Jack gets back. He is good with these things." Elizabeth tried to reassure herself. Actually, Jack wasn't a good handyman, but it made her feel better to say it.

"It's nothing but a thing," Rita grabbed Elizabeth by the arm. "Let's have a look-see, the men can't have all of the fun."

Elizabeth shook her head from side to side emphatically. "I don't want to go down there. It's really creepy."

"Sweetie, I've been in the cellar fifty times since this house went on the market. The only thing scary down there are the field mice you get in the fall."

"I realize that, but—" She stopped protesting. "Wait, we have mice?"

"Yes, come on, let's go downstairs. Seriously, probably nothing worse than the house settling or something falling off the shelf." Rita let Elizabeth by the hand and opened the door to the cellar. She found the light-switch and illuminated the cave-like stairwell. "See, nothing to be afraid of."

"Yeah, except for serial killers and clowns. Oh, and serial killing clowns," Elizabeth laughed at her own joke. Rita seemed so confident, so powerful. It also helped that the spider was no longer guarding the entrance. "Fine, but you go first, maybe the serial killer is only killing Realtors this week."

The two descended the stairs, Rita in front and Elizabeth looking over her shoulder.

Elizabeth wasn't sure what she was going to find. Part of her expected to see a dead body or something. Their cellar stretched out before them exactly as it had before. Trash cans, the plastic trash bags, and the old paint cans were stacked exactly as they had been. She dared a glance over to the workbench to see the ax was still where she had left it the day before. With the exception of where they had disturbed the dust, everything looked just as it had.

"See, everything's fine down here. Nothing to worry about." Rita was looking at the collection of old paint cans on the rack. "You need to take these to the hazardous waste dump. They're pretty much worthless, based on how old they are."

"Mice?" Elizabeth said, looking around the room.

Rita chuckled at her. "Don't worry, these are cute field mice. Put out some traps and you'll keep them under control. They come in from the fields during the fall, looking for somewhere warm to winter over. They're going to have a shock with you guys here. Probably used to having free reign of the place."

Shivering at the idea, Elizabeth said, "Yuck. Okay, maybe my imagination ran away with me a bit. Let's get back upstairs and finish putting stuff away."

Just then, footfalls squeaked their way across the kitchen floorboards. "Lizzy? Rita?" A voice called from the kitchen.

"Your stallion has arrived," Rita said.

Elizabeth rolled her eyes at her new friend. "You are unbelievable, Rita." The two ascended the stairs and met Jack, who wore a dumbfounded expression.

"Wow, Rita, you got my wife to go back downstairs with you? Is there anything you can't do?"

Rita flexed her arms to accentuate her accomplishment. "Nope, and don't you forget it!" She picked up her cup of coffee from the table. "Hey Jack, how was the first day at the campus? Pretty impressive, huh?"

"Actually, it's smaller than I'd remembered it, but it's really pretty nice. I can see myself being comfortable there. Not sure if it's where I want to build tenure, but it'll do for now."

"Glad to hear it," Rita said. "Well, I'll let you two love birds be. Jack, go easy on her, she is still a little sore." She gave Elizabeth a wink and made her way outside.

"Sore? What on earth is she talking about?"

"Don't worry about her, she's just ... being Rita." Elizabeth shook her head.

"G'night you two."

"Night Rita," Jack and Elizabeth said in almost perfect unison.

Outside, Rita climbed into her car and they watched her tail lights disappear into the evening dusk. The sky had taken on a pink-purple color. This afternoon, with no clouds or summertime haze to obscure their view, they could just make out the top of the corncrib of the farm across the road.

Elizabeth gave Jack a deep kiss. "Welcome home, honey, you'll find that I blew all of your next six paychecks today."

"Well, as long as we have steak, I'm good with that."

"We do," She said. "Just name the cut."

"Something big and with a glass of red wine so dark I'd think I was drinking blood."

She pointed at the cabinet, newly stocked with an assortment of wines she and Rita had gotten from the store. "I had to improvise wine storage until the rack gets here, but I think I can find something to your liking."

Jack sat down at the table, opened up his satchel, and pulled out several blank forms to be filled out. "You should see the size of my office. It's huge. The largest office I've ever been in. Thankfully, the computers and stuff are all set up. Tomorrow, I can go to IT and get my login credentials and get a university laptop to work from home."

She turned from the wine rack to face her husband. "Excellent! Hey, that reminds me, when are we going to get Internet? I'm going to leave you for the first guy that offers me their wifi password."

"Before you leave me, you may want to know they're coming tomorrow. I got a call today. Can you be around?"

"Hell yeah, I need to get my *Real Housewives* fix, so the internet situation has to improve toot sweet." She moved to the refrigerator and pulled two steaks out of the refrigerator.

Jack came up behind her and gave her a kiss on the neck. "Be right back. I have to grab some information from upstairs."

He took off up the stairs, running up two at a time.

Elizabeth seasoned the steaks in the pan. It was not her favorite way to make steaks, but their new barbecue grill was in the back of a moving van, somewhere between central Illinois and Northern Virginia. It would be a few days before the delivery truck brought the rest of their belongings. She had just finished turning the steaks in the pan and adding onions when she heard a loud crash from upstairs.

Elizabeth waited for Jack to call down to her, cry out, or offer some sort of reaction to the loud noise. There was a small voice in her head telling her, *Don't worry about it. Nothing to see there.* The noise was muffled, like it had been played on a television set from somewhere in the house. Thirty seconds went by, and her concern got the better of her and she ran upstairs.

"Jack? Jack, I heard a crash. Is everything okay?" She was out of breath as she reached the top of the landing.

Why hadn't Jack said anything? Certainly he would have cried out if he'd dropped something.

Panicked, she ran into their bedroom. Jack was on the floor, holding his head. Next to him lay an old picture someone had put on the wall years ago. Glass and blood were everywhere.

"No, don't come in," he said, waving her away.

Jack's head gushed blood while he tried to hold the cut closed. Blood stubbornly oozed from between his fingers. She quickly ran from the room, finding a pair of boots she used for garden work in the hallway, she pulled them on and then grabbed Jack's tennis shoes. "What happened, Jack?"

He stared groggily up at her. "I don't know. I was changing my clothes, and the picture fell on me. It was so sudden. Hit me hard, like someone threw it on me."

Elizabeth grabbed a hand towel from the bathroom and gave it to him. The way he was speaking sounded slurred and confused. There was blood all down the front of his dress shirt. "I think we need to get you to the hospital, Jack."

He nodded, pressing the towel to his head. "Whatever you think is best."

Now she was really worried. He hated the hospital. There was pretty much nowhere on earth he'd prefer to be less.

Fifteen minutes later they were walking through the door of the clinic, which was in the same set of buildings as the library and the pizzeria. Unlike the other buildings in town, the interior of this building looked fairly modern. The large waiting room suggested more patients than Elizabeth thought possible for such a small-town. The room was filled with white plastic chairs and small coffee tables containing a vast array of old magazines. Fronting those, were three reception desks with two small chairs. Only one of the stations looked like it was ever in use as the others were filled with boxes from medical supply companies.

The nurse, sitting at the only occupied reception desk, immediately stood up, trying unsuccessfully to stifle her shock at Jack covered in blood. Elizabeth helped steady him, while he lowered himself into a chair. The nurse hurriedly handed them some forms and a clipboard before rushing to get the doctor.

It's probably not too often they see someone walk through the door wearing boxer shorts and dress shirt, soaked in blood, holding a towel to his head.

Elizabeth was shook so hard she found filling out the forms difficult. Jack looked vulnerable sitting there, covered in blood. Remembering details like his date of birth, medications, past surgical history and even spelling his name correctly proved Herculean.

The nurse, looking more composed, reappeared. "The doctor will see you now, Mr. Milburn." She brought them through a door on the side and led them to a small room. It was cold, medicinally white, and had a single chair and a padded examination table, where Jack was advised to sit. The nurse quickly took his vitals using a portable machine and left the room.

After a few minutes, an old man entered the room, wearing a lab coat and a stethoscope. "So, I see we have the Milburns here with us tonight. I'd say it is a pleasure to make your acquaintance, but under the circumstances I'm sure you would rather not be meeting me while covered in your own blood. I'm Dr. Gold."

"Good evening Dr. Gold. Sorry about the late hour," Elizabeth said.

The old doctor leaned in and took a closer look at the wound on Jack's head. "No worries, that's what we're here for. Let's have a look. What happened Jack, you forget your anniversary?"

"What?" Jack said.

"Well, looks like your wife hit you over the head with a frying pan." The doctor laughed at his own joke.

"Oh, no," Jack said humorlessly. "I'm not sure what happened. One moment ... this damn picture hit me on the head."

"Good sized abrasion too. These things always bleed like crazy. But, I don't think it'll need stitches. A good butterfly bandage will close it up. You're going to want something stronger than aspirin for the pain, though. Gonna knock you on your ass for a few days, to be sure."

The doctor quickly finished his examination. Then he gave Elizabeth printed instructions he kept in a file cabinet, leaving Elizabeth to wonder how many head injuries they got that they needed pre-printed instructions amass. The instructions covered keeping the wound clean and how to keep it from bleeding again.

"Is he going to be alright?" she asked.

"I'm concerned about a concussion," said Dr. Gold. "But I don't think there's any permanent damage. I'll give you some information about what to watch out for and a list of symptoms. If you see them, you need to call me right away. I'd like to run a couple more tests, just to make sure he's all right. Why don't you hang out in the waiting room for a while, and I'll call you?"

Elizabeth, suddenly feeling more reassured by the doctor's lack of concern toward the injury said, "Can I go get something to eat and come back?"

Dr. Gold said, "Sure, give us about forty-five minutes and just leave your number with the receptionist so she knows where to find you."

Elizabeth walked out of the building and turned toward the pizza shop. She wasn't sure she would be in the mood to cook steaks by the time she got home, so she ordered an Italian sub to go. The boy behind the counter said it would be ready in about fifteen minutes.

While waiting for Jack, Elizabeth went to the library. She only had ten minutes before closing time.

An old woman stood up from behind the main desk where she was working on a stack of books. "Hello, young lady, can I help you?"

Elizabeth wondered how old you had to be before people stopped referring to you as 'young lady'. "No thanks, I'm just looking around."

The woman, who looked like a quintessential librarian, sat back down in her chair. "Alright then dearie, let me know of you have any questions."

The county library occupied a space that used to be an old clothing store. The floors were covered in an oriental style rug which looked out of place for this little town. There was a section for fiction and an area for reference materials. In the corner, under a large chandelier which looked ridiculously out of place, stood a collection of newspapers. Next to that were three computers.

She sat down at one computer and double clicked on the Icon for the Farmers Daily World newspaper. She knew, from what Jack had told her, their new home was once called the Anderson farm, so she tried searching on that and found nothing. She then tried searching for the address and a dozen articles came up.

Her phone buzzed, and in the quiet of the library, it startled her. "Yes?" she said tersely.

Dr. Gold's receptionist spoke to her from the other end. "Mrs. Milburn, you can come back now. I think we're done here."

Without reading any of the articles, she closed the browser. Research would have to wait for another day that didn't include her husband bleeding all over the floor of their bedroom. She thanked the librarian on the way out with a promise to return for a library card later on in the week.

BRYAN NOWAK

Dark Dreams Reveal Darker Fears

Jack remembered going up those stairs to get their birth certificates out of their small fire safe. Some of the information needed for the forms the school required were not things either of them would readily remember. The stairs creaked under foot reassuringly. It reminded Jack of an old movie he'd watched where someone went upstairs to confront someone about a mystery. Those were his last truly clear thoughts of that evening.

After Elizabeth left to get some dinner, Dr. Gold's voice became serious. "Jack, you're sure your wife didn't hit you with a hammer or something?"

If Jack's head wasn't hurting so much, he would've laughed at this insinuation. Elizabeth had a hard enough time killing spiders, let along hurting him. Instead, he just replied, "No, I'm sure, she was downstairs. Why?"

"Quite a bit of force behind that blow to the back of your head. More than just a picture falling. Back in my younger days I worked in an emergency room in Chicago and it was pretty obvious when someone was attacked with something rather than just simply a fall or being hit."

Jack shook his head slightly. "We just moved into an old house to renovate it. My guess is, the nail in the wall failed and the picture fell. I just happened to be in the wrong place at the wrong time."

"Old house, you say," the doctor said, shining a light in Jack's eyes. "Whereabouts?"

"Mr. Gulliver called it the 'Anderson farm.'"

The doctor switched off the light and took two steps back. "You mean Donald Anderson's place?"

"Yes, that's it."

Dr. Gold knitted his eyebrows and let out a sigh. "Wow, I haven't seen the inside of that place in thirty years."

"Mr. Gulliver told me Donald Anderson killed some people."

"Yeah, that is a bit of an understatement. His whole family, then himself."

Jack stared in disbelief at the old doctor. "I mean, did they ever find a note or anything?"

"Nope, nothing like that. But the bank was on the verge of foreclosing on the property. It was a bad time for farmers. Especially corn farmers. The price dropped, and suddenly the seeds weren't worth the ears they grew. Lots of people around here lost their farms. I guess going crazy made sense to him."

"Where did they find the bodies?" Jack asked.

Dr. Gold shook his head. "Tell you what, let's change the subject. That day isn't one I'll likely ever forget, and not one I am terribly keen on remembering."

"Okay, but I have a lot of questions—"

Dr. Gold put his stethoscope down on the table next to the examination table. "Look, Jack. If I were in your shoes, I'd have tons of questions too. I'm sure you can find answers at the library if you want them, but you won't get them from me. Donald was a friend and a patient. His whole family was. On that day I lost a lot."

Jack could see he'd touched a nerve with the old doctor. He was going to protest, but he thought better of it. The doctor's face had taken on a sad countenance as if, in the old man's mind, he was replaying old conversations, seeing old friends.

Dr. Gold turned from Jack and opened the exam room door to the hallway. "I'll go write you a prescription for the pain."

"I'm actually feeling a lot better."

Dr. Gold chucked at the insinuation. "Jack, as your new doctor, I can tell you, it's going to hurt like a son-of-a-bitch in the morning. That's the medical term for how you're going to feel tomorrow. Take the meds. I'll tell the nurse to call Elizabeth to come get you."

A few moments later, the doctor returned with a few pills in a small white envelope and a little paper cup of water. He also had a prescription for antibiotics and painkillers. "Take two now, and one at bedtime with a light snack. The script is for tomorrow and the next day."

Jack took the items with a relieved smile. "Thank you, doctor."

"You're most certainly welcome. If that head wound doesn't improve, come back and see me. I want you to take it easy for a couple of days. No work tomorrow. Take the prescription over to Bacon Drug Store across the street. You go see the druggist, Todd. He's waiting for you. I already told him what I was going to write the prescription for, so he'll have it ready."

He walked into the waiting room again just as Elizabeth was coming in.

"Good as new?" she said. Elizabeth cringed as she inspected the bandage the doctor put over the wound.

"Oh yeah, we are signed up for doubles handball tomorrow morning, and then go a few rounds in the ring after lunch."

"I would definitely not advise that," the doctor said, smiling. "Elizabeth, you keep him nailed down to a bed tomorrow. I don't want to drive by your house and see him out in the yard unless he's in a lounge chair. If you need anything, you can come back and see us."

"Thank you, doc." Jack walked arm-in-arm with Elizabeth to the door. As they left, Jack cast a glance toward the nurse's station. Both Dr. Gold and the nurse were staring at him and Elizabeth. The look was one of confusion, fear, and perhaps a little pity.

Walking out of the clinic, the pain seemed to renew its assault on him with the sun shining in his eyes. Sitting at the dining room table, Jack ate half of Elizabeth's sandwich and took the drugs the doctor gave him. Working quickly, they made him drowsy. He only remembered Elizabeth undressing him, and some joke about it not being erotic undressing a man who has a gaping head wound. Then sleep took him.

Jack stood in a field of green. Out in front, he could see a world of corn. It swayed in the Illinois breeze. The green leaves of the plants shined against the sun like a rhythmically undulating ocean. The road, which would normally have been in front of him, was no longer there. Only fields of corn approaching harvest season.

He was aware of the house behind him. Turning around to see it, their two-story farmhouse grew into a six-story monstrosity, which leaned precariously toward him, threatening to fall over. The sky had gone from a deep blue to a tangerine orange. The wind picked up, and the temperature dropped.

The house had taken on an angry demeanor, if a house was capable of such things. It laughed at him mockingly, daring him to enter. In the place of their door, a giant mouth grinned at Jack. Two circular windows made up eyes on either side. The other windows looked to have their own ghostly faces inside them.

This is crazy, I'm not going to be afraid of my own home.

Part of him knew he could never enter the house, or that would be the end. Still, he was drawn to it. Jack's mind flashed to the memory of an old cartoon with a cat floating into the kitchen, drawn by the magical scent of a fully cooked ham, only to have a mouse drop a bowling ball on his head as soon as it entered.

"No way … you aren't going to fool me," he said. "I know what you're up to."

The house smiled back at him, as if it knew something he did not. An unspoken secret the house knew and Jack had to work to unravel.

"I see through your tricks. I'm staying put out here."

Wind rose from the corn fields, the shiny green leaves battered one another in a chorus of vegetative applause. The sky behind the house faded from orange to angry blood-red like the applause from the corn field angered the sky itself. Dark and foreboding clouds rose up from beyond the fields forming a vapor army, with Jack as their General.

The house let out a deep, growling, mechanical sound. Jack knew homes should never make sounds like that, it reminded him of his old uncle Joe's belly laugh. It was terrifying and defiant.

For a moment, man and house sized each other up. Blood-red sky and dark clouds stood at opposition. Two armies, facing off on the field of battle, neither side giving the signal to attack, but both knowing that the command was coming, preparing for bloodshed.

The house laughed again, with its deep mechanical roll. From deep within its frame, a noise rose above the din. A cry for help, a plea for Jack. The only thing on earth which could get him to go inside. It was his soul mate, Elizabeth, begging for rescue. No matter the cost, Jack had to save the one he loved. The house looked on approvingly, knowing his life was meaningless without her.

Plunging through the door, Jack suddenly found himself in a world stuck in 1984. In the living room, the one he already knew well, sat a man in overalls. He was drinking coffee from a faux-china cup, looking at him over the fold of his newspaper. For a moment their eyes met. Jack's gaze wandered to the top of the man's head, which was missing the upper right quarter. The farmer's clothing was soaked with blood, as was the couch and the floor surrounding him.

"Jack, great to see you," he said. "Terrible weather out there, isn't it? I suppose I ought to get going. Lots of work to do on a farm. Lots of work indeed."

The farmer folded the paper, dropped it onto the coffee table, and stood up. Grabbing a shotgun from behind the couch, he vanished, disappearing into a white vapor as he walked out the door.

"Jack, please help me!" Elizabeth's pleas became more insistent. He shook himself from his momentary fixation on the old farmer's apparition and ran through the house in search of his wife. In the dining room, laid out on the table in suits, were two teenage boys. Although one was older than the other, neither one was older than eighteen. They were side by side, eyes closed, surrounded by flowers like they were laid out for an old-time funeral. Neither one of them moved.

"So, what do you think of Jack and Elizabeth?" one of the boys said.

"I kind of like them," said the other. "He seems nice. Not wild about the fact that he's a teacher, though. I mean, it would be cooler if he was a rock musician or something."

"Sure, because a lot of rockers move to central Illinois farm country you idiot."

"What? It could happen."

The older boy smiled wryly. "What do you think of that Elizabeth, huh?"

"I would love to get my hands on that body of hers." His brother responded.

"You haven't even had your first kiss yet. You would have no idea what to do with a woman if you got one in your room."

The younger boy continued, "Oh, I dunno, I'm sure I'd like to give it a shot."

The swinging door separating the kitchen and the dining room exploded open, throwing the doors off their hinges and onto the floor at Jack's feet. Looking enraged, a woman in an old house coat stood glaring at Jack and then the boys. The woman would have looked like a mom from one of those 60s television sitcoms had it not been for the gaping hole in her chest, from which blood spurted making a sickening noise as the deluge hit the floor. Dark rings sat around her eyes in contrast to the pale grey color of her skin.

"I told you boys, that's no way to talk about a lady! You dirty little boys are growing up to be dirty little perverts, and I'll have none of it!"

An ax appeared in her hands in a puff of smoke any prestidigitator would have been proud of. Raising it high above her head, blood dripped down the handle and onto her hands and arms. The woman swung the ax down hard and it buried itself deep into the chest of the younger boy. Blood splattered onto Jack and the boy said nothing. Jack wiped the crimson fluid out of his eyes to see the walls dripping with the boy's fresh blood.

She seemed to have a hard time pulling the ax out of his chest. After a couple of attempts, she wrenched it free of the boy with the sickening sound of crepitus. She turned to the second boy and regarded him for a moment. She swung the ax into his chest, just as deep and with just as much effect. Blood streamed over the table, covering the flowers and the boys' suits. Both remained motionless through the whole affair.

"We're sorry, mommy." The boys now spoke in unison to assuage their mother's anger. "We love you, mommy, and we promise to do better."

Jack was taken aback by the sudden sounds from the decimated corpses. Stepping farther away from the enraged woman, he tried to make any kind of sense out of the horror playing out before him.

"There … that's my sweet boys." the zombie-like woman said. She lowered the ax head. "I love you boys so much. You know that, don't you?" She locked eyes with Jack. "I would never let anything happen to you."

"Help me, Jack, please!" Elizabeth yelled, momentarily breaking Jacks attention from the grisly display.

"And you," the woman said, yelling at Jack. "You're responsible for all of this. We were happy. Now I have to finish you too!" Once again, she raised the ax, this time to her shoulders, and took a swipe at Jack. The baseball swing was easily avoided, the head of the pernicious tool burying itself in the wall to his left. She strained to extract it, but it remained intransigently stuck. "As soon as I get this out of the wall, I'm going to chop your dick off ... make you a fucking eunuch!"

Jack wasted no time and shoved her out of the way, running into the kitchen. Half expecting to see Elizabeth chopped to pieces, he was relieved to find she wasn't there. Turning once again into the dining room, he ducked, allowing the blade of the ax to swing over his head with the woman's next attack. She shrieked as the weight of the ax threw her off balance and Jack shoved her to the floor. Leaping away, she tried to grab his ankle but missed.

The sound of Elizabeth's pleading was louder and more anguished. It was coming from upstairs and Jack bounded the steps two at a time. One of the smaller bedroom doors sat wide open. Inside, he could see a naked foot dangling off the side of the bed. It was still attached to the leg, but only by sinew and skin. Parts of it had been hacked off. Other body parts also lay on the bed, which was soaked in blood. Carefully placed on the pillow was Rita's dismembered cranium. Her eyes opened, staring at him with a piercing glare.

Rita's mouth suddenly opened and said, "What's the matter, Jack? Not really in love with your remote, three bedroom, two bath, fixer-upper, starter home? Located in a quiet neighborhood in farm country, with a little elbow grease, it could be the perfect place to start a family. The back yard is perfect for—"

Jack slammed the door shut and ran to their bedroom. On the bed, dressed in the "Jane of the Jungle" outfit she wore to last year's Halloween party, was Elizabeth, tied to the bed posts.

"Oh, God, honey. Let me get you untied," he said, working at the ropes.

"Hurry, we have to get out of here before they come back," Elizabeth pleaded.

"I know." As the last restraint was untied, he moved to the door. "Come on, we have to run for it."

Opening the door, he heard a movement behind him. Although Jack was certain the only other person in the room with him was Elizabeth, a distressing feeling overtook him. In the brass of the door knob he could just make out the image of Elizabeth glaring at him. He turned to face her just in time to his wife bring down a picture frame over the top of his head, sending him crashing to the floor.

Jack shot up out of bed, letting out a forceful scream which ended in a cough. He could hear Elizabeth's footfalls running up the stairs in response to the scream. The force of the nightmare, or perhaps the scream, made his head suddenly throb uncontrollably. He felt hot and suddenly nauseous.

Elizabeth burst through the door with a look of concern on her face. It was morning, and she was wearing a pair of shorts and one of his old tee-shirts from college. "Jack, are you alright?"

He leaned back on the pillows, the memory of the horrible dream flooding his head. "Wow, yeah. What a terrible nightmare." Jack held his head to try and calm down the throbbing, with little effect.

"Poor baby. Well, you can tell me all about it if you want." She sat down on the bed.

"Not really. This was one I'd like to forget as quickly as possible, but I doubt I will."

She sat on the corner of the bed with him, as he tried to will his blood pressure and pulse rate back to normal. He felt like his heart was going to beat out of his chest. The dream was so weird and real, it felt like he was actually running through the macabre world his mind had created.

"The doctor did say the meds can give people odd dreams," she grimaced at the sight of her stricken husband.

"I know, but that was one hell of an odd dream, but I am starting to feel better. Well, except for the massive gash on my head."

Elizabeth put her hand on Jack's shoulder. "Doctor Gold also said, you should eat, so I'm making you some ham and eggs for breakfast. Would you like a couple of pieces of toast?"

He leaned forward, rubbing the sides of his head. "Sure, I'll have to call the university secretary and let her know I won't be in today. I still have a ton of paperwork to fill out anyway."

"Don't worry about it, I already called them."

"Okay, great. You take such good care of me." Jack looked at his wife turned nurse and thought silently about how wonderful she truly was. "Toast, huh? I think I can get up for that." Jack tried to get out of bed. Pressing his first foot to the floor seemed to be his brain's signal to introduce the full effect of the pain. The doctor was right about the pain. Suddenly he felt like he'd been repeatedly beaten over the head instead of just having suffered a single blow. Elizabeth, seeing Jack's anguish, helped him get out of bed and dressed. She cleaned his wound and replaced the butterfly bandage.

Putting on his slippers, he looked down at the broken remains of the picture frame. Maybe it would be worth having it repaired. It was all wood, beautifully done, perhaps it was even hand-crafted. Really a nice piece of work. He read somewhere that the frames themselves can sometimes be worth more than the paintings they were built to hold. Or maybe burning the damn thing in the backyard would be the better way to go. It would certainly make him feel better.

He stood up slowly, but that didn't stop him from feeling a little woozy. He steadied himself. Maybe the hit he took was more severe than he thought.

Downstairs, Elizabeth had just finished spreading butter on his toast. "Here you go, my love. Try to eat slowly. I'll get you a cup of coffee and your medicine."

He ate his eggs slowly, trying to forget about his horrible dream. It made him feel cold inside. Jack had nightmares before, but never one so vivid. He felt every splatter of blood, heard every step on the stairs,

106

smelled every acrid scent. His own dearest Elizabeth killed him.

He took a sip of the coffee, letting the warm liquid roll down his throat. It was an elixir, a connection to the real world. Magically it undid the perceived evil of the dream. Not even the sock-puppet, which had consistently haunted his nightmares as a child, scared him as much as that nightmare.

Taking a bite of his toast, he chewed its crunchy, buttery goodness. It was just the way he liked it. Toast never tasted so good.

He had just resolved to rid himself of the horrible memory when Elizabeth jumped up from her chair, almost knocking it over. He looked at his wife, who suddenly became very excited. The toast was good, but it was still just toast. Something else had caught her attention.

"Oh it's here! I'd almost forgotten."

"What's here?" Jack snapped out of his internal monologue, amazed by her sudden burst of physical energy.

She put her hands on Jacks shoulders and stared into his eyes. "Now Jack, you know our agreement?"

"Agreement?"

"You know, that I'm only allowed to buy you one thing a year? Well, this is my one thing, sweetie. So no fussing. I'm not going to sit here all day and wait for you to come home so I can go out." Although he could only see a small part of the driveway, the flash of red color stuck out like a neon sign. "What did you do?"

They walked to the doorway, and outside was parked the largest pick-up truck he had ever seen.

The Road to Recovery

"What did you do?" Jack repeated.

Much, my love. I have done much.

She'd almost completely forgotten about the delivery of the truck when it pulled into the driveway. In between the medicine, breakfast and generally worrying about him, there wasn't any time to really worry about the new vehicle she'd purchased.

Elizabeth previously steeled herself against the inevitable tongue-lashing for buying him such an expensive gift. She had her reasons lined up one right after another and they were good ones. It had four-wheel drive, which they would need during the winter, there was no way on planet earth she was going to sit in this house all day. So really, one could argue it was a gift for her as much as him. With his injury and the medicine he might not be in a mood to ague.

The truck was a deep cherry color with exterior accents and in all chrome. The bed liner was top of the line, sprayed in, and the tires were all-weather. Indulging in his love for old time radio shows, she had a satellite radio installed so he could listen to his heart was content. It was a beautiful thing.

Jack said nothing; his eyes were huge. She could tell he was mentally calculating what something like that would cost. She could also see, given the opportunity, he'd jump inside and drive it around town just to show it off. Her mind flashed back to Rita's comment about Hal killing her for spending that much money, but keeping the truck.

She leaned over and said, "Just say thank you, Jack."

The delivery driver had them both sign the paperwork and gave them the temporary title. Another car was waiting to take the driver back to the dealership and as quickly as the truck showed up, the two men were gone.

"I don't know what to say," he stammered.

"Don't say anything, honey. We need a truck for the winters out here and with the renovations, this fits the bill. It's my one gift to you for the year."

"But what about an electrician?"

She frowned at him. "Sweetie, that isn't a gift. That's making sure we all don't die in our sleep from an electrical fire." She kissed him.

He sighed and stood staring at the large vehicle in front of him. "Thank you, honey. I'm going to take it for a spin."

"Ah … no, you're not. Doctor's orders. Those drugs you're on are elephant-strength. No heavy machinery, and that beast qualifies." She pointed at the truck. "Plus, you need to rest. Maybe in a couple of days, you can play with your new toy."

"Yes, mom," he said, making a mock-pouty face.

"Good boy. Now, if you want, you can sit in it."

It wasn't exactly a consolation prize and she knew it. Jack really wanted to go for a drive. But Elizabeth could tell that just the walk to the truck proved to be almost as much exertion as he could handle at the moment.

He pulled himself up behind the wheel. She saw him testing out every knob and button he could find. Elizabeth thought Jack looked like a ten-year-old suddenly let loose at an amusement park. Turning the ignition key and revving the engine, Jack looked at her expectantly. Elizabeth stomped her foot and wagged her finger at him, closing the door to any further negotiations. She was right, of course, but he loved to push the envelope when he had the chance.

He climbed out and stood next to her, looking at the new truck.

"So, do you like it?" she asked. It was a rhetorical question.

"Are you kidding me? It's the sexiest thing at this house. Next to you, of course." He kissed her cheek.

"Good boy. You were treading on thin ice there for a second."

A yawn broke through his smile. "I hate to admit it, but that was more than I can handle right now. I think I need to lay down for a bit."

"Yeah, another side effect. Don't worry, tomorrow's dose is far less. These are just to get you through the worst of it."

A few minutes later, he was zonked out on the couch in the living room. She covered him with a blanket. *Men are truly just kids with car keys.*

After cleaning up the dishes, Elizabeth retrieved the full garbage bag from the kitchen. Outside the house, she dropped it into the metal cans for the garbage truck to take away. Turning to go back in, a flash of movement caught her attention. Had she not known better, she might have suspected it was Jack, but there was no way he could possibly move that quickly in his current condition.

"Hello, is anyone there?" No answer came. She walked over to the corner of the house to investigate. She suddenly felt foolish for being afraid. They lived in Middle-of-Nowhere, Illinois, and it was probably just a cat or one of the large black crows that seemed so prevalent here. But her mind also flashed to the idea of the 'mice' Rita mentioned. Elizabeth was sure they weren't as cute and harmless as Rita supposed.

Still unsure, she cautiously peered around the corner of the house. Although the coast appeared clear, she heard a thumping noise which sounded like two pieces of wood hitting each other. It seemed silly to worry about any animals near the house. Their biggest concern around here were skunks. Her sudden disquiet over the noise made her feel silly.

On that side of the house, there was only an old garden, overgrown with weeds, and the outside door to the cellar. Farther away, in between the house and the field of corn were the remains of the burned out barn. She remembered Jack moving a couple of pieces of wood around the day before, when he was checking it out. Maybe the noise she heard was one or two pieces of the wood settling.

Cautiously she approached the twisted pile of wood. It was only thirty feet from her, but it felt like a million miles. The cement foundation of the barn gave away its overall size, when it dominated the landscape. It was massive: maybe fifty feet on the long side and thirty feet wide. Not simply an old barn like you would see in westerns, twisted metal tubing and the remains of wires indicated it had been wired for electricity. In the refuse of the retired inferno, she could make out rusted tools and melted glass. As Jack suggested, she could just make out the hood of an old tractor sitting in what would have been the far corner of the structure.

Something about it made her sad and on-edge; although, Elizabeth had no reason to be. It was impossible to put her finger on, but it felt like profound and catastrophic loss. The remains of the barn told a story. It had once been a sturdy, strong building. Likely painted red, but she had no way to know. It seemed to her that a barn of this type should be red.

In her mind's eye, she saw it standing at its full height. The farm tractor, perhaps a hand-me-down, sat in the corner while a man in overalls, stood in the open door of the barn teaching his kids how to properly measure and cut wood. He prepared them for a time when they would use those skills to make repairs around the farm they would one day inherit.

The man looked on while the boys put their new skills into practice. "Measure twice, cut once, boys. Remember that. Always measure twice. Wood is expensive and if you take care, you can make the most out of it. We don't waste so much as an inch."

She could almost see the boys rolling their eyes at their father.

The boys groaned in unison. "We know, Dad."

Looking at one of the boys sawing a piece of wood in half he said, "Good job, boys. That's as perfect a cut as you're ever going to get. Maybe, someday, you'll be just as good as your old man."

"Maybe even better," the older boy said.

The younger boy chimed in, "Hey Dad, can I go now? I want to play with Peter down by the creek for a while."

"Sure, Robbie, just be careful. Stay out of that Massasauga nest down by the creek. I don't want to be running anyone to the doctor today with some snake bite."

"We'll leave em' be. Not sure why we don't just kill them."

"You haven't been listening to me then, Robbie. That's their home. You have about as much business being there as they have lounging around our living room. Besides, they eat rats. Let them eat the rats, they'd be doing me a favor. Now get, I'll see you later."

"Hey Dad," the older boy said as Robbie ran off to meet his friend. "I was thinking about something."

"Uh-oh, this is gonna be scary."

Matthew huffed. "Stop dad, I'm being serious."

"Okay Matthew, what is it?"

"I'll be fifteen when I blow my candles out next week."

His father scratched at his whiskery chin. "Okay, don't tell me. You're thinking of moving out and joining the circus?"

"No, Pop, I want to talk to you about buying Mr. Bransford's old Dodge."

"Fixer-upper farm truck, huh?"

"Yeah, we could use another field truck, and I'll be old enough to get a farm license. Who knows? By the time the trucks ready, I'll be old enough to get my regular license."

"I don't know Matthew, a truck like that's a big responsibility. You'll have to spend lots of time working on it. It needs an engine rebuild in the worst way. It'll limp along for a while if we work on it, but I don't think you know how much trouble it'll be in the end."

Matthew pointed into the garage, in continuance of his plea. "But, Dad, I can already take apart the tractor and put it back together blindfolded. I could just about do the same to your truck. Mr.

Bransford's truck is nowhere near as complex."

"You're kind of young to be driving around in a truck, Matthew." He broke out into a big, satisfied smile as those last words tumbled out of his mouth. He wanted to string his son on a little longer, but Matthew was putting up a good show. "Matthew, your mother and I already talked about it. We asked Mr. Bransford for the slip last week. He's giving it to you as a present. The old coot is going to bring it over and tell you Happy Birthday himself. Just be sure to act surprised, he loves that old truck, and he knows you'll take good care of it."

"Thanks Dad!"

On the other side of the barn the sky turned tangerine in color. Lightning bolts shot from the sky, tearing into the ground around the barn. For a brief second, both the man and the boy vanished and then reappeared with a flash of lightning. This time the father had an ax in his hand and his face was contorted in anger, like he was fighting off a wild animal. The other end of the ax was buried deep into the chest of the boy, whose eyes were wide with fear and his overalls covered in a river of blood.

Elizabeth stifled a scream and stumbled backward, tripping over a branch and falling to the ground. Opening her eyes, the building sat as it had. The remains of the barns burnt out timber sat in a pile, twisted and unrecognizable to anyone except those determined to retrace its history. She felt a little red-faced from her sudden child-like daydream.

That was it, nothing more than an odd little daydream. She had them sometimes, but never one so vivid. It didn't even seem like a daydream at all, more like watching professional actors interacting on stage. It was so full of detail; she could see the holes where the nails were countersunk on the barn doors and the deep gash in the boy's chest.

A daydream is all. I need to get more rest and stop worrying about Jack so much.

The man at the barn bore a striking resemblance to Jack. It was all just a part of the stress of worrying about him. It will pass soon enough.

She was brought out of her inner dialogue by the sound of car doors slamming. Elizabeth stood and dusted off her jeans and after casting a weary glance at the pile of wood, she spied Rita standing next to the enormous truck, admiring it.

"Whew, Lizzy, you got good taste in trucks. That's one hell of a piece of machinery. If you are this good at picking out everything you buy, remind me to take you dildo shopping."

"You are something else Rita," Elizabeth said, patting the truck on its quarter panel. "The dealership really helped me pick it out. And the Internet, of course."

"Oh naturally, we don't do anything without the Internet these days. I'm here to check in on you two kids. Doc called me and said Jack hit his head or something?"

"In a manner of speaking. More like a picture fell off the wall and hit him on the head. I was downstairs when it happened, so I didn't see it."

Rita frowned, "Poor guy. I was hoping to get through some of the things you don't want today. With that new truck of yours we can haul away some of the old stuff. But I know Jack is resting and it can wait

BRYAN NOWAK

till another day."

"I think it'll be alright. Let's just be quiet. He's on some super medication. Besides, I'd kind of like the company." Elizabeth said. In truth, after the barn, she didn't want to be alone.

The two worked for the remainder of that afternoon. Smaller furniture items, knickknacks which didn't fit their style, and pictures from the wall were all carefully loaded into the back of the truck. Rita gave each picture and knickknack a cursory check to make sure they didn't have some hidden value. She would do a more thorough job when she had the chance. Elizabeth remarked that she looked like one of those guys who bought abandoned storage units and sold the contents afterward.

Elizabeth wondered, not for the first time, about the people who used to live here. Who were they, and what were they like? She knew, from what Jack said, they were a farming family. How true were the stories? Was someone really killed in the house? It seemed a little far-fetched to her, but stranger things had happened.

The walls told stories of innumerable discussions taking place under this roof. Here they lived, dreamed, had sex, gave birth, and made clothes all within these walls. Elizabeth could feel them. They were a part of this house. She could feel their souls here. Maybe they were gone, but their essence still pervaded every corner of the house.

Rita finally said goodbye and headed back to check on Hal. It was getting late and he'd be wondering about dinner.

Elizabeth made a pitcher of lemonade and poured herself a glass. Walking past her sleeping husband to the patio, she sipped on the cool

117

liquid. The doctor advised her Jack would likely sleep most of the day away, and it was probably best. If he were awake his head would hurt, no matter how strong the medicine was.

On the porch swing, she sat and watched the corn fields wave in the wind. The house was surrounded by fields on all four sides. On the left, at the end of the driveway, was a stand of three trees. Sturdy maples, whose leaves seemed to twirl around in circles from her view on the porch. They were just on the inside of the property line where the drainage ditch ran along the road. To the right of the driveway, a large oak stood along two aspen trees. The oak had a long, thick branch reaching toward the house like an arm.

Studying the tree, she could see the remains of an old rope which had been tied in two places on the branch. Directly under the remains of the rope, not fully covered with grass, was an indentation in the ground. She could almost see a little boy, sitting on a swing, with his feet dangling in the indent. The tips of his shoes just touching a well-worn dirt patch below.

Elizabeth heard a sound to her right. Jack was up and moving again. He looked the worse for wear, but still better than earlier in the day. The sleep had been therapeutic for him.

"How ya feeling?"

"Like reusable toilet paper. Shit on, wrung out, then shit on again."

"Wow. Needlessly graphic, but an effective metaphor. That good, huh?" She motioned to the seat next to her and handed him her lemonade.

"Well, at least I'm starting to feel hungry again."

Elizabeth smiled at his acknowledgment of his hunger. "Good. The information the doctor gave me said we should worry if you didn't have an appetite by tonight. Funny thing: sitting out here, I noticed those trees just before you came out. Do you see that oak tree out there? Look at the branch extending out toward us. See the rope?"

"No," Jack studied the tree, shielding his eyes against the sunlight. "Oh, you mean the green stuff? I see it. Maybe they had a tire swing or something."

"Could be. They must have had kids."

He scratched his chin. "Two, as I recall. Husband, wife, and two kids."

"You didn't tell me that," Elizabeth said. She wasn't sure why, but she felt a little slighted. Jack had been holding out on her.

He shrugged his shoulders. "Never really came up before. Family of farmers, property passed down from generation to generation before being foreclosed on. Apparently someone died here, but I really didn't look into it. Not a big deal, our house now." He beamed. "By the way, you and Rita sure did move a lot of stuff out of the house while I was asleep."

She returned a proud smile of her own. "Yep, we worked our butts off. As the old saying goes Jack: if you want someone to talk about doing something, send a man. If you want something done, send a woman." She leaned over and gave him a kiss. "Still, part of me feels guilty about selling all their stuff. I feel … I dunno … like I am selling off their lives."

"I can understand that. I was told their kids were teenagers when the family left the house, so the parents are either dead or happily installed in some nursing home by now."

"I just hope no one ever comes looking for something. Legally, we may be fine, but I would feel awful if we accidentally sold the urn containing beloved Aunt Edith to some guy from Des Moines, who thought it'd make a cool ashtray." She stood up. "Anyway, I'm going to head back in to start dinner. Meatloaf and potatoes, I think. Maybe green beans ... not sure yet."

"Sounds great. I think I'll just sit out here and relax for a while and drink the rest of your lemonade."

She went back inside, and brought out the meat, spices, and other ingredients for her famous meatloaf. Try as she might, Elizabeth couldn't find the meatloaf pan. They had one, because it was on the top of the stove earlier while they were getting things moved out to the truck. But now it was nowhere to be found.

Then she remembered Rita had moved a bunch of things back down to the cellar. Elizabeth froze in fear at the idea she might have to go downstairs to find it, but she had to get used to the idea that some things would have to be stored in the dark, terrifying bowels of the house. They couldn't keep everything upstairs.

Opening the door to the cellar and switching on the light, Elizabeth expected the spider Jack killed to return from the dead to jump out at her, seeking vengeance for its murder. Peering around the corner, there was nothing unusual to be seen; only the lights reflecting off the rocks at the bottom of the stairs. For a moment she thought about maybe calling for Jack and asking him to go get it. Chasing away that idea almost immediately, she imagined him passing out at the bottom of the stairs from the exertion. She would never be able to get him back up the stairs.

Put on your big girl panties, Lizzy, she thought to herself. *That meatloaf pan wasn't going to march its way back up to the kitchen all by its lonesome.*

Elizabeth took a deep breath and descended the stairs. With every step, she felt her heart jump into her throat.

She was briefly reminded of being dared to enter the supposed 'haunted house' as a kid. Every town has one. A house abandoned by time, and occupants, which took on a legend of its own. The story of a foreclosure morphed into a foreclosed property where mysterious murders took place. According to legend the father had been carted off to an insane asylum, where he promptly escaped and now waits in the house for fresh victims. All across the country, in every town, the story ended the same way. The house was possessed by evil spirits, looking for children to kill so they could add to their collection of souls.

When she was a teenager, sitting in that same 'haunted house', she kissed Denny Beckerman and smoked her first joint.

She felt the reassuring crunch of the rocks under foot as she reached the bottom of the stairs. The lights cast a dim glow over the subterranean portion of the house. On the opposite wall from the paint cans and the rusting gardening equipment, she spied the box Rita brought down earlier. She'd placed it on the workbench, maybe not realizing she'd brought the meatloaf pan with her.

Her hand absently brushed against the ax. She looked at it again, closer this time than before. She picked it up and felt its heft. It was a formidable tool. It was easy to imagine someone in the backyard splitting wood for a fire pit or removing a large branch fallen from one of the trees.

As her fingers moved across the outside of the metal, she could see it was only a fine layer of rust coating it. Steel wool and some elbow grease would give it a new lease on life. Her finger traced the edge of the blade. It was time worn, but it had been razor-sharp at one point. Maybe Jack would know how to sharpen it.

"Honey, are you down there?"

His voice startled her, "Oh yes, sorry. I was just looking for the meatloaf pan." She couldn't take her eyes off of the ax. It seemed to call to her. She envisioned it shiny, with a fresh coat of protective paint and a well-sharpened blade. She saw Jack, in the back, maybe his shirt off, chopping wood for their fire in the backyard. Maybe Sangria in the moonlight.

"Are you coming back up? I'm kind of surprised you went down there."

Her fixation on the ax was broken by the sound of his foot on the first step. "Don't come down here, Jack. I'm on my way back up." She put the ax back down on the workbench and picked up the meatloaf pan. She made a mental note to get some steel wool to clean off the rust. Maybe a thick paint for the ax head to protect it.

Moments later she was in the kitchen, mincing onions and garlic for her famous meatloaf, but she found her thoughts drifting back to that ax, and the tender loving care it cried out for.

Out with the Old

Jack hated the feeling of spending the day in a drugged stupor. The alternative was worse. He'd feel like he had been mauled by a lion and then subjected to a violent beating with a rubber mallet. The sleep was his salvation.

When he did finally wake up, he felt better. His head felt clearer, and the throbbing had gone down. No longer overwhelmed by the immediate urge to take another pill, Jack knew he'd take one before going to bed anyway.

Elizabeth's lemonade tasted good against the warmth of the day. The cool sweetness of the lemon, punctuated by a tangy twinge at the end of the sip was exactly what he thought lemonade should taste like.

She pointed out the trees, towering over the house like giants making their way out of an ocean of green, onto dry land. He thought it funny he'd not really noticed them before. One of the limbs stretched out over the yard toward the house but lacked leaves to really provide much shade.

Looking to his right, just past where the house ended, Jack saw the tip of one of the cross beams of the burned out barn. Its charred end poked out of the pile, reaching for something or someone to hang onto, not realizing its usefulness in this world had come to an end.

Yesterday, when he looked at the remains of the barn, he saw an old tractor. It made him wonder why anyone would abandon something like that. Maybe it had outlived its usefulness too. Maybe it was like the charred piece of wood: searching for relevance in a world where it was no longer needed.

He didn't want to tell Elizabeth about the murders of the family quite yet. He'd told her there was indeed a murder here, but not that everyone was found dead. Really, he hadn't lied to her as much as he only told her what he knew for certain. At this point, he only had Mr. Gulliver's story and some vague notions from the doctor, who seemed less inclined to tell him more. Maybe tomorrow or the next day, he could get into town and hit that library up for some information. There had to be more to what Mr. Gulliver told him. He wanted cold, hard facts to tell Elizabeth instead of half-truths and speculations.

The sun had been working on its downward journey for a while. They had a few hours of sunlight left. He watched the leaves on the corn stalks wave in the slight breeze. Up on the porch, he didn't feel much of the wind, and the sweat rolled down his back and neck. Ordinarily he hated the heat, but today it had a comforting warmth. It was the perfect counterpoint to the lemonade Elizabeth had left him.

With the blaze of the sun starting to give a little and the lemonade now gone, he soon fell asleep in the chair swing. Only a catnap, but a nap his injuries had insisted he take. Carefully standing up, he moved back into the living room to investigate the suspicious quiet of the house. Elizabeth would have had more than enough time to get the meatloaf into the oven by now.

Elizabeth wasn't standing in the kitchen, but the door to the cellar stood curiously open. Maybe she fell down the stairs, he wondered with sudden panic. "Elizabeth?" he said fearfully. "Honey, are you downstairs?"

The idea of his wife voluntarily going into the cellar seemed absurd. He approached the door, listening for sounds from the basement. Calling out for her again, the result was the same. He pushed open the door to its full extent. The lights in the basement were on but it was still curiously quiet. If Elizabeth were moving around in the basement, he should hear her feet moving across the rocky surface of the floor.

He moved down a step and could just make out her shoes. She was standing in front of the workbench on the opposite wall from the stairs. The noise of him coming down the stairs and calling to her seemed to jar her from whatever thought she was presently lost in.

A few moments later, she thumped her way up the stairs. In her hands, she had the meatloaf pan. "Rita tried to hide it from me. I really must have a talk with that girl."

"You were down there for a while. I was worried the spiders had eaten you."

"I walked around a little bit, looking at the old cellar. It's not as creepy as I first thought."

He made a comical face at her. "Okay, so who are you and what did you do with my wife, you body-snatcher?"

"What?" she retorted. "I'm not saying I want to move our bedroom down there, but with some plastic tubs and some shelving, we could really make it work. It's reasonably dry, and the spiders aren't so bad."

She pushed past him and started washing the pan in the sink.

Jack stared at his wife for a few moments. As long as he knew her, she had a fear of the creepy crawling things of the world. Could Rita really have that profound of an effect on her? Unsure if he was more worried about her or impressed with her sudden ability to get over her fears, the sudden change in his wife was perplexing.

A short time later, the house was filled with the odor of garlic and onions. The meatloaf had been utterly decimated, along with two baked potatoes and the remains of some bread Rita brought over the day before. Jack sat back on the couch and let out a self-satisfying belch. "Come sit with me, honey."

"I can't, I have to do the dishes," She turned toward the door.

"What's the hurry? I'll do the dishes."

She patted him on the thigh. "You can barely stand up. No, that's alright, I'll get them later."

"Thanks babe. I really appreciate all your doting. I promise, once I'm better I'll make it up to you. By the way, I have to say that was one of the best meatloaves you've ever made. It was pretty spectacular."

"Awww, sweet. You know how to charm a girl." She sat down in the chair next to him and slipped her arm through his. "So, what time is the dumpster being delivered tomorrow?"

He had forgotten all about the dumpster with the activity of the last two days. The work would be harder to get done now that he had to take it easier.

He put a finger to his lips as he tried to remember. "It should be here around eight or so. Two grad students are coming over to help who need some money." It was common practice for professors to hire college kids to help out with odd jobs they had around the house.

126

She looked at him and said, "Jack, I don't want you overdoing it tomorrow. You need to take it easy. Doctor and Elizabeth's orders. You don't have to do anything."

He knew Elizabeth would do some running tomorrow. There were some things they needed from town. He still couldn't drive because of the medicine, but he could go with her.

Sleep found him easily that night.

Jack woke up to the sound of something crashing into the driveway. At first, he thought it sounded like another picture falling from the wall. Then he heard the revving up of a truck engine. Whatever was going on outside of the house, it was making one hell of a racket.

Getting out of bed, and walking over to the window. Outside he saw a big diesel rig dropping a dumpster in the center of their driveway. Not exactly where he wanted it, but it was close enough.

Elizabeth and Rita stood next to their new red truck with the two students Jack hired from the university. Elizabeth and Rita turned to the window and waved. He waved back, suddenly realizing his robe was open.

A few minutes later he was standing on the porch, dressed in jeans and a tee-shirt, looking at the dumpster. A formidable metal box, it was bigger than he'd imagined. Jack briefly mused about the possibility of burying such a thing and then waterproofing the inside to use it as a pool. They had lot of stuff to throw out and it was better too big than too small.

The two students came over to him. "Good morning, Dr. Milburn," one of them said.

"Good morning, gentlemen, hope you came excited to work. We got lots of stuff to get rid of and, as you can see, I am going to be out of commission for a few days," Jack said, pointing at his head. "So, what should I call you two?"

The taller of the two students said, "My name is Chester, everyone calls me Chet. And he's Taylor."

The other student nodded at Jack and said, "We're ready to get started when you are."

Jack sensed their eagerness was partly their need to make a good impression on the faculty and partly the incessant need of a broke college student for income.

Elizabeth grabbed Jack's hand hanging down at his side. "Good morning, honey. You slept like a rock. But you look a million times better."

"Thanks, I feel better. I see you have the whole gang here this morning."

"You bet, and if you hadn't gotten up, I was going to throw you in the dumpster and run away with one of these strapping guys here." Chet and Taylor both turned beet red in response.

Jack ate a quick breakfast and took a half a pain pill as instructed. Although he was not at full strength, he could move some things around. He tried to restrict himself to light loads, but when he tried to do too much, Elizabeth or Rita would yell at him to take a break and let the young guys handle things. He couldn't help but feel old, and a little useless. Even a half dose of the medicine was wearing him out.

Nearing lunch time, Jack called into town and ordered pizzas. Elizabeth volunteered to go pick them up as she had to pick up a few samples from Gullivers anyway.

Redecorating was Elizabeth's thing. Jack often half-joked that when she was done redecorating the last room, she would likely start all over again. She was always ready to pick out new colors for the walls. Rita was happily removing wallpaper, something she seemed to be a natural at. Jack took to calling her the Wallpaper Whisperer. He tried to help, but only managed to tear off little shreds.

As the morning wore on, Jack's head began to throb. The medicine, at only half strength, only dulled the pain and didn't stop it completely. Dr. Gold was worried about stomach problems if he took too much of the strong narcotic pills he'd prescribed for the worst of the pain. Jack dropped into a chair in the living room, exhaling as he did. He'd reached the end of his usefulness sooner than planned and had to wave off the chance to join Elizabeth on the run into town.

In between her time removing wallpaper, Rita tended to Jack. She didn't have to help them as much as she did, but Jack suspected it was in her nature. The more he knew of her, the more he liked her. As she continued to remove strips of old wallpaper, she told him stories about Hal. It made Jack more than curious about any man able to keep up with a woman who was so full of energy.

Jack watched the lights from his new pickup truck disappear out of the driveway and onto the main road. Pizza was on the agenda for lunch and he had to admit he was beginning to crave a thick piece of mozzarella between his teeth.

"Be right back, Jack. I need to run upstairs for a couple more sponges," Rita frowned a the sponge in her hand which accumulated more than its fair share of wallpaper paste from a bygone era.

"No, no," Jack waved to Rita. "Let me, I need to get up and move around for a little bit. Sitting around is making me stiff as a board." Jack struggled to his feet and stretched. Starting up the stairs, they let out an oddly satisfying creak with every footfall.

On the upper landing, it occurred to him how deeply quiet it was. Life in central Illinois can be strangely quiet, but this was different. As if something, or someone, was absorbing all of the noise. The supplies sat in one of the extra bedrooms.

At the end of the hallway, the closet looked firmly shut. Every time he had an occasion to walk down that hall, he'd push on the door to ensure it was latched. It made him feel foolish for harboring such fears. He was a learned man, after all, but he found solace in reasoning that even the wisest of men harbored occasional irrational fears. And fearing the unknown was not irrational at all.

Walking by the bathroom, he resolved to fill up the tub with water and take a relaxing, unnecessarily long bath. The thing looked like a swimming pool with clawed feet. It would be his reward for spending the day with an achy head and still managing to be more of a help than a burden.

After retrieving a packet of sponges from the spare bedroom containing the cleaning supplies, Jack made his way back to the landing. Just before he put his foot on the first step, he glanced to his left. The door to the closet sat open a few inches.

Only open a crack, but definitely open.

Old News Made New Again

The mass dumping of the farmhouse was a huge undertaking, Elizabeth thought as she turned the huge pickup out of the driveway. There were piles and piles of clothes to be gone through; and, if need be, disposed of. Most of them were fodder for the dumpster. Years of use, neglect, and moths ensured they were pretty well unwearable. The ones that could be saved would be given to charity.

Chet and Taylor worked their butts off. Being farmhands since they could walk, they were strong, well mannered, and didn't spend any time slacking.

The combined exhaustion from that morning's work and the buffeting air from the open windows of the truck were intoxicating as the truck sped up to highway speed. Time passed quickly and she found herself having to bring the truck down to a more reasonable speed as she entered the little town. Pulling into the small grocery store, she picked up a couple of cases of soda and a bag of ice. Attached to the grocery store was a small pizza and sandwich shop called Anthony's. Elizabeth mused that half the pizza shops in the nation were called Anthony's or some variation on that name. Either way, Anthony had a market on the pizza and sandwich business in town, by virtue of being the only one.

"Good afternoon," she said. "I have an order to pick up for Elizabeth."

"Ah, yes, Mrs. Milburn. Sorry, I would have called you, but I didn't find out until just now. There was a small problem, and I had to remake your pizzas. I'm really sorry." The older man behind the counter, wearing a ball cap, shrugged his shoulders.

"Oh no, what happened?"

"They fell off the counter." The man shot a glance at a guilty-looking boy working in the kitchen. She felt sorry for the kid. She had a feeling that he'd get a good tongue-lashing, or worse, as soon as she left the building. Whatever happened to the pizzas must have been the boy's fault.

"It's really not that big a problem. How long do you need to remake them?"

"I just put them in the oven. They should be ready for you in about fifteen or twenty minutes if you have a couple of other things to do."

There wasn't much else to do in town. She might sit in the truck and read, but then Elizabeth remembered her truncated visit to the library. Maybe she would make good on her promise to get that library card.

"Thanks. I'll run over to the library while I wait." She looked to the kitchen area and could still see the kid cowering in fear from the impending verbal abuse his boss was about to unleash on him. "Go easy on the kid, huh? No harm done really."

"Oh sure, I will." For some reason, Elizabeth really doubted he would. She shot the boy a smile and he risked returning one, breaking it off as soon as the owner glared at him.

She walked down the street and into the library. A small buzzer rang out somewhere behind the checkout counter. From behind the stacks, a serious-looking girl came to the front desk. She was a young woman, but she had one of those faces that Elizabeth suspected could look perpetually young. With long brown hair, pulled through the back of a University of Illinois ball cap, high cheek bones, and a splash of freckles across the bridge of her nose, Elizabeth imagined what a stunning figure she would make in a cocktail dress.

"Can I help you?" the girl said, making no attempt to speak with the quietness one usually associated with being in a library.

"Yes, I'd like a library card please," Elizabeth whispered to the girl, trying to maintain her supposed sanctity of the place.

"There's no reason to whisper, Mrs. Milburn. We're the only ones here. As a matter of fact, you're only the third person to come in today."

"Really? Where is everyone?"

She shrugged. "Lots of people working, but now that people can renew their books on-line or drop their books into the book return outside, you only need to come in to check the books out. And also, you can register online and just fill in the form. I can pull the books and have them waiting for you. Pretty slick."

"Remarkable," Elizabeth said. Instantly a troubling thought hit her. "How did you know my name?" A complete stranger identifying her with a single glance would certainly garner more than just suspicion in northern Virginia.

"You're kidding, right?" she scoffed. "Everyone knows who you are. You're the new family in town. Bought the Anderson farmhouse. Believe me, no one keeps that a secret for long. I knew you'd be coming in to see me, even before you did."

Elizabeth looked her over, her eyes narrowing a little. "Little young to be a librarian, aren't you?"

"Only summers and weekends. The rest of the time I'm a college student. But, truth be told, I'm pretty much here most of the time anyway. Just me and my one volunteer, my mom." She reached under the desk and pulled out an envelope. "Okay, I just need to see a photo ID."

"That explains the older woman I saw here the other day. I have my old driver's license, but it doesn't have my current address. Sorry." Elizabeth handed it over.

She smiled at Elizabeth and glanced at the out of state license. "It's okay, here's a card for you and your husband. Already filled out. Just go on-line and register."

"It's alright? You trust me?" Elizabeth said, somewhat surprised at her willingness to bend the rules.

"Well, I run the place, so I'll flog myself for not following procedure. Anyways, I drive by your place every morning so, I know where you live. And besides, this isn't exactly New York City, I think I can trust you."

"Thank you ... umm, I didn't catch your name."

"Penny, Penny the Librarian."

Elizabeth reached out her hand, which Penny shook. "What are you majoring in, Penny the Librarian?"

"Library Science."

"I should've probably guessed that." She gave her a quick eye-roll. "I'm Elizabeth, but you can call me Lizzy."

Penny smiled. "If there's anything you need, let me know. I'm usually in the back doing library things … or studying. Either way, I'm here to help. And if I'm not, my mom is here four nights a week. I think she just likes to hang out with me."

"Great, I'm just going to look at the old newspaper clippings about the house. I started looking at them last time I was here, but I had to leave."

She motioned to the back, "Have at it. If you need to check anything out, let me know. We still don't have an automated kiosk for that, but I'm working on it."

Elizabeth made her way back to the three computers containing the newspaper data. She clicked on the icon to bring up the newspaper holdings which had been scanned into the system. After a few clicks, she found herself faced with the same listing of newspaper articles outlining the history of the Anderson farm she had seen before.

She learned that the Anderson family owned the farm for generations. One article from the early 60s talked about the fourth generation working the farm. On the front page was a yellowed photo of the house. It pretty much looked like it did when she and Jack moved in.

Another article talked about how the house was being featured in a real estate magazine for being a traditional U.S. farm home. The feature had a set of photos showing the house and the barn.

"Hey, Penny?"

"Yep?" Penny yelled from a few stacks over, where she was shelving books.

"Can I print from here?"

"Yep, you can print here or send anything to your smart phone as a pdf."

Elizabeth thought about how much the world had changed so much from the first time she went to her elementary school library. She found an icon of the program which said, 'E-mail PDF'. She hit it and was immediately prompted to enter her e-mail address. Moments later, her cellphone beeped as she received the e-mailed file.

"Wow, magic," she said, impressed.

Penny, obviously still nearby, said, "Yeah, that's magic alright. This place wasn't always so high tech, you should see what the county library board said when they were trying to decide to buy their first copier. You'd thought they were introducing witchcraft or something. The librarian at the time, who'd been here for like fifty years, actually retired over the scandal. Now we don't even have to make copies, we just send the electrons to the phones."

"Handy," Elizabeth said. She continued scrolling through the listing.

Several other articles talked about various children being raised at the house and how extended members of the family were visiting the home.

The things they publish in small town newspapers is fascinating. Even repainting the mailbox was apparently newsworthy.

She jumped as her phone rang. "Hello?" she asked.

"Mrs. Milburn, your pizzas are ready," came the pizzeria owner's voice.

"Okay, thanks." She felt like she needed to ask about the welfare of the cook, but thought better of it. "I'll be there in a few minutes. Let me just finish up here."

"Sure thing. Don't wait too long, though, or they'll get cold." Staring at the selection of documents on the screen, they all seemed to be pretty normal stuff. Articles about the 4-H ribbons won by the boys and other accolades. She knew she had to get going, but there was one article from May 8th. The title of the newspaper article was obscured. It read simply, "Nightmare Scene at the Anderson Farm".

Elizabeth tried to hit the send key on the screen, but nothing seemed to happen.

Oh well, I'll have to come back to read it I guess.

Standing up to leave, she grabbed her purse and phone from the table. Leaning over the desk she yelled toward the office, "Have a great rest of your day, Penny. See you next time."

"Lizzy wait, you're forgetting your print." Penny came out from the side with a piece of paper. "Ordinarily, I'd charge you forty cents, but your first is on me."

Elizabeth stopped short of the door to the street. "Oh, I didn't even know I printed it. That explains why it didn't go to my phone. Are you sure about the forty cents?"

"You're kidding, right?" Penny had a huge grin on her face. "This is actually the longest conversation I've had with any living human being this week. I'm thrilled to do it. Granted, I like the solitude of working alone, but sometimes it's kind of nice to talk to another human."

"Thanks, Penny." She grabbed the paper and shoved it into her purse.

Walking across the street, she felt the Midwest heat beat down on her. True to his word, the guy from Anthony's met her at the door with her pizzas. "Here you go Elizabeth."

"Thanks, what do I owe you?"

He squinted at the slip of the paper taped to the box. "Let's make it fifteen even."

"Really?" Elizabeth stared at the man in disbelief. "Seems pretty cheap for five pizzas."

"Well, you had to wait."

"Really, I didn't mind. I went to the library and met the librarian."

He laughed. "Oh, that's my Penny."

"You're daughter?" Elizabeth asked, handing him a twenty.

"Nope, my niece. She's a good kid."

She climbed into the truck, shoving the pizzas toward the passenger seat. "Keep the change, Anthony."

He looked puzzled. "Why do you think my name is Anthony?"

"It's on the sign, I just figured."

"Oh no, Anthony was my pop," he said. "He's making pizzas for Jesus now. We tried to get him to take care of himself, but he liked the pizza business a little too much, if you catch my meaning," he said, patting his belly. "My name's Red. The kid is my boy, he's Anthony. And don't worry, I went easy on him. He's a good kid. Not real bright, but makes a pretty good pizza."

"Thanks, Red. Tell Anthony I said thank you as well."

She pulled the truck back out into the street and turned the radio up. Being away from the house made her feel lighter. Maybe it was the dark dampness of the place which seemed to hang on it like a wet blanket. The sooner she could slap some paint on the walls, the sooner she could combat the dreariness.

Pulling into the driveway, she saw the work crew drinking lemonade and sitting on the porch. As she got out of the truck she said, "So, what's all this? I leave for a an hour, and y'all decided it's break time?"

Chet and Taylor shot a terrified look at Jack. Elizabeth was doing her best to look serious. "I'm just kidding, guys. Sheesh. Have some pizza."

Chet and Taylor tried to hide the fact that they were just terrified of a woman who was roughly half their size. They tried to recapture a little of their coolness, as they tore into the pizzas.

Jack, slumped in a chair, looked like he'd had it. "Are you okay, honey?" Elizabeth asked.

He sighed. "Oh yeah, just beat is all." Brightening slightly, he added, "Rita tried to put me to work the second you left."

She gave him a kiss. "Yes, that Rita, what ever will we do with her? Tonight we can draw you a bath and you can relax a little. Say, I stopped by the library while I waited for the pizzas."

"Funny you mentioned the bath, I was thinking the same thing. You stopped by the library?"

She showed him the cards Penny had given him. "Yes, the librarian, Penny, gave me our library cards. Apparently, everyone knew we would be coming to town and got our papers in order for us. I'm kind of surprised Rita didn't have her buddy at the DMV make us new drivers licenses." She smiled at Rita, who was negotiating a piece of mozzarella which swung precariously from the tip of her slice.

She laughed at Elizabeth's comment. "I would have, but I didn't have any recent photos."

By late afternoon, four of the five pizzas had been eaten and the work crew had dispersed for the evening. They would return in the morning to help finish up.

Neither Jack or Elizabeth were particularly hungry for dinner so they just snacked on a couple of things from the kitchen. She took off everything but her tee-shirt and filled the bathtub with water. She wanted it warm enough for a good soak, but not hot. She was worried about Jack's head wound. But the swelling had gone down and now he only had a nasty patch on his head where the doctor had to shave the hair to close the laceration.

Jack came in behind her. He had taken off all of his clothes. "Hey there, sex kitten."

"Down boy, you need to take it easy for a few days. But, don't worry, I'm like your trusty rubber ducky, I make bath time lots of fun."

He put his arms around her and gave her a kiss. "Oh, I love it when you talk dirty. Get it … bath time … dirty?"

"Yeah, Jay Leno, I get it. Someone got a new bad joke book, didn't they?"

He turned on the shower and climbed inside. "I'm going to jump in for a second and rinse off the day."

She did the same following his exit from the shower, then joined him in the tub. For a while, they just laid there in the bath, hot water playing over their skin as the cares of the day regressed. She felt the rise and fall of his chest. He wrapped his legs around her, and it made her instantly feel safe. He always had that effect on her. A single touch was all it took to make the world seem safer. Tomorrow would be more work, but for now, the combination of Jack and the warm water chased her cares away.

Things that go Bump in the Night

Jack had to admit, even with his injuries a limiting factor, they put in a good day's work. From the porch, he saw over the edge of the dumpster and could just barely see the top of the junk pile.

With a good portion of the extra stuff out of the house it felt like it doubled in size. Rita made a couple of runs to the storage facility, and what didn't make the cut went into the dumpster. The weekend would soon be here, and so would the moving truck. As poor as he'd felt, it would be good if they could delay things for a day or two, but the moving truck needed to be unloaded and kept on schedule.

As tired as Jack was, sleep seemed to evade him. Elizabeth, suffering from the opposite problem, fell into a steady rhythm of light snoring.

In the darkness of their room, thoughts of children occupied his mind. Rita had a point, it really was a great house for children. Plenty of space inside, a huge yard on a not so busy street, and even that awesome tree for a tire swing.

He could almost hear the pitter-patter of little feet somewhere in the house. For a moment he was tempted to yell out, "Get back to bed," to his non-existent children. He sat up in bed as he realized he wasn't hearing the sounds in his dream. They were coming from inside the house. Someone was inside.

He whispered, "Lizzy, wake up." Not getting any reaction out of her, he whispered again, "Come on, Lizzy, wake up."

"But I'm not done with the shopping yet, and the cartoon

characters aren't here …" She murmured from somewhere in her dreams. He wished she wasn't such a sound sleeper.

He listened again, and the footsteps sounded like they were right outside the door. He got up from the bed. On the dresser was the old revolver Elizabeth had found earlier. It wasn't loaded, but he grabbed it anyway. It looked mean enough to scare someone away. At least he hoped it was.

Jack reached for the knob, but hesitated, debating the wisdom of just throwing the door open and trying to scare the person out in the hallway. Thinking better about it, a quieter approach made more sense. As he cautiously pulled the knob toward him, he peered out into the empty hallway. In the moonlight, the door to one of the spare bedrooms moved.

Did someone go in there?

Jack stepped into the hallway, creeping along the carpeted runner toward the bedroom door. There had to be a reason it moved. Maybe a window had blown open, but that wouldn't explain the footsteps. His hand tightened on the pistol as he took each careful step. Somewhere, in the back of his mind, he realized that it was probably more useful as a club than a revolver, but that thought didn't translate into any specific action.

The bedrooms didn't lead anywhere, and the fall from the window would land a burglar in the hospital. If someone was in there, they were trapped. He reached up and put his hand against the wood door frame. This time, he would just throw it open and switch the light on. In his mind, he saw himself doing all of this much faster and with far greater skill than he knew he could pull off, but it was worth trying.

Pushing open the door, he reached to turn on the lights. In his haste, he forgot that there was an old bed behind the door. The door bounced back and hit his shoulder. It didn't hurt, but in the dark, it startled him. Dropping the revolver, he bent over to grab it while still trying to turn on the lights. He head-butted the door, sending it, once again, bouncing against the bed. He finally switched the lights on, thankful Elizabeth was nowhere near him to see the cartoonish antics.

His eyes adjusted quickly to the blinding light and the sudden embarrassment of an empty room.

The window was open with the single nylon shade dancing around in the light breeze. Picking up the revolver, he shoved it in the pocket of his robe. Glancing out the window, he saw the corn stalks waving in the light breeze. Standing their nightly vigil, but nothing else.

Just his imagination playing tricks on him, maybe that and a combination of the window being open. He turned and looked out the door of the room, toward the hallway. A black shape soundlessly and smoothly raced past.

"Crap," Jack yelled and instinctively grasped for the gun.

Thinking better of it, he picked up a baseball bat laying on the floor where undoubtedly one of the Anderson kids had left it years before. Slinging it over his shoulder like a club, Jack ran out the doorway just in time to see the shadowy form race noiselessly down the stairs. Following as quickly as he could, the form proved far faster and more agile.

It tore through the kitchen and into the stairwell leading to the cellar. Jack reached the top of the cellar stairs, pausing momentarily to check his resolve. He knew the outer doors to the cellar were held closed from the other side by a large brick, to keep them from flapping in the wind. If anyone tried to open those doors, they would make one hell of a racket in the process.

He put his hand around the corner, and into the stairwell, feeling for the switch. As the lights of the cellar snapped on, he listened for a moment and didn't hear anything.

"I know you're down there. I have a …," he was about to say 'bat', but instead continued, "… a gun. I don't want to hurt anyone, but you're in my house and I need you to leave. So how about we make this easy? You can push the outer doors open. I'll hear it when you leave. What do you say?"

He gave whatever it was a brief pause to decide. "Alright, then I'm coming down for you." Descending the stairs, he kept the baseball bat at the ready. Sweat poured down his back. Jack was a college professor, not a gladiator. In a fight, he could probably hold his own, but he knew if he came up against a skilled assailant, he would likely be on the losing end of the confrontation.

Stepping on the gravel at the bottom of the stairs, his foot gave a reassuring crunch on the river rock. He remembered reading somewhere he was supposed to pick one side and search in that direction. However, the cellar wasn't a big place. There were a lot of shadows someone could hide in and the lighting configuration wasn't the best.

Taking a step forward, he thought he heard the sound of something immediately behind him, he turned to face it.

Nothing. Only the stairs he just descended.

With a noise sounding like someone was torturing a wild animal, the outer doors of the cellar made a deafening hiss. Jack knew, instinctively, it was the sound of a cinder block being moved off of the aluminum door.

But how could that be? Did the thing get past him, only to try and get back in?

The door burst open, sending them crashing against the ground. Outside, a storm raged, lightning flashed, and the wind blew so hard he was sure he saw pieces of the house and corn stalks flying through the air.

Under the terrifying commotion of the storm raging outside, a voice growled at him. It grew in intensity, laughing. Each shrill interlude grew louder until it even drowned out the howling wind and the thunderclaps. Staring into the raging storm, a figure formed out of the growing maelstrom. The bursts of lightning silhouetted the figure against the sky. In its hand, it held an ax.

The form was female, he could tell by the voice and her body. He knew that form well. That laugh, although somewhat demonic and cold, belonged to Elizabeth.

Hefting the ax over her head, she glared down at him. This was an enraged version of his wife, something he'd never seen before. With every step down the stairs, Elizabeth's eyes glowed with a seething hatred. Her hands, which Jack could see as soon as she stepped into the light, were taught and white as she squeezed the wooden handle.

"Elizabeth, what the hell are you doing?" Jack backed away from the stairs.

Not seeming to be in any particular hurry, Elizabeth refused to even acknowledge him. Her face was locked in an evil grin, eyes drilling into Jack's soul.

Fearing for his life, Jack turned to run. In his haste, he ran into the wall on the side of the stairs. For a brief moment he could have swore Elizabeth made a lurch toward him. And then, everything went black.

The Real Housewives

Elizabeth was not sure how or when she fell asleep, or even if she really did at all. The world slipped away into a haze, only to be replaced by the front yard. A wind buffeted her from an unknown corner of the property, off to an unknown destination. The sky darkened behind the house in testimony to an impending storm. It filled her with a sense of dread, but also a sense of excitement. There was a feeling of anticipation, like something significant was about to happen.

Looking up toward the house, she saw images of people standing in the windows. They flickered momentarily and then were gone. Only lingering long enough for Elizabeth to make them out before they changed. The upper left window, where their bedroom was, featured an image of a tall boy. He was there for a moment in overalls, the next moment in jeans and tee-shirt, the next in pajamas.

To the right side of the house, in the upper story window, there was another boy. He was younger than the first. Wearing pajamas one moment, then a suit that looked like it could be for confirmation, finally a bathing suit with a towel over his shoulder.

In the open front door stood a woman. Her image flashed from dress to dress. Elizabeth could tell some were for working around the house, one was for church, and then she wore the red dress Elizabeth found in the closet. Behind her, lightning flashed through the open window, giving momentary light to the scene. The images changed again, but this time, all three were skeletons. They paused long enough for her to see their skulls staring at her with their piercing dark

151

recesses. Then they flashed back to the images she'd seen before.

A voice rang out from behind her. "Do you know what it's like to lose something so dear to you that you want nothing more than to get it back?"

Elizabeth found herself unsurprised by the sudden voice. Some part of her expected it, even anticipated it. It was far less disconcerting than the images of the three people flashing in front of her.

"Why am I seeing this?" Suddenly feeling scared she added, "I want my husband. Where's Jack?"

The woman said matter-of-factly, "He isn't here now. It's just you and me. The real housewives that make it all happen. Men don't appreciate the role we play."

A lightning bolt jumped from the cloud and disappeared into the cornfield. The sudden noise made Elizabeth shiver. She couldn't take her eyes off the flashing images in the two windows and the door. They reminded her of a fun-house she got lost in when she was ten. Panels would swing out to scare you as you walked along a pre-determined path, marked by lights. But these weren't panels, and her path was anything but clear.

"You don't need your husband. He'll betray you. They always do."

Elizabeth finally pried her eyes from the house and looked toward the source of the voice. It belonged to a woman who Elizabeth guessed to be in her forties. She had beautiful, slightly graying auburn hair, thin but not anorexic, and slightly shorter than Elizabeth. She wore a simple white cotton sun dress.

Elizabeth glared at her. "You don't know Jack; he'll never betray me."

She looked back at the house, but the flashing images of the people were gone, replaced with poster length photographs put up in the windows. They were of the same two boys and the woman, but this time they were covered in blood. All of their mouths were agape in a silent scream, and their eyes looked out toward the cornfields in a vacant stare.

This was all too much for Elizabeth. She put her hands up to cover her eyes from the horrifying images.

"Elizabeth, it's okay. No one is going to hurt you here. I want to show you something. You are very ... very important to us."

Elizabeth asked, "Us?"

"Yes, us."

The woman grabbed Elizabeth by the arm and led her across the grass toward the house. The images in the window were gone. She wanted to stop and look for Jack. Her instincts told her she should do everything to resist this woman who filled her with terror. It was like being in the presence of someone you knew would want nothing more than to kill you.

Elizabeth recognized the interior, but all of the old furniture they had removed was back. In the dining room, the two boys sat at the table, eating cereal. Elizabeth stared at them for a moment before the other woman broke the silence.

"Jack wants to kill them, you know."

"I'm sorry, what did you just say?" Elizabeth asked.

"Jack, wants to kill my boys. Don't act so surprised, you know they all do. All husbands do. They can't really help it."

The two boys seemed ambivalent to the women standing there. They were transfixed on the cereal box. It said something about a prize or toy. The woman handed something to Elizabeth, and she took it reflexively without looking at it.

The woman said to Elizabeth, "Here, try it out for yourself."

It was heavy in her hands. Just based on the feel of the object, she knew what it was. She glanced down to the ax. The head was dripping with blood. Each drop spattered to the floor.

Drip ... Drip ... Drip ...

"I can't kill anyone. I'm just not capable of that."

"You will, or they'll kill you. You know it's true. All men want to kill their wives. It happened to me, it'll happen to you. But the kids, there's no need for the kids to die. They're innocent. I need you to save them, Elizabeth. If you don't, no one ever will."

Elizabeth ran her hand over the handle of the ax. The wood was smooth and had been cared for. It felt reassuring to her. She shuddered at the thought of anyone killing another human being with something like this. An instrument made for splitting wood could do unspeakable damage to a human body. It was so very wrong. But at the same time, she felt compelled to swing the tool over her head. To feel its full weight and power slam down on something. The blood, the warm blood everywhere would be her reward. She needed to feel the swing.

Elizabeth raised it above her head.

The woman, standing next to her, looked on approvingly. "You need to learn this lesson Lizzy."

She felt slightly off balance as she held the ax head directly over her. Her hands gripping the wood so tight she could feel her fingers burning with tension. Her arms, while not strong, felt suddenly empowered by the massive piece of carbon-steel above her head. Elizabeth was in control of life and death; she could easily end their lives by the simple downward force. It wouldn't take much; the momentum would do the rest.

Elizabeth swung the ax down with terrifying effect.

Elizabeth woke up with a moan. She found herself hitting the comforter with her hands, completing the swing of the ax. She sat up straight in bed, looking around the room. It was morning. Just another nightmare.

"Holy crap," she said to no one.

She half expected to see Jack enter the room, but he didn't. His side of the bed was already cool to the touch. He must already be awake. Outside, the sunshine was creeping up on the back side of the house.

Downstairs, she heard some rustling of dishes and some things being moved.

Didn't anyone hear me scream? Why didn't Jack come to check on me?

She got up from the bed, put her pajamas on, and made her way downstairs. She saw Chet and Taylor working in the living room. No one seemed to have noticed.

Had she screamed? Was it in her head?

"Good morning Mrs. Milburn," one of them said.

"Good morning, guys." A sudden image flashed in her head of both of them laying in a pool of blood with an ax stuck in their chests, their dead eyes transfixed on her. The image hit her hard, and she felt light headed. Elizabeth had to sit down on the stairs.

"Are you alright, Mrs. Milburn?"

"Yeah, fine. I just didn't sleep well last night. Maybe I got up a little too quick this morning. No worries."

A man walked in through the kitchen door carrying a large canvas bag. He looked like he was about fifty and badly needed a shave.

"Oh, good morning," he said.

Elizabeth, shocked by the sight of the stranger, said, "Who are you?"

"Names Fred, from Globocast."

She was suddenly self-conscious about being in front of the men in her pajamas. "Okay, just wait one second. I'll be right back." She turned from the trio and ran upstairs to put her work clothes on. Rejoining the men in the living room she stammered, "Okay, let's try this again. Who are you?"

He chuckled at her odd demeanor. "Fred, from Globocast."

She still looked at him with a gaping mouth and confused eyes.

He offered her his hand. "Internet ma'am, I'm doing your install today."

"Oh, you're the internet guy! I'm sorry I just expected … you know."

He pointed to the students, who were no longer working and just watching the odd exchange. "You were expecting someone like them, huh?"

"Well, kind of. Yeah."

Fred smiled at her. "No worries, I've been in communications for years. Started out installing phones for Illinois Bell Telephone back in the day, so you can bet I am more than qualified. By the way, I'm just about done. I need to run another cable outside the house, and then you'll be in business. Pretty easy these days. Wireless and all."

Elizabeth smiled back at him. "And I can finally get caught up on my television watching?"

"These little farm houses don't look like it, but we can get some good internet service out here. I'll get back to work. I got about six installs today, and it'll be hot as a beast out there so I don't want to waste too much time."

"Excellent, it'll be nice to have the internet up and running."

She worried silently about Jack's whereabouts. He wouldn't have gone off without telling her. The truck was gone and it seemed likely he'd taken it into town.

She glanced out the window and watched the two students sorting tools on the front lawn. They took careful inventory of what should be kept and what tools were rusted beyond the point of usefulness. Maybe there were a few things worth keeping.

The internet guy cleared his throat from behind her. "Good morning again, ma'am. I just need to know where you want the box?"

Elizabeth was dumbfounded. "The box?"

"Yes ma'am, the box. You know, for the router."

"I really don't know, my husband Jack handles those kinds of techie things. What do you think?"

He pointed to the bookshelf behind her. "Probably the best place for now. Your husband can move it later if he wants. Not that hard to do."

She shrugged her shoulders. "As long as I can watch my shows, I'm good."

"After I leave, you should be able to watch all the television you want," he said, handing her a card.

"What's this?"

"The card with all the log-in information. Naturally, you can change the pin number after I'm gone."

Elizabeth chuckled. "That's why I have a husband. He's here for killing spiders, opening jars, and making sure the Internet is working."

He smiled. "Back in my day it was making babies and chopping wood."

Fred returned his tools to his kit. There was a deep chill that came over her as he zippered up the bag. She felt silly, but she didn't want him to go. It was like he was going to be her last link to sanity in the strange house. Once he was gone, it would be only her. She looked out the window, hoping beyond all hope that she would see the return of the shiny red truck and its occupant. Maybe it would be just a few more minutes.

Fred picked up his bag and started toward the door. "If you have any issues, ma'am, you have my card. Just call me. Charges for service calls are listed on the back of the receipt."

"Would you like some coffee before you leave?" she said, hoping he would linger a little longer.

"No thanks ma'am, got a bunch of calls today. Lots of people wanting to watch *The Real Housewives*," he said, laughing.

The screen door slammed shut with a cold wooden thud. Alone in the house, the only visible movements were that of Chet and Taylor in the yard. Out of the corner of her eye, she could swear they were not the grad students, but the two boys from her dream.

She shook her head at the images. Hopefully, when their stuff arrived, her sleeping patterns would return to normal and the crazy dreams would stop. Turning toward the kitchen, she vaguely heard the sound of the coffee pot chirping, telling her it was about to shut off. It also reminded her that she still hadn't eaten breakfast.

The coffee came out of the pot with a satisfying gurgle as it filled the cup. Maybe that was all she needed, some coffee and a bowl of cereal. The table, the same table the boys were sitting at in her dream, filled the center of the dining room. It was big, too big for the room, and it would be nice when they had a chance to get it out of the house. She thought Rita said the buyers would be by tomorrow to pick it up.

The temperatures were supposed to soar above ninety degrees that day and it already looked stifling outside. Even with the heat, the house felt cold and cavernous. The cup of coffee was reassuringly warm. Maybe she would sit outside and watch the students work. They had done a great job. When Jack told her he had hired students to help out, she imagined children instead of fully grown people. It was funny how the fact that they were students made her think of them as kids rather than adults. Almost as if being married automatically made unmarried people younger than them.

As she reached for the front door handle to go outside, she heard something upstairs. It sounded like water sloshing around in the bathroom.

Odd, no one besides me is inside the house right now.

She released the door handle and turned toward the stairs, listening intently to the house. Outside of the distant hum of the refrigerator and the guys throwing old tools into the dumpster, there was nothing. Just as Elizabeth became convinced she was just hearing things, another sloshing noise came along with a person laughing. It was a faint laugh, but unmistakable.

Her fear froze Elizabeth in place. There was someone else in the house with her. How could that be? It wasn't that long ago that she left her room. The guys hadn't come back in, and she was sure Fred the internet guy left as soon as he was done. The truck was still gone, so there was no way it could possibly be Jack. There was no logical explanation, unless someone had snuck into the house through a door or a window.

She was a runner, not a fighter. In a physical confrontation, there was no way she could match a man's strength. Her normal common sense was somehow being overruled.

At the very least, I should bring in the guys and have them come up the stairs with me. But would I be willing to risk the lives of others? This is my house, damn it!

Elizabeth surprised herself when her foot touched the top of the first stair. She didn't even remember leaving the door and walking toward the staircase. Her foot hit the next stair, ascending each riser in a slow but consistent pace.

Above her, the sloshing noise continued. She could swear she heard a man talking. It sounded familiar, but then again, completely unfamiliar at the same time.

Slosh ... slosh ... slosh ...

"Oh yeah baby, that's it. Bleed for me ... bleed for me!"

Another voice, this time from inside Elizabeth's mind spoke up. *I tried to warn you, I really did. You wouldn't listen. You stupid bitch.*

She felt like she was watching an old black-and-white movie where the audience pleads with the woman on the screen to stop walking toward the door they know the villain is hiding behind. Although the steady march toward a closed door which could harbor and intruder felt illogical, her feet didn't seem to mind. Running outside and getting help made the most sense. Logic and sense were no longer taking an active role in her decisions.

"Oh yeah, baby, this is better. You like it this way. Yeah, you do, I saw the way you begged for this." Whomever was speaking was panting heavily now. If Elizabeth didn't know any better, she would have sworn she was listening to the male side of a porno being shot in her bathroom.

All men cheat, dear, all men lie. They all want the same thing. To see you bleed.

The water sounded like it was sloshing over the side of the bathtub and onto the floor. The male grunts and groans were amplified by the cavernous tile bathroom.

It startled her when her foot touched the top stair. To her left was their bedroom. She shot a glance toward their closet, expecting to see someone standing there watching her, but the room was as empty as she left it. Then she looked down the hallway toward the bathroom. The man was still making groaning noises. Now that she was up close, she heard the unmistakable sound of gurgling.

Three steps and she would be at the door. She resolved to throw it open and see what was going on inside. If someone was using their house for a sexual escapade, it had to end right now. She could not abide by uninvited guests.

This is madness, she thought.

Her instincts screamed at her to run. Her common sense told her to get as far away from that bathroom as possible. But still, she couldn't. There was an attraction to the bathroom door handle she just couldn't overcome.

On the floor, soaking into the carpeting, water leached into the hallway, presumably from the tub. It was stained red, giving it the color of a rosé wine.

The cold of the door handle stood in sharp contrast to the sudden warmth of the air on the second floor of the house. She could feel its metallic form in her hand as it turned.

Tools of the Trade

Jack crawled through a semi state of consciousness. His head, feeling like a concrete block, rested on a cold and sharp bed of river rock.

Had Elizabeth done him in? Was this the final taste of consciousness before he passed into whatever his version of the afterlife was?

No, that made no sense at all. Elizabeth would never hurt me.

Moving his hand toward his face, he picked a piece of rock out of his skin where it had implanted itself. Blood, most likely from his wounds, covered one of his eyes, making them hard to open. Gradually, with every muscle in his body screaming for mercy, Jack sat up and looked around the room.

The door to the outside, which previously had been opened, sat closed. The lights to the basement were on, as he had left them. Was it possible this was all nothing more than him hallucinating because of those damn drugs? Was it possible the drugs had taken an hallucinogenic turn for the worst?

Still, how did he end up on the basement floor?

Standing, he remembered what happened, or what he thought happened.

What did he really see though? It was ridiculous to think of the love of his life trying to kill him in the basement of their home. It had to be the medication, there was no doubt in his mind. And still, some.

Jack stood up and grabbed the wall for support. Surprisingly, spending a good portion of the night laying on the damp, cold, rock strewn floor really didn't leave him any worse for the wear. Maybe a little stiff, but other than that he felt just fine.

Stepping into the kitchen, he snapped off the lights of the cellar and closed the door behind him. Jacks' brain swam in a torrent of thoughts and ideas about the night before. Every idea left him with the idea that it was nothing more than an odd side effect of the weirdest dream he'd ever had, combined with sleepwalking. Something he was never prone to, but still wasn't out of the realm of possibility given the heavy and continual dose of pain medicine. And still, doubts lingered.

The clock on the wall read 6:00. Far too early to wake Elizabeth up and far too late for him to go back to sleep.

Stepping gingerly up the stairs, he pushed open the door to the bathroom and took a look in the mirror. The wound on his head hadn't been bleeding at all, but a small abrasion above Jack's eye did the lion share of the bleeding. Washing his face off in the sink, he stared down at the wisps of reddish color the blood made in the water.

Thinking back to the story of the farmer killing his family, Jack thought about what it must have been like for a man who would do such a thing.

Certainly a terrible tragedy, but how close was anyone to possibly slipping a proverbial nut and doing the unthinkable?

After cleaning up a bit, Jack slipped into their bedroom and grabbed a pair of pants and tee-shirt off the floor. Sneaking out of the room and back downstairs, Jack wanted to find out how much fun it would be to finally drive his pick-up truck.

With the exception of a slight headache, he felt really good. A couple of aspirin, and the pain began to subside. He wondered if it was truly more of a psychosomatic affect or was it really the work of the drugs.

He left Elizabeth sleeping restlessly in bed. He knew, from previous experience, that waking up his sleeping wife in the morning was akin to taking his own life into his hands. As he left the bedroom, she murmured something and turned away.

Downstairs, he made a pot of coffee and then poured a to-go cup. Grabbing his keys, he climbed into the cab of his new truck. As he did, the two grad students pulled into the driveway.

"Good morning, Dr. Milburn," said Chet, climbing out of the car.

He waved to them. "Morning, guys."

"Are you going somewhere, Dr. Milburn?" Taylor asked.

He smiled unconsciously, this was the first time he got to drive his truck. "Yep, heading over to the university for a bit."

Chet pulled a pair of work gloves out of his back pocket. "Where should we start?"

"Elizabeth's still sleeping, so stay away from the second floor if you value your lives. She hates to be woken up early. Why don't you start in the cellar? I want all of the tools brought out. Let's do up an inventory and figure out what goes and what stays. I should be back in two hours."

"Okay Dr. Milburn, see you later." The students started toward the cellar door on the side of the house.

He shouted to them as he started the truck's engine. "Oh yeah, and if the internet guy shows up before Mrs. Milburn wakes up, let him in and have him do his thing."

With the freshness of the air along the county road, the coffee, and the aspirin, Jack started feeling like his old self again. Switching on the radio, a tune originally recorded in the thirties belted out from the speakers. The song seemed to whisk away any lingering concerns over what had happened at the house. Perhaps it would be better to let this little incident just slip from memory. Elizabeth had enough on her mind and really there was no harm done.

He thought again about the repairs to the house. Today was supposed to be stifling. At one point, the house had a central air conditioner, but it had long since stopped working. *Perhaps it should go on my short list of things to have repaired?* Bonny, the department secretary, told him that the August temperatures could be deadly around here. Without air-conditioning, they would likely melt.

The university was only about a twenty-minute drive from the house and his need for fresh air and a nice drive gave him the perfect excuse to go to his office for a while. He wanted to check in, get his messages, and turn in some forms. While he was there, he shelved some of his books and tried to rearrange his office. Even that little exertion took its toll on him. Sooner than he wanted to, Jack left to head back home.

Back on the road, he had planned to stop by Gullivers and pick up a new paintbrush. As he drove through town, he saw the CLOSED sign in the window of the library being flipped to OPEN. He remembered he needed a book on basic wiring.

Entering the library, Jack heard a distant buzz somewhere from behind the front desk. From the back room, someone yelled, "I'll be right out."

An attractive young woman came from out of the office. "Can I help you?"

Jack was looking out into the rows of books in front of him. "Yes, I need to check your stacks for something."

"Well, I never! I'm not that kind of girl."

Jack's face turned red. "What? I didn't mean what you think I—"

The young woman laughed at Jack's reaction. "Chillax, Dr. Milburn. I'm just yanking your proverbial chain." She extended her hand. "Penny the Librarian. I met Elizabeth the other day and, seeing how you are the only new man in town, I just guessed you were Dr. Milburn."

He felt like an idiot. He'd forgotten they were no longer in the tight-as-a-drum academic world of New England. He'd have to get used to the more relaxed world of the Midwest.

"Well, it's nice to meet you Penny."

"Likewise. You and Elizabeth are the first new people to move to town since the fifties; and I do mean the eighteen-fifties. You guys moving here made the papers, and I'm not kidding. The sale of the Anderson farmhouse was literally front page news."

"Wow, slow news day in our little town here. Seems fitting for this place."

"Oh, you have no idea. Literally we had no mayor for two years because no one was eligible in town. Everyone interested in serving had already done two terms and rules say they can't serve more than that." Penny made a sweeping gesture around the building. "So, this is the library. I'm the librarian. And yes, I'm not some old doddering woman with white hair. This place gets pretty busy when school's in session. My Mom runs the joint when I'm in class, but I'm here most other times. It's kind of my home."

"Wow, interesting to find someone your age who is willing to do this."

Penny's demeanor changed, and she took on a more professional tone. "Dr. Milburn, Library Sciences has changed a lot since you were a kid. Being a librarian has only gotten more complex over the years. You not only have to be good at research, but you have to be your own IT department, and in some cases a master grant writer. There's a lot involved in keeping an operation running like this."

He smiled at her. "Wow, you're very impressive."

"Thank you very much. This place is about the only thing I take seriously. By the way, you're going to have to get used to my rapier-like wit. You'll be hearing a lot more of it."

"Oh really," Jack said. "Why's that?"

"Starting in September, I'll be in your Tuesday and Thursday classes. I'd better get a good grade, or all of your library books will have late fees!"

He rolled his eyes at her. "Rapier-like wit?"

"Always."

As she gave Jack the grand tour, he couldn't help but wonder if she was really an old woman living in a college student's body. Penny's commitment to the books was laudable in a world that didn't seem to understand their value.

"Oh, can you bring something to Elizabeth for me?" Penny said.

"Sure, what is it?"

"She printed something the other day. I gave her the first page, but the second page got caught in the buffer and when I turned on the printer this morning it came out."

She reached over the desk and produced a piece of paper with a sticky note indicating it was for Elizabeth.

It was part of an old newspaper article.

…although no suicide note was found, the police have noted that Donald Anderson may have murdered his two sons and wife before killing himself. The police are still searching the scene. The next of kin, Charlie Anderson, Mr. Anderson's brother, has been notified. Although multiple attempts were made, the family is unavailable for comment.

The ax used in the murders was …

Jack felt sick to his stomach. He purposely hadn't told Elizabeth about the murders because she could be a little squeamish about these kinds of things. Judging by the final page of the print-out, she probably knows the whole story by now. She'd be pissed.

"Do you know what she was looking for when she found this?" Jack hoped the other part of the article didn't print clearly. Either way, he had to get home sooner rather than later before this all blew up in his face. However, if she did have the full article, it could answer some of the particulars of what exactly happened in the house.

"Yeah, she was looking for information on the Anderson place. She wondered about the history."

"Okay, thanks. By the way, any books on basic wiring?"

She rolled her eyes. "Oh, come-on, give me something hard to do! Too easy." She pointed to a small shelf of materials under a placard labeled "Do-It-Yourself" and had an amusing picture of a cartoon character hitting his thumb with a hammer.

He quickly picked out a book labeled *Wiring for Dummies* and had Penny check him out.

"Thanks, Penny!"

"You're most welcome, Dr. Milburn."

"Please, call me Jack. Dr. Milburn makes me think I should be a character in an old western."

"Jack and Elizabeth, you guys are totes adorbs." She handed him the book and a cloth book bag with the library's name on it. "We got these from some endowment, so I give them out. You can have more if you want."

He hugged it in an exaggerated gesture. "Thanks, Penny the librarian. I'll treasure it always. I think one is enough for now."

Walking back to the truck, Jack thought it best to put off the stop at Gullivers. He needed to go home and make sure his wife wasn't ready to kill him.

Pulling into the driveway he found the students looking over an impressive assortment of tools and things from the cellar. The sheer magnitude of the tools Chet and Taylor had pulled out of the house was staggering.

He shook his head at the piles. "That all came from the cellar?"

"Yep, sure did, Dr. Milburn," Taylor said. "There were a few cubby holes filled with tools, spiders, and a few mouse nests. We cleaned those out too. There are three piles. Stuff to throw out, stuff you could sell or give away if you want to, and then stuff you should keep. You know hammers, saws, screwdrivers, pliers, stuff like that."

Jack was admittedly not as handy as he should have been for having taken on such a daunting challenge as this house. However, he knew where to look for information and he was relatively good at following directions. It also helped that almost any home repair was easily researched on the internet. "Wow, I'm impressed. Tell you what, I trust your judgment. Throw out what isn't useful anymore, let me look at the stuff you think I should keep, and you can decide what to do with the rest. I don't really care."

They went over and above their mandate. He couldn't have known they were going to be that thorough but they were grad students who were out to make a good impression on the new professor. Ascending the stairs, onto the porch, he saw an old ax leaning up against the door.

"Hey guys, what's this?"

Chet shot him a confused glance, "That'd be an ax."

"Okay, sorry for not asking the more precise question. What's it doing up here?"

"Weren't sure if we should throw it out or not. That's a pretty good ax, but it needs some work. You should hang onto that. Not really worth selling, and it could be used again if you cleaned it up a little."

Jack remembered, it was the ax he had seen on the tool bench in the cellar. He was planning on throwing it out. He wasn't really the type to chop wood, no matter his delusions of grandeur. But still, they might be right and it could be a good tool to have around. If that large tree in the yard ever fell they'd have to chop the thing up. But, then again, maybe just buying a new one would be easier.

He put it down, leaning it up against the railing of the porch, and went inside.

There's a Ring in the Tub

Elizabeth felt the door handle twist under her grip. Somewhere inside the mechanism, the springs which made up the ancient door latch were being tensed. Elizabeth's heart beat out of control, her breath quickened, and sweat poured from every available pore in her body. There was a part of her that needed nothing more than to see inside of the bathroom and a whole other part that knew this was a huge mistake.

This is insane, I can't be hearing this.

The voice in her head spoke up, *Of course, you're hearing this, Elizabeth. I understand your hesitation. I really don't think you understand the gravity of the situation you're in.*

Turning away from the door as if her body was filled with lead, Elizabeth overcame her own inertia. Maybe it was time to get a head scan or talk to a shrink about the sudden lapse of her senses. The weight of the world crushed down on her as the stairs, and what felt like common sense, beckoned her away from the room and out of the house. She put one foot in front of the other and started down the stairs.

One foot in front of another, that's right. I can do this. I'm in charge.

The voice spoke up again, but this time it seemed to be coming from right next to her and not inside of her own head. "Oh, dear sweet Elizabeth, that's where you have it all wrong."

On the fifth step, Elizabeth froze, as if a force locked her knees in place. Seemingly shoved outside her own body, she floated above herself. She watched in horror as she turned back toward the bathroom and started back up the stairs.

How could this be?

The voice shouted at her, "You think you're in charge? You stupid little bitch. I can take control of you whenever I want to. I own you now, like my own whorish puppet on a string."

Elizabeth could feel it all. Every footstep, every grasp of the railing. Her disconnected fingertips reported every texture and her feet reported every shift of her disembodied weight as she ascended the stairs. She recoiled in fear as she found herself back in her own body, her hand reflexively reaching for the door.

"There's something behind this door you need to see. Something to help you understand. Do you really think I am doing this just for kicks, Elizabeth. No, dear sweet child, I am doing all of this for you. There are things you need to learn, things you need to understand."

"Who are you? Why are you doing this?" Elizabeth screamed out with tears forming in the corners of her eyes.

"Oh, come-on now, I'm your ally here. I want to help you, but you need to figure out who's the real enemy. This is your home now and you have a responsibility for it, as it has a responsibility to you. Just sit back and let Marylyn take care of you."

Elizabeth's mind searched feverishly for any recognition of the name. Coming up short of a face for the name, she thought about the history of the house. The Anderson farm, she believed it was called. Marylyn was the matriarch of the family. But how was a deceased woman from thirty years ago was talking to her now? It didn't seem possible. This had to be another dream.

But what if it wasn't?

On one point she had to concede that the voice was right. This home belonged to her and Jack. It was theirs to defend. Whatever was happening inside that bathroom was definitely not something she approved of.

Steeling her resolve, she felt Marylyn's control loosen. It waned in response to Elizabeth's acceptance that she had to open the door.

Admittedly, the sloshing sounds were terrifying. Occasionally a splash of water hit the tile floor. She only imagined what could possibly make the water so red. The voice inside the room was panting and screaming.

"Oh baby, that's right, you know how I like it. Oh God, yes!"

A spark erupted into burning anger inside of Elizabeth. Whatever was happening in the bathroom was inexcusable. This was her house. It was their home. Whoever it was had no right to use their bathroom in that way. The door would open freely now, all she had to do was push. Swallowing her fears, she flung the door wide with a flourish.

Centering herself in the doorway, she took in the devastating scene. Inside the claw footed bathtub was a man and a woman in the middle of a sexual encounter. He had his arms wrapped around her torso. He thrust his manhood, over and over again, inside her. The man was fit and at once familiar, but also unfamiliar at the same time. The woman was older and not as fit as he was. The man had her knees bent while the rest of her body hung against the side of the tub like a rag doll.

That was when Elizabeth saw what was making the water red. Her breasts had been torn apart. Loose flaps of skin and fat hung down where her breasts should have been. In the man's hand, he held a straight razor. It dug into the flesh on her hips. Blood streamed down the side of the porcelain tub, mixing with the water accumulating on the floor.

Elizabeth wanted to run. Somewhere, a voice shouted out to her. Like body and mind were completely divorced from one another. She tried to call out, scream if she could. No voice could be found.

Staring at Elizabeth for a second, the man grabbed the woman by the hair and pulled her head toward him. With his other hand he ran the blade of the razor deep across her throat. Blood gushed from the wound and onto the floor. He released her head and it lolled to one side as he continued to thrust his erect penis into her, each time with an accompanying moan.

She looked into the woman's eyes … the dead eyes of Rita. She shifted her gaze up from her dead friend to the man. It was the contorted face of her own husband.

"That's right baby, you're next … I'm gonna gut you like a fish. You little bitch. You get all that you deserve," Jack screamed while pointing the razor blade at Elizabeth. She hadn't recognized him right away because they were not the kind eyes of the man she loved, but eyes filled with hatred and anger. He looked like a beast, bent on vengeance for some sort of perceived offense.

Finding her voice, she screamed and tried to back away but slipped on the pool of blood stained water that collected on the floor beneath her feet. She needed to get away … run for help, but the world seemed to vanish from underneath her. Elizabeth hit her head on the wall as she crashed to the floor. Everything went black.

* * * *

"Elizabeth, sweetie, are you okay?" A voice pierced Elizabeth's abyss. "Elizabeth, honey, can you hear me?" The voice floated down through the entrance of a cave impossibly dark and indescribably deep. Cold enveloped her like a blanket of ice. Jack's voice pleaded with her from the void. The only thing she could feel was the warmth and familiarity of his hand on her forehead. That link chipped away at her frozen state.

The awful memory of Jack and Rita made her want to pull away from his touch, but found no extremity of her body would respond. She feared she was in the bath with her husband. Even now her blood draining from her body, the sudden sensory deprivation a sign of impending exsanguination. The images of Rita, laying there dead and mutilated in the tub, flashed through her head. What evil overcame Jack, making him do such a thing?

If Jack could turn on her, then why even bother fighting him? Perhaps it would be better if she were dead. If the very foundation that you build your life on couldn't be trusted, then maybe death was preferred. What had she done to deserve this? Maybe Marylyn was right?

"Elizabeth!" Jacks voice cut through the blackness, this time with a lilt of concern.

Light pierced the dark of her unconsciousness. She could make out shapes and forms, but they were out of focus. The warmth of someone's hands, holding her up, registered. Perhaps her situation wasn't as dire as it first seemed.

"Elizabeth, what happened?"

The shapes began to take focus. She could make out door jambs and the knobs. The fuzzy shape of what she knew was her murderous husband was above her, but she lacked the strength to run.

She pushed him away, "No ... no ... no!" she screamed.

Jack had a confused look on his face. "Elizabeth. It's me, Jack."

"I saw ... I saw ... you ... I saw what you did."

He pleaded with her. "What are you talking about Elizabeth? Honey, please, talk to me."

The stairs creaked as someone rushed up them. Rita appeared. "Jack, I called the doctor. He's on his way."

Elizabeth looked at Rita with sudden disbelief. "Rita, how are you standing there? Jack, I thought you had ..."

But, what had she really seen? What did she really know for sure? She was lying on the floor of the hallway. She just watched her husband commit necrophilia with Rita's freshly murdered corpse. Who was, as of this moment, very much alive.

Rita put her hand on Elizabeth's forehead. "Elizabeth honey, are you alright? Tell us what happened."

She sat up slowly and looked into the bathroom. "I don't know." No blood, no water, nothing to indicate the tragedy she witnessed being played out in there. Jack did not even own a straight razor that she was aware of. Elizabeth had never seen Jack with one.

What the hell is going on?

"Come on sweetie, let's get you to your feet." She allowed Jack to help her up. Her legs were shaky and weak from her ordeal. Jack and Rita helped her down the stairs and onto one of the dining room chairs.

A few minutes later, Dr. Gold's green Buick pulled into the driveway. Upon seeing the car, Elizabeth instinctively tried to get up, but her leg muscles protested. Rita ordered her to sit down while Jack opened the door to meet Dr. Gold.

Her head still felt decidedly in a fog. Elizabeth went through what she was so sure she had witnessed. It all seemed so real. If it were, Rita would be dead, and likely so would she. The more she thought about it, the less sense it made. Elizabeth was sure Marylyn had taken control of her body, but that idea was ludicrous. How could anyone do that? Surely that wasn't possible.

Dr. Gold examined Elizabeth. He asked her a series of questions designed to assess her state of mind. She felt like a child answering questions about where she lived and what day it was. Elizabeth began to suspect she was the victim of an elaborate hallucination.

The old doctor asked, "Elizabeth, when was the last time you had anything to eat or drink?"

"Coffee this morning, I think I went to eat breakfast, but skipped it."

"Okay, and how about yesterday. What did you have for dinner?"

Elizabeth thought about the day before. They hadn't eaten anything after the pizza except a few chips and some soda. "Not much after lunch. Snacked mostly."

"Mmm-hmmm," Dr. Gold mumbled while examining Elizabeth's

eyes with a light. "Thankfully, I don't think this is anything serious and the treatment is simple. You, my dear, are suffering from exhaustion and dehydration. How have you been sleeping?"

"Pretty poorly, actually."

Dr. Gold took off his stethoscope and put it back in his black bag. "Classic symptoms, really. Too much moving to stop and eat or drink properly. Working yourself to death around the house. Jack and Rita, you're both responsible for making sure she sits here and drinks a whole glass of water. I want her to drink it slowly, no gulping. Then I want you to make her something to eat while she drinks another glass of water. After that, you can have some fruit juice or a sports drink to get some sugar back into your body. You kids these days think you can run around on soda and skip meals. The human body doesn't work that way."

"That's it? Dehydration?" Elizabeth was shocked the doctor thought it was something so simple. She hallucinated that the love of her life had committed a heinous murder, mutilated a body, and had sex with it. And it'd be chalked up to simple dehydration? Was it even possible that dehydration could force such an elaborate hallucination? She took the glass of water Rita handed her. She didn't tell them exactly what she saw, only that she imagined someone was in the bathroom.

Dr. Gold shrugged his shoulders. "Yep, seen it happen a million times. These old farmers go out into their fields and work through breakfast and lunch. Pretty soon you find em' sitting in the corner of the barn, thinking they are back in the war, fighting the Chinese or some damn thing. Dehydration does some strange things. I've no reason to suspect it's anything different. However, I want you to come in for a complete physical in a few days. If you're not feeling better by tomorrow morning, have Jack run you out to the clinic."

"Thanks for the house call, doctor," Jack said, giving the old doctor's hand a shake.

"No problem, that's what I'm here for." Dr. Gold took in a deep sigh. "Haven't been in this house for years. I kind of hoped I would never have to again. But, on the bright side, you two are going to make up a whole other revenue stream for my practice if you keep this up. Got to see both the husband and the wife in one week. That has to be a new record."

"Thanks again, doctor." Elizabeth took a long sip of the water. She hadn't felt thirsty all day, but suddenly it overwhelmed her. It was like the doctor's suggestion of dehydration had magical powers, and she needed water desperately. The traumatic event had taken a lot out of her. She watched the grizzled old farm doctor for a moment as he got up to leave.

Dr. Gold stood momentarily, staring off at an old card table which had been left sitting in the corner. For a moment she thought his eyes had welled up with tears. His look was distant. Like a man who was pulling a memory from long, long ago.

"Alright, if you kids need anything, make an appointment." Dr. Gold turned from the three of them and walked out the door.

"Elizabeth honey, should we go sit on the couch?" Jack said.

He was obviously shaken by what he saw. But, try as she might, she couldn't shake the image of Jack in the tub, having sex with Rita's corpse. A corpse which was presently holding her hand and about to make her a sandwich.

What is wrong with me? Am I losing my mind?

Ever since coming to the house, Elizabeth sensed an undercurrent of something. She never believed in spiritual energies, or the paranormal before. But she had to admit to herself that the house seemed to want something, but she had no idea what it was.

No dear, you just need to kill Jack.

She closed her eyes against the thought that forced its way into her head, dislodging thoughts of dehydration and sandwiches. It was random, like standing in line at the amusement park to get on a ride when you remembered you forgot to put away a tee shirt you left on your dresser at home.

She looked at Jack. "I'm fine really. I need to rest, I think. Maybe sit out on the porch for a while. Get some fresh air."

"Okay." He reached down to help her up.

Try as she might, she couldn't push the image of his hands, wrapped around Rita's waist, out of her mind. It supplanted all other thoughts.

With those hands he did the unspeakable, you know that. He'll do the same to you, Elizabeth.

"No, I've got it. I'm alright." She waved off his offer to help her up. Elizabeth meant it, she did feel better. Maybe the doctor was right, she just needed to drink more water and have something to eat.

Elizabeth stood up and looked at Rita. She found herself annoyed with the way the older woman was looking at her with eyebrows knitted with concern, almost pity. She could see it in Rita's eyes. Worry for this poor young kid who had moved here from the East Coast, expecting some sort of idyllic life on the open prairie.

The voice forced its way back into her head. *You saw what they were doing. You know he didn't just pull her in there. She had to jump in there with him. She doesn't understand what murdering pigs husbands are. But we do, don't we Lizzy?*

Reality Sets In

Elizabeth made her way outside and sat down on the porch swing. Fresh air from the prairie hit her full force, instantly making her feel better.

Maybe there's something about the house that's affecting me? Maybe a gas leak or something? Elizabeth mulled this idea around in her head.

The sun's angle chased the shadow of the porch enough that the sunlight bathed her ankles in warmth while the rest of her was in the relative cool of the shade. The fresh air felt good as it buffeted her from the fields.

"Elizabeth, when you started to wake up, you were really confused," Jack said.

She felt a twinge of panic as she had no idea what she'd said while coming out of her delusional state. Although it scared her to death at the time, the idea of her husband cheating on her was only slightly less ridiculous than him cheating on her with Rita, a woman who was almost double his age.

"What did I say? Do you remember?"

He shrugged her shoulders. "You just babbled a little."

"I had a weird hallucination. You were … well, it doesn't matter." It would be better to just stop there than relate the grim details. It would hurt Jack if he knew she even thought him capable of such ghastly acts. It was only a hallucination brought on by lack of water and food. The longer she sat outside, the more she was convinced the doctor was right. Really, the idea of her husband being a philandering murderer was beyond ridiculous.

Rita, dear sweet Rita, came out of the house carrying a tray of sandwiches and more water. "I'm sorry to have to leave you guys, but I have to go home. Hal will never remember to take his medicine if I'm not there." She grabbed Elizabeth's hand again. "Are you going to be alright?"

"Yeah, I'm fine. I'm going to have to keep a closer eye on what I'm eating and drinking from now on. I feel silly for having worried everyone."

"Oh sweetie, this is nothing. I once had to pick up Hal from the police station after a night of partying with the boys. They found him naked in a town square ... in Ohio."

Jack laughed. "Oh yikes, I won't tell him you told us that."

"Oh, that's the kicker with Hal. If you ask him ... he'll tell you the whole story. He's proud as a peach about it."

Rita loved Hal. Elizabeth could see that love written all over her face and she'd never cheat on him. He was her reason for living. Although she complained about his spending too much time on the couch and not enough time in the yard, her love was unmistakable. Elizabeth watched her friend walk to her car and then drive away. Rita was a friend. Probably their best friend.

What was happening to her? She remembered stories of settlers contracting "prairie madness" where the isolation of living on the prairie would get to them after a while. They would be found frozen to death in a wheat field after being convinced they could walk home to the East coast. But that was before *The Real Housewives*, and delivery pizza was available.

Elizabeth felt an overwhelming hunger. She tore into the stack of sandwiches. The cheese, meat, and lettuce made a satisfying crunch in between the pieces of wheat bread.

"Tell you what," Jack said. "I have an idea. The internet is working; we have the television plugged in. Why don't we spend the rest of the day indulging in our need for mindless television watching?"

She had to admit, the idea sounded pretty good to her. She was feeling a bit better. She knew there would be multiple episodes of her favorite shows just waiting for her. Maybe he was on to something.

Tomorrow was going to be a big day. The moving van had gotten caught in traffic somewhere in Indiana but would arrive early the next morning along with the people interested in buying the table. Jack had sent the two students home while Dr. Gold conducted his examination. For the moment, it was just Jack and Elizabeth in the house.

Maybe it's time for just us, she thought.

"Jack Milburn, you may have hit upon the perfect idea. A little time in front of the 'idiot box' could be the thing for us both." Just then, a roll of thunder issued from a cloud overhead. It was going to rain soon, with the promise of cooler temperatures. "Let me run upstairs and change clothes into something a little less … hot and sticky."

She was still feeling a little shaky, but reached the top of the stairs on her own. Having accepted the doctor's theory, she only cast one nervous glance toward the bathroom door. It was still open. She could see a foot or two into the doorway. No water on the floor, no sloshing, nothing.

In the bedroom, her purse lay open on the bed where she threw it. Reaching into the pocket to pull out her lip balm, her hand hit a piece of paper. It was the paper from the library. She'd forgotten all about it after Penny handed it to her.

Laying it on the bed, she took off the shirt she put on that morning. They would both need showers after the heat of the day. But for now, she would just throw on something more comfortable. The mid-morning sun was still baking the house, but the impending storm hinted at some relief. Sitting down on the bed, she picked up the news story.

May 7th, 1985

By: Lauren Preston

Tragedy shocked our little town today as the deaths and apparent suicide of a local family was discovered late Sunday evening. The McClean county sheriff's office was called to the Anderson farm, on county road 7, after neighbors became worried when the family didn't show up for church.

Authorities are not disclosing the nature of the injuries, but the medical examiner believes it could be a murder-suicide. The official report won't be available until next week. Donald Anderson, the family patriarch, was found next to his slain wife, in bed. He appears to have died from a self-inflicted gunshot wound.

The two Anderson boys were also found dead at the scene. One in the barn, and another inside the home. The Sheriff is unsure why Mr. Anderson would take such extreme measures ..."

Elizabeth sat in stunned silence.

She'd heard the rumors and the stories. But somehow, seeing it in print made it real. It was no longer a nebulous local legend that had been embellished over the years. The realization made her shiver.

She felt like she was being watched and turned around to see Jack standing behind her.

"What's the holdup, babe?" Jack asked.

"This ... did you know about this?" Without meaning to, she looked at Jack with accusing eyes. She knew he'd never intentionally keep something like this from her, but it wasn't reassuring. Someone should have said something. Like, maybe, 'Your house was the scene of a grisly murder-suicide.'

Jack quickly scanned the paper. His long sigh and guilty face confirmed her suspicions. "Sweetie, I was waiting for the right moment to tell you. Today was obviously not the day. I was going to wait until tomorrow." He sat down on the bed next to her.

"Oh my God, Jack. I can't believe it." She cast a glance at the bed they had been sleeping in. Something about it suddenly nauseated her. It was here the medical examiner found the bodies of Donald Anderson and his wife.

"It doesn't change anything, Elizabeth."

"Doesn't change anything?" She wondered silently how this new information couldn't possibly change the situation at all. This was not inconsequential. Then, part of her knew he was right. There was nothing they could really do about the situation. The home was cheap enough that she knew a court wouldn't give them much in compensation for failure to disclose, or if the sellers are even legally required to disclose something like this.

She looked into Jack's eyes. Elizabeth saw real disappointment. There was no way he could keep a secret like this from her. He waited to tell her and there had to be a good reason. "We need to find out more about this. I wonder if there was anyone in town who could tell us more about what happened here?"

Jack folded the newspaper article into fourths, giving each fold a sharp crease. "Well, I know Mr. Gulliver knew the Anderson's. He told me about the murders, but the story seemed so fantastical that I didn't really believe him. I'm really sorry about not telling you. I think the doc knows more than he is letting on about this." Jack patted his pants pocket. "Oh wait, I almost forgot. I have the last page of the printout. Penny gave it to me when I stopped into the library this morning."

Elizabeth unfolded the paper again and scanned down the page. Maybe there was more information to be had. Perhaps the person who discovered the bodies would know more? The bottom of the page ended with the words,

The doctor, who was called to the scene, indicated all persons in the home were dead. In a follow-up statement Dr. …

The rest of the sentence must have been on the next page that Jack had. "You said you had the rest of the printout?"

"Yeah, why?"

She looked at him with renewed purpose. "The rest of the paper has the information on what the doctor found when he made his way to the house. Something about declaring all the victims dead at the scene."

Jack frowned at her, seeing where she was going with this line of reasoning. "I'm not sure we really have to even look, do we?"

Without even looking Elizabeth knew there was a one hundred percent chance the paper would indicate the doctor on the scene was their new family physician, Dr. Gold. That could be why he seemed so distant and sad when he was there earlier.

"When we were at the clinic, he said we would have to look up the information ourselves if we want to know what happened here. I guess we did that alright."

Elizabeth had felt it the first time she walked into the house, it was a dampening of her spirits. An inconsolable sadness descended upon her. Normally something like this would not bother her, but this news shook her to the core.

"Jack, you know I—"

Jack grabbed her hands and looked deep into her eyes. "Look, Elizabeth, I've told you before, I'll do anything you want. If you want out of this house, we can just walk away from it. No problem. In a moment, in a heartbeat. I love you more than anything on this earth. If you want we can run away to the Caribbean and teach islanders to speak English, I don't care."

She kissed his hand. "Jack, let me finish. This house is ours and nothing is going to change that. Okay, so something awful happened here and we have had a rough go of our first week. I'm not willing to let that dominate our lives. You need to work at something you love and makes you whole. That's who you are. I would never ask you to give that up for anything. So, we are going to stay. Until this big ole creepy house falls down around us, we're staying right here."

"I love you."

"You damn well better. So, let's go watch some TV, you know it's been almost a week since I had any dose of reality TV."

Jack stood up from the bed and pulled her up with him. "Okay, let's go downstairs and rot our brains."

They spent the afternoon in each other's arms watching episode after episode of reality television. Afternoon turned into evening. Elizabeth allowed the mindlessness of television wash over any remaining negative thoughts in her head.

Bandits

Jack cast a downward glance at Elisabeth, he could see the back of her head, resting on his shoulder. The warmth of her body was reassuring. She was finally at peace and resting. It had been a hard day for her.

Before the realization that she suddenly knew more about the murders than he thought, Jack was prepared to tell her about waking up in the basement. Seeing her incapacitated body laying in the hallway shoved every other thought to the back of his mind. All he could comprehend was the idea that the love of his life was in trouble.

Coming out of her blackout, he could see a certain distance in her eyes. Her eyes lit up every time Elizabeth saw him and this time they were cold and distant. There was something in them difficult to comprehend. Elizabeth, the love of his life, feared him.

He was worried about her and hoped the decision to bring them both out in the boonies was not adversely affecting her. Jack would gladly give his own life to keep her safe and the thought of her suffering, even a little, was too much for him to bear.

Jack resisted the urge to say anything to Elizabeth about his feelings. The first time they stepped into the house, it seemed to take control over her. It made her depressed. Granted, this was their first time really being away from the East Coast they both knew and loved. Could it be a simple case of homesickness?

The choice to spend some time on the couch together was the right one. They needed to be together.

"You know, we could, if you want to, take the time to have

someone completely gut this place and redo it all. We could make our home in the motel down the road while a local contractor wreaks havoc in here. New paint, new rugs, everything. We make it our own."

Elizabeth sat in silence for a moment, some commercial playing on the screen for haircare products. "No, I don't think so. Besides, it'll be good for Rita and me to do the work. Maybe we can enlist some of the other ladies. We could form a club. Chicks with hammers!"

He smiled. "I'd hire you. Maybe only because I'd demand you work in a negligee."

She faked being deep in thought. "I'd definitely have to charge you extra for that. Mostly because negligees are hard enough to clean, but getting paint on them? Ugh! Seriously, though, what should we do with this place? Do you like the colors I brought back?"

She had indeed brought back every conceivable color from Gullivers Hardware. Everything from 'Brightly White' to something called 'Zebra Black', which didn't even sound like a real color to Jack. She carefully tacked the colors up to each of the walls.

He thought it was so cute that she asked him his opinion on the color schemes of the house. She wanted him to feel included. But they both knew he didn't care either way. Ultimately he'd let her paint the house any color she wanted to. His job was to go pick things up from the hardware store.

Jack shifted uneasily in his corner of the old couch. "Yes, I certainly do."

Elizabeth eyed Jack suspiciously. "Really? You really like the colors?"

"Yep, absolutely."

"Okay, smart aleck," Elizabeth said. "Exactly which ones do you like the best?"

He swept his hands out in a grand gesture. "Oh sweetie, I love them all. You have the best taste in home decorating. I love every one of those colors you selected."

She laughed at him. "You're so full of shit, you know that. You can't even tell me what any of those colors are. Can you?"

"Sure, I can. Blue. Blue? Yeah, blue."

Elizabeth jabbed him in the ribs. "Oh wow, you are such a man."

He held his hands up in surrender. "Sorry, honey, but I remember our wedding vows. I'm supposed to open jars, kill spiders, and rock your world. At no point did those vows include anything about knowing the colors."

"So, your kindergarten teacher taught you what exactly?"

"He was a gym teacher, he made us run laps."

Elizabeth cocked her head to one side and looked at him. "I changed my mind, you're such a boy."

Just then, Elizabeth's phone rang. She stood up and grabbed it off the end table. "Hello? Oh hi, Rita. Yes, I'm feeling better. What's that? Oh no, Jack was just sitting here doing inappropriate things to me. Yeah, we're going to post it all on the internet. I simply must do something to make a living, and internet porn seemed like the most logical choice."

Jack stood up. The show they had been watching was done. He poured himself a glass of water from the sink and went out to the patio to sit on the chair swing. The evening had promised rain, and it had delivered. The grass was soaked, and the driveway had turned a couple of the ruts into mud holes. He would have to go get some more gravel to fill them in eventually.

Elizabeth came out the door with a glass of water and sat down next to him. The rhythm of the rain was soothing and temperatures had finally abated. He knew the storm only bought them a slight reprieve from the summer humidity. It would be back in full force as soon as the rain stopped.

As Elizabeth planned out grandiose projects on the phone with Rita, Jack stretched back on the swing. Looking over his shoulder, something leaning up against the railing caught his eye. He remembered the ax the students found while doing their cleaning. Maybe it would be best to just throw the old thing in the dumpster and leave it there. If they needed an ax for anything, Gullivers had a wide selection to choose from. Then again, Jack thought to himself, a tool like that could be very useful and it seemed a shame to throw the thing in the dumpster if it still had so much life in it. Although Jack really didn't envision himself in the backyard chopping wood, it could be useful for any occasional chores around the house.

"Thanks, Rita. We'll see you in the morning. I'll have to make Jack put on clothes. You know, I ordinarily make him walk around naked with a leash on until noon. My mom always told me to treat a husband like a dog."

Elizabeth laughed at Rita's response. Jack loved to hear Elizabeth's laugh. It was infectious. She hit the big red disconnect button on the screen. "I think I may have convinced her to start treating Hal like a dog."

"Oh, I'm sure of it. Say, what do you think of that old ax? Keep or throw?" Jack wondered about the value of the old tool since he returned home. It seemed to be a shame to throw out such an impressive tool.

Elizabeth's strange and suspicious attraction to the thing bothered him a little. It also worried him that the thing figured prominently in his own dreams. On the other hand, it was irrational to be afraid of wood and steel. Something about the old tool spoke to Jack, compelling him to rescue the thing.

"I think we should keep it. I actually want to go talk to Mr. Gulliver about it. See if he can tell me how to clean it up," Elizabeth said.

"Well, you could always look that up on the internet. I'm sure there are about a dozen videos posted on how to maintain an ax blade."

Elizabeth sighed. "You're probably right. Sharpening an ax might be fun!"

"Oh sure, creepiest fun ever."

"Well, you know my love, you keep me at home barefoot and pregnant, I will likely have to find some hobbies to occupy my time between hanging out the washing and canning fruit."

Jack yawned and stretched out his feet toward the railing. "Monday I'll go back. For now, we need to get this house in order. Once the semester starts, I'll practically be living in my office at the University. Tomorrow the people are coming for the table and the moving truck will be here. Lots to do."

Nodding in agreement, Elizabeth said, "I suppose that's true."

As they stared out at the cornstalks, Elizabeth watched the rain beating down on the plants. It's beat settled into a gentle, hypnotic patter. A slight wind blew through the fields. The smell of rain and soil and cooler weather made an oddly refreshing combination. The sound of the water rushing through the drainpipes made an almost riverine sound.

Jack reached out with his foot letting the water splash on his toes. Elizabeth reached out with her foot as well, but could only manage to reach the handrail. She put her leg over his.

Elizabeth looked to her right toward the charred timbers of the barn in the distance. "I've been thinking about something. What do you say to the idea of rebuilding that old barn this fall?"

Jack kissed her hand. "I think that could really add a lot of storage space if we do it right. I looked at the foundation, and it seems largely intact. Not much damage from the fire. It wouldn't take much to rebuild. Maybe we can restore it to the way it was."

"I think that's a great idea. I saw a photo of it at the library and I think it would be a fun project. Every farm needs a big red barn."

He stood up and went back inside the house. It had been a long and stressful day. Standing in the living room stretching his back, Jack suddenly had the feeling of being watched. Up the stairway something moved in the darkness. Although he was convinced this was a figment of his imagination, he shivered against it, remembering his odd dream the night before. Blinking the exhaustion from his vision, he cast another glance at the top of the stairs to see a thankfully empty landing.

He yawned against his own sudden sense of exhaustion. "Honey, I think I'm going to shower and hit the sack. I'm pretty tired."

"I suppose I will too. What time is the moving van going to be here?"

Jack looked reflexively at his wrist as if it would tell him the time although he wore no watch. "I think they said it would be here around ten."

Jack was the first out of the shower. Elizabeth busied herself by looking over the paint swatches she bought for their bedroom. The fresh Midwestern air had exhausted both of them. As he shampooed his hair, he thought about Elizabeth and her fainting episode earlier. He heard all the doctor had to say, but still worried. What if it's something more serious?

Jack's mind, being left to its own devices, imagined the worst. What if it was a brain tumor or some other kind of cancer? Or it could be some disease they didn't know about. Dr. Gold was undoubtedly good at his job, but he still was essentially a country doctor. Likely, the old man was good with broken bones, lacerations, and common ailments around the farm but something like a brain tumor was not necessarily his area of expertise. He had not run extensive tests. Perhaps they should consult an expert in a larger city.

Elizabeth walked into the bathroom.

"Hey, there hotness," Jack said, his eyebrows raising and lowering.

She scowled at him. "Oh stop! Don't men ever stop being horny?"

"I can't speak of the afterlife, but I know that here in the corporeal world, not really."

"Ah, that explains it."

Jack stepped out of the shower, grabbing his towel off of the hook near the stall before giving her a kiss. "Shower's all yours."

Elizabeth gave him a queer look. "What is this cut on the side of your head?"

She was referring to the abrasion on his head from the night before. "Oh, that thing? I hit my head on one of the walls downstairs. I guess I forgot all about it." A little omission of details was better than facing the inquisition on why he ended up on the floor of the cellar.

Jack thought the shower would invigorate him, but it just seemed to make him more tired. He slipped between the sheets. Their bedroom window was open, the breeze blowing through the room. It was just cool enough for their bedsheets, but not enough for their comforter. *Perfect sleeping weather.*

He woke up when Elizabeth climbed into bed. She grabbed him by the waist, which would have ordinarily turned him on, but tonight the need for deep sleep overruled all impulses.

Jack woke with a start at the sound of a terrifying scream. He looked down at Elizabeth, who was now fully awake. Confirming she wasn't the source of the shriek, Jack jumped out of bed, grabbing his robe and the old baseball bat. "Stay here. If I scream, call the cops!" Without another word, he threw open the door and plunged into the hallway.

Turning the lights on as he went, he saw nothing out of the ordinary. The area rug, which lay on the hallway floor, was exactly where it had been. Doors to the upper floor bedrooms were wide open and, though he was sure he'd closed them earlier. Jack thought the sound had come from the second-floor hallway, but he wasn't completely sure. A sudden panic overtook him as thoughts of his previous nightmare flashed though his head.

He stood still for a moment, matching the sudden grave-like silence of the house. Even the rain which had persisted until after they fell asleep issued no sound.

At the end of the hallway, there was a door leading to a small walk-in closet. Jack could swear he saw the door move slightly. *Or was it just my imagination?* He froze as he considered it. Maybe his mind was playing tricks on him.

"Jack, are you okay out there?" Elizabeth's voice rang out from the bedroom.

"So far, so good. Just stay there, alright?"

He took several more steps, passing the stairway and stopping just short of the bathroom door. Pushing it open, he risked a glance inside. Thankfully nothing but an empty room. Next, he moved to the other bedrooms and was pleased to find nothing inside them except some of the supplies they'd bought for making repairs. Moving further, he approached the door of the small storage closet.

Jack was sure this door had moved. With the end of his bat, he pushed the door open slightly. It was dark, almost impossibly so. Something inside was absorbing every last ray of light and hiding it away. He needed to reach in and turn on the one naked light bulb hanging from an aged electrical cord. Cautiously, he reached for the string and gave it a tug.

For a second, nothing happened. The old wiring in the house took its time to deliver promised electrical current. As the wires in the light bulb finally warmed, it cast a glow on the small storage room.

The flash blurred Jack's vision, but what he saw when the light illuminated the depths of the closet made him jump back, almost tripping over his feet in the process.

In front of him stood a man, a little taller than Jack, dressed in overalls. Blood was spattered over his entire body. In his hands, he held a shotgun. His head was cleaved in two, like he had lost a medieval battle against a seriously pissed-off swordsman.

Two mice ripped pieces of flesh off his bare feet while blood fell from his hands, hitting the floor with a sick dripping sound. Judging from the swarm of flies that covered him, he had been dead a while; however, no-one had bothered to tell the unfortunate corpse.

Jack, terrified beyond reason, backed down the hallway toward their bedroom. His hand gripped the baseball bat as if it were a talisman against the grisly sight before him. He brought it up like he was preparing to hit an inside slider. He had to protect Elizabeth. No matter what.

Elizabeth yelled, "Jack? Everything okay?" He must have let out a shriek as he beheld the creature in the closet.

He tried to get more words out, but only managed to say, "Just stay there," before choking on his own tongue. Jack's mind raced. If there was something inside of that closet, still alive, there was no way it was in any condition to fight him. He forced himself to calm down. Whatever was in there still hadn't emerged.

202

Stories of deranged meth-addicts breaking into houses and doing violent things occupied his mind. Jack held the bat at the ready, approaching the closet door again. Daring a peek around the corner, he instantly felt like an idiot. Instead of seeing a bloodied zombie farmer, there was a collection of mops and some old blue fabric. On the floor were two mice, but they were children's toys that hadn't been thrown out when they were emptying the house. The combination of the early hour and his own overactive imagination conspired against him.

Jack snapped off the light just as he heard a woman scream, this time from downstairs. He yelled out, "Elizabeth!"

She yelled back from the bedroom, "That still wasn't me!"

Jack ran to the stairs. There was no way he misheard that. Snapping on the stairwell light, he made his way to the living room. Seeing nothing out of sorts, he turned toward the kitchen. Possessed by the need to find the source of the scream, he plunged into the dining room. He could see the light they left on in the kitchen just beyond the doorway. Then came another scream, this time from the cellar.

How the hell could anything be down there?

He threw open the door and turned on the lights. Peeking around the corner he saw the stones at the bottom of the stairwell. For the moment, nothing seemed to move.

"I warn you, I've got a bat!" Jack's mind raced through the events of the dream again. He remembered the form of Elizabeth standing at the top of the stairs as the storm raged behind her. Icy tentacles gripped his spine. "I'm warning you!" Something darted across the bottom of the gravel, like it was being chased. The gravel crunched lightly under its feet. But it definitely was not human.

A flash of darkness stumbled across the bottom of the steps. Another dark mass joined it, and the two tussled for a bit. One of them let out a shriek. Similar to the sound of a screaming woman, it occurred to Jack what the screams were. It was something far less than supernatural.

Jack put on some boots and descended the stairs. He hit the gravel floor just in time to see the two figures, who had chosen their cellar as a battle arena, or romantic getaway, jump through a small hole in the brickwork. He'd have to fix the hole sooner rather than later. But for now, he took one of the boards laying on the floor and shoved it in the hole. Maybe that would keep them out, maybe not, but at least he'd solved the mystery.

A few minutes later, he strode through the bedroom door. Elizabeth let out a stifled scream.

Jack put the bat down next to the door. "Sorry honey, I'll put bells on next time."

She glared at him. "God, you scared me. What was all that?"

"Well, nothing lethal, if that's what you mean." He took off his robe and slid into bed. "But, ask yourself this question, you were freaked out by field mice; do you really want to know what I found in the cellar?"

She grimaced at him. "Jack, if you ever want to fondle another breast in your life, you'd better tell me what the hell is living in my house."

"Okay, Mrs. Milburn, you've got a bit of a raccoon problem."

She quickly yanked up the covers like they were a force-field against wildlife. "Crap! Raccoons? I thought a woman was being murdered downstairs."

"To be fair, I gave you the choice to not know. That's the sound they make when they fight or mate."

"Well, at least tell me they're gone."

He sighed as he laid back against his pillows. "Yes, they're gone, but we have a hole we have to board up, or they'll be back. Raccoons can be skittish, but they are really determined critters. Once they figure out we aren't going to shoot, then they'll take up residence in our cellar. I'll run up to the store and get a trap tomorrow."

They went back to sleep, but Jack was never completely successful. He kept his ears open for the rustling sounds of animals.

Letting the Ax Fall

Raccoons. How could anyone sleep with raccoons living in their house? Elizabeth pulled the bedsheets up close as if they had been treated with magic raccoon repellent. Jack, seemingly undeterred by the furry intruders, fell right back into a restless slumber. She was sure there was no way she would ever get back to sleep, maybe ever. She surprised herself by drifting off.

Elizabeth woke to the sound of wind buffeting the house. Out the window, grey clouds raced across the sky in search of something on the horizon. Checking the weather on her phone, it told a dismal story. They could expect a chilly, cloudy day. But it'd be a good day to spend working on the house. Few things would change her happy mood this morning. Today they'd get their own stuff back and maybe return to a bit of what she considered normal. It would be a huge load off her mind to see their own belongings again.

Pulling on a pair of sweatpants and a tee-shirt, she came downstairs to see Jack sitting at the table. Dressed in a pair of slacks and tee-shirt, he looked far more ready for the day than she was. He read his newspaper and slurped coffee.

"Morning, honey," he said.

She leaned over and gave him a kiss. "Good morning."

"Don't get too comfy. The people buying the table will be here in ten minutes."

"Too bad, it's kind of grown on me."

He looked over the top of his newspaper at her. "It is kind of a cool table, but we really don't have room for two of them."

"True. With this thing in here, we barely have room to move. Besides, the cash from the sale can go into window treatments."

Jack looked up at the article he was reading, "Into? They are giving us enough to basically cover all the window treatments. How much do you think you are going to spend on blinds and shutters anyway?"

"Oh Jack," Elizabeth gave him a wink. "Silly boy. I think your naivete about home decorating is cute."

She got up from the table and crossed the room to the corner. Since moving in, she hadn't actually taken the time to look at the small folding table abandoned by the previous owner. There was nothing special about it. It looked like one of the old folding tables her grandmother kept around for when the family came over, or when she invited the ladies over to the house to play cards.

Pulling it away from the wall, the back of it made a slightly sickening noise as spider webs and years of neglect conspired to keep it in place. Sliding it across the floor, a sudden plume of dust rose into the air making her cough and sneeze. Her head felt light, as if she were about to black out, but she didn't. Instead, she felt suddenly warm, like she was standing in the sun.

With the dust irritating her eyes, she closed and rubbed them. When her sight returned, the mostly emptied house lay repopulated with the furnishings they had removed. The home looked just like when they first moved in. The pictures, couch, chairs, and coffee table were suddenly there again. Even the items they'd brought with them in their overstuffed car disappeared. Jack even vanished.

The folding table was no longer in her hands. It was set up before her, in between the living and family rooms. On top stood a collection of books and papers, obviously as someone's desk.

The world had gone still. The normal smells of the house were replaced by a stagnant odor of stasis. Like a world filled with air incapable of, or simply refusing to move.

Outside, the light had gone from the overcast grey of the wet summertime low-pressure system to a pale, almost dingy-looking orange. It reminded her of the sepia tone images she'd seen in her grandmother's old photographs.

Daring to take a few steps forward, toward the staircase, even her feet seemed to make no noise at all as she walked across the floor. The throw rug was firm under her, but when she tried to move the tassels around on the floor, they failed to yield; stuck in place by some unimaginable force.

She dared to touch the top of the couch. It felt soft, but also hard at the same time, like a couch was screen-printed on the top of a hard rubber form. At first glance, the world seemed normal, but upon closer inspection was surreal.

"You aren't dreaming, Elizabeth. You know that, don't you?"

She turned to face the owner or the voice. In front of her was a demure woman, a little shorter than she, but older than her by about ten years. She wore a blue apron, and her hair was up in a conservative bun. Elizabeth recognized her instantly from the sound of her voice.

"If I'm not dreaming, then where am I? What is this place."

Marylyn looked around the room. "This is where I'm forced to live. Or rather, this is where I'm forced to die. I'm sorry I had to do this to you, but I am borrowing you from your own reality for a bit."

"You can't do this to me, Jack will miss me. You can't just steal someone."

"Oh, don't get your girdle in a bunch. He won't notice and time for you won't pass at all. What I have in mind will take but a short time in my world and seem instantaneous in yours. As a matter of fact, in your world, that old folding table slipped from your fingers and hasn't even hit the floor yet."

Dismissing the odd statement, Elizabeth asked, "You're Marylyn Anderson, aren't you?"

"You guessed right, sweetie. I am."

Elizabeth's stomach tightened into knots. She felt the distinct burn of acid in her lower throat as her stomach threatened to force the coffee she drank back through her esophagus. She fought to keep it down.

"Or rather, I *was* Marylyn Anderson. I'm not sure if you're are legally married anymore if your husband kills you. Pretty sure that violates the 'love and honor' portion of the vows."

Elizabeth's mind flashed an image of her lying in bed, blood streaming from her chest where an ax had crushed her chest cavity. She shook her head to clear the image. "What do you want with me? Why did you bring me here?"

"I want some understanding, and maybe to help you. Before I send you back to Jack, I want to have a little heart-to-heart. You know, some girl-talk."

Elizabeth was pretty certain, taking someone from their own reality didn't constitute either girl-talk or a heart-to-heart chat. For the moment, she was seemingly trapped here so she swallowed her fear. "Okay, tell me what you want to talk about."

"Oh, my dear, I'll do better than that. I'll show you what I want. Follow me, please."

As Marylyn walked past Elizabeth, she couldn't help but touch Marylyn's arm. She expected to reach through skin and bone. But her arm was warm and as solid as she was. The Marylyn she was seeing was no ghost.

"Oh, I am really here Lizzy, I assure you of that," Marylyn said, walking out of the house and into the yard. Elizabeth, although terrified, couldn't help but follow. The compulsion was undeniable. Her terror was overruled by the sheer curiosity of why Marylyn, who had been dead for thirty years, would drag her into this. Whatever *this* was.

As she walked across the rock-strewn driveway, she was shocked her feet failed to make any noise at all. She felt the unevenness of the driveway under foot. The rocks and dirt refused to give way to the pressure of her footsteps, as they would have in the real world. They stopped halfway between the house and the highway. To her left was the tire swing, restored to its rightful place, hanging from the old oak tree. Like the rest of the world, it hung motionless.

Elizabeth must have had a look of confusion on her face as she looked at the tire swing. Elizabeth said, "This is how everything looked the day my husband ... well, the day it happened."

Off in the distance, to the right of the tree branch, stood the barn. Not the burned-out husk of a barn, but a true farmer's barn. It stood tall and proud, silhouetted against the fields behind it. The large barn doors were open, and inside she could see the front end of a pickup truck sticking out.

"We owned all of this back then. The fields behind the house and the fields across the road. We had this barn and two others spread out across our four-hundred acre operation. Lots to keep running. Do you want to know what keeps a farm running, Elizabeth?"

"Corn?" Elizabeth asked.

Marylyn laughed at her odd statement. "No. The thing that keeps a farm running is the wife. I know I don't seem like much, but Donald and I were married for twenty years. Our second year of marriage, I gave him his son and heir to the family farm. For twenty years I did everything. I even went without most times. I didn't mind, really. It was my duty to make sure my boys had it all. They were my pride and joy. Family over self is the unwritten code of the farm wife." She seemed to drift off into her own thoughts for a moment.

"So, what happened?"

Marylyn shot Elizabeth an annoyed glance. "Well, things are never that simple, are they? I wish I hadn't been so blind. Men, you know, are funny things. They'll turn their back on you."

"Oh, my Jack never would do a thing like that," Elizabeth said.

Marylyn Anderson glared at Elizabeth with eyes filled with rage. In a sudden movement which almost happened too quick to be seen by the naked eye, Marylyn pushed Elizabeth to the ground. "What makes you so damn special, sweetie? You think you're different somehow? You think you're going to give him a couple of babies and you'll live happily ever after on the farm? Is that what you think? Trust me, you are nothing but a fun little hole to him. I bet you all just love to fuck your brains out in my house, don't you? You're nothing but a two-bit whore!"

Elizabeth put her hands up over her face, afraid the enraged woman was going to hit her. She considered running into the house and hiding from Marylyn, but she had no idea how to get back to Jack. This world pressed down on her more with each passing moment.

Looking up through her fingers, she saw Marylyn standing there with a suddenly serene demeanor. "I'm sorry, Elizabeth. I got a little carried away and I apologize. You're not a whore. Not sure why I said that. I am sorry about pushing you. This is just so frustrating sometimes and I can't help myself."

Elizabeth was stunned, and confused, at the sudden change in her demeanor. Ignoring Marylyn's outstretched hand, she picked herself up off the ground and instinctively brushed herself off, but found there was nothing of this alternate world to brush off.

"Well, alright," Elizabeth said, cautiously. "Marylyn, you have no right to shove people and I am not going to tolerate being treated like that." Marylyn's mood swings convinced Elizabeth that she didn't have a complete grip on reality. For now, she had to play along.

"I said I'm sorry. The polite thing to do would be to accept my apology and we can move past this. At any rate, follow me. There's something I want to show you. I want to … convince you of something."

"Convince me of what?"

"You'll see, come with me."

Elizabeth couldn't move for a moment. Her instincts screamed at her to stop, like at the stairs before, Elizabeth's feet betrayed her as they began moving against her will, despite her best efforts to freeze her feet to the ground.

Elizabeth trailed Marylyn as she continued toward the barn, her fear growing that she might remain in this strange netherworld forever. Maybe she could simply find out what it was that Marylyn wanted her to see and then she could go back to her world. Back to Jack.

She reached the slight incline of the ramp leading into the pristine barn. Tools hung from the walls in designated places. The ground was clean, almost sterile. Elizabeth was seeing a version of the barn that Marylyn wanted her to see. A version that might have only existed in Marylyn's version of reality.

Marylyn came to a stop beside the truck. The hood had been left open, an old prop-rod holding it up. It was an older truck. Elizabeth remembered seeing one like it at an antique vehicle show Jack insisted on taking her to. In spite of the truck's age, it appeared to be in good shape. Marylyn looked pensively into the open engine compartment, motioning for Elizabeth to join her.

"What am I here to see, Marylyn?"

"Oh, please come closer. Don't be afraid, my dear. There is nothing to fear. Everything that is about to happen already has and will happen again."

In spite of her reassurances, Elizabeth's instincts told her to be terrified of what lay in the engine compartment. She could tell that something in there deeply disturbed Marylyn, in spite of her reassurances that there was nothing to be afraid of. Whatever it was made her profoundly sad. Elizabeth saw it in her eyes.

Elizabeth pleaded, "Marylyn, what am I doing here?"

"You're here to learn. I have things I need to teach you. They're hard lessons, to be sure, but they're good lessons and I really want you to learn them."

Elizabeth bit her bottom lip in an attempt to try and keep her composure. "I want to go home and see Jack. I don't want to play these games. Why can't you just say your piece and let me go?"

Marylyn drew in a ragged breath. "You want to see your precious Jack again, then you'll come up here and join me, right now. Maybe you're right to be scared. That's not for me to judge." She seemed to contemplate the idea for a moment. "Maybe I was too stupid to be scared. I should have known better. You have the chance to understand what I failed to understand until it was too late."

Elizabeth couldn't help herself. Her feet compelled her forward, ignoring her continual pleas to stop moving. In a few steps, she stood next to Marylyn and looked into the engine compartment of the truck. What she saw terrified her.

The engine compartment was shaped like a coffin. Inside, ringed with flowers, a small boy lay, dressed in a suit. In his hands he clutched a handful of dandelions. The boy's delicate head was supported by a small satin pillow. The interior of the coffin was lined with white silk,

215

and seemed to generate its own ethereal light. The boy looked peaceful, like he was in a well-earned slumber.

"Is he your boy?" Elizabeth tried to remember what she read in the newspaper. There was something about two teenage boys being killed. This boy could have been no more than six years old.

"That's my Matthew. He was much older when he was taken from me, but I really can't remember him that way. Its guess that's a mother's curse. We have no choice but to see our boys at their most innocent. It's always that way with mothers. Not that you'd know." Marylyn spat out the last sentence as an indictment against Elizabeth for not having any children.

Elizabeth said, "Someday I'll know." She was still unsure what kind of unholy game this specter was playing.

"All kids do is break your heart." Marylyn reached inside the engine compartment and straightened his tie. She leaned over and gave him a gentle kiss on the cheek. Then she pulled out the prop-rod from the hood and let the large piece of sheet metal fall closed with a dull metallic thud. She pushed the hood down for good measure.

Marylyn brushed the non-existent dirt from her hands and looked Elizabeth in the eyes. With a sigh, she said, "Whether they die on you or they leave, they'll break your heart eventually."

Terror gripped Elizabeth as she heard the panicked voice of the little boy inside screaming to be let out. His pleas seemed to rise in intensity as he hit the metal lid of his coffin.

"Daddy ... Daddy ... no! Mommy, stop Daddy, please. He's gone crazy. Mommy help me!"

Marylyn stood stoically, refusing to move a muscle.

Elizabeth jumped toward the truck and began pulling furiously on the hood to free the tortured child. "Help him! He's your child, for God's sake!"

"You don't see, Elizabeth; it does no good. No matter what happens, they all break your heart."

Elizabeth grabbed Marylyn by the shoulders. "Why the hell aren't you doing anything?"

The large eight-cylinder engine roared to life. Matthew's cries went from being screams of panic to ones of intense pain. Elizabeth heard the sounds of crunching and mashing from inside the engine compartment, but was powerless to stop it. Blood, bone, and tissue fell from the bottom of the engine compartment and onto the floor, making a sickening sound as it did. The giant engine acted as a pulverizing machine.

The boy's cries went silent as the blood from under the truck pooled around Elizabeth's shoes. All the while, she continued to pound on the hood, tears filled her eyes. Matthew was dead.

Elizabeth turned toward Marylyn with an accusatory glare. "Why would you bring me here to see this?"

"Because you have lessons to learn, Elizabeth. If you are going to live in my house, there are things you need to understand."

"But, this isn't your house, it's *mine*."

Marylyn suddenly erupted in anger. "Listen you stupid bitch. I have had enough of your backtalk and childish stupidity. Do you think I like it this way? Every day I stand here and watch the same thing.

Don't you think I would do anything in my power to stop this? I have stood here, thousands of times, and pounded on that hood. Do you have any idea how hard it is to watch your own child murdered over and over again? No? Then shut the hell up! Quit being a little self-centered whore and pay attention. You might learn something."

"Why are you doing this to me?" Elizabeth ran past her and back out into the grass, doubling over while vomiting. Shock took over as the reality of what she witnessed settled in.

Marylyn shook her head at Elizabeth. "I'm sorry, I lost my temper. For the last thirty years I've relived this day in an endless loop. This is my way of trying to help you. I know you don't understand it yet, Elizabeth, but you will. Get up, it's time to move on anyway." Elizabeth could feel the blood, which had soaked through her canvas shoes. She wanted to take them off and wash her feet, but after what she just witnessed, the idea of touching the blood repulsed her.

Between the house and the barn, Elizabeth dared a look back. To her surprise, it was no longer the fully constructed barn she saw, but the burned out husk. The timbers were exactly as Jack left it. The truck and the blood on her shoes were gone as well.

"The barn, it's—"

"Gone, yes I know. You saw what I needed you to see. We don't have much time left. Come on, we need to see the rest and then you can go back to your precious Jack. That's if you still want."

The way she said "precious Jack" sounded angry and condescending. Once again, Marylyn spit her words out of her mouth like they were an unexpectedly bitter piece of fruit. Elizabeth's mind raced. What did they have to do with any of this? She got the impression Marylyn harbored some resentment against Jack, but the source of that resentment was unclear.

Elizabeth asked, "Did you drop that picture on Jack?"

Marylyn stopped for a moment and made a half-turn toward Elizabeth. She appeared to regard the fields for a moment and let out an almost imperceptible smile. Then, without a word, she turned back toward the house and continued walking.

"I asked you a question," Elizabeth said.

"I'll tell you what," Marylyn said. "Since you're in the mood to suddenly ask questions, I'll make you a promise. If you just do what you're told and come with me, then I'll answer all your questions when this little tour is over. How does that sound?"

"Promise me," Elizabeth wanted to hear her say the words.

"I just did, darling. All you have to do is agree," she replied stoically.

Elizabeth had about enough of Marylyn's dodgy answers, "Say the words, Marylyn!" Now it was Elizabeth's turn to spit her words out.

Marylyn's face turned red and her mouth curled into a sneer. For a moment, Elizabeth worried she might be attacked again. "Fine," Marylyn said. "I promise as soon as we are done I'll tell you if I had any hand in dropping that painting on your precious Jack."

Elizabeth knew that ultimately this ghost, specter, hallucination, or whatever it was had the upper hand. There was little she could do but comply. "Fine, let's get this over with."

"Excellent, then let's go inside." Marylyn motioned toward the house. They walked up the stairs to the porch. For a moment, Elizabeth hesitated.

"Something the matter? Need I remind you of our promise? Is your memory really that short?"

Elizabeth needed a moment to collect her thoughts. Four people had lost their lives, including Marylyn herself. She stared out into the yard, hoping she wouldn't be witness to the other three killings that day. Looking off in the distance, toward the trees, she saw the empty branch where the swing had been. Perhaps she'd learned what she needed to learn, and the facade of Marylyn's world no longer needed to be maintained.

"Let's go." Elizabeth stepped in front of Marylyn and entered the house. The room looked the same as it had before they went outside, except that there was now a young boy sitting at the folding table. He was hunched over some homework that looked like it was probably too advanced for a child his age and seemed to understand it anyway.

He looked up from the work and regarded them seriously. "Hi, Mom."

"Hi, Robbie, honey. How's the homework coming?"

"Good, Mom. It's going well."

"Look at me, baby. Look up at momma." Robbie did as he was told. "Do you see the nice lady standing next to me? This is our new friend, Elizabeth."

Robbie regarded her for a moment. "Is this the lady you were telling us about?"

"Sure is, baby. She is going to free us from all of this."

Elizabeth remembered the newspaper article. Robbie was the second boy it mentioned. He was about sixteen when he was murdered. Just as the last boy, this one appeared to only be about seven.

Panic suddenly rose in her chest. She realized what was about to happen next. "No Marylyn, I can't watch this. You can't let this happen."

"But I have to die, lady," Robbie said. He regarded her solemnly. "I have to die because that's what my daddy wanted. For all of us to die. And it happens every day. Mommy says only you can stop it."

Marylyn put her hand on his shoulder. "Shhhh ... baby, look at your papers now. You know you shouldn't talk to adults that way. You have homework to do."

She tussled his hair as he picked up his pencil again. "Yes, ma'am."

Elizabeth looked away for a moment. Did these people really have to die every single day? Is that what was wrong with this house?

One look into Marylyn's eyes confirmed the awful truth. Every morning, the tragedy of that fateful day replayed itself where the Anderson family is viciously murdered by its patriarch. Or, at least, some version of that horror takes place.

As she turned her eyes back to the scene, On the opposite side of the table, a man stood next to Robbie. An ax hung high above his head.

Elizabeth tried to scream out, to tell him to stop, but couldn't move. She was stuck in place. The ax swung down with frightening ferocity. It was quick, wordless, and bloody. She watched as the body of the boy fell off his chair and onto the floor next to the table. His head rolled onto the table and stopped when it hit a pile of textbooks.

The eyes of the slain boy stared at Elizabeth for a moment. His mouth fell open and the severed head said, "You are the only one who can stop this, you know? It goes on and on, day after day."

Marylyn's voice rang out, suddenly from somewhere upstairs. "You know you shouldn't talk to adults that way." The man had vanished from the room as well. Elizabeth was alone with the slain child. The boy's eyes closed.

Elizabeth stood in frozen panic. She wasn't sure what to do with herself. There were still two more people in that house, and it was up to her to try and avoid seeing their demise.

"Oh Elizabeth, please come join me upstairs." Marylyn's somber voice called from the bedroom.

"I want to go back now. I can't stay."

Marylyn yelled down from the master bedroom. "I quite agree, you can't stay. We are almost at the end, let's get this over with and you can be on your way."

She fought against her own feet. But part of her also desperately wanted to be free of the grisly sight of the dead boy. She turned toward the staircase. At the top, instead of the dark hallway, she saw the warm hue of a light streaming from the bedroom.

Elizabeth felt like a chain was pulling her up the stairs. She strained against the pull while daring to look back at the body again. To her surprise, the body was gone. The blood, the books, even the pencil the child had been using were gone. The table remained, empty of any evidence of the horror that took place.

Why would anyone kill those children? She wondered to herself, while her feet stubbornly continued to pull her up the stairs. They did nothing to deserve such a fate. Really, neither did Marylyn. *But why was she showing me these things?*

"That's right honey, now you're asking the right questions." Marylyn's voice rang out from upstairs, in response to Elizabeth's thoughts.

Elizabeth yelled up toward the bedroom. "Why did Jack kill them?" Suddenly she realized her mistake. "I mean; why did Donald kill them?"

"Oh, Jack or Donald, it doesn't really matter, does it? Men are murderers." Marylyn shrugged her shoulders as if Elizabeth should have seen it just as clearly as she did. "Look, I've had thirty years to think this through. Thirty years of people coming and going through my house and I've come to a conclusion. Donald, my dear sweet husband, needed me to die. It's in his DNA. He can't help himself and it's the same with your little Jack too. Excuse my foul language, but you're nothing more than a pussy and a set of boobs to them. Hell, if a hand could orgasm, the fate of the human race would be in peril. Oh sure, an occasional blow-job will give you some control. Outside of their own sexual pleasures, men need blood."

It certainly wasn't that way with Jack. But with each step, she felt less sure of herself. Images of Jack having sex with Rita's mutilated corpse continued to flash through her mind. She was so sure that wasn't real. Or was it? Elizabeth questioned what she really saw, what she knew to be true. Had she actually watched her husband having sex with a corpse in their bathtub? Was she really willing to accept that?

After seeing the two in the tub, she'd blacked out for a time. Could it have been long enough for Jack to move the body *and* clean up the bathroom? Jack was a terrible housekeeper, but Elizabeth supposed there was a first time for everything. The blood would have been all over the place. On the other hand, if he managed to keep the blood in the tub it would have all been rinsed away.

But Rita, there was no denying that she saw Rita. Jack and Rita never actually interacted, or did they? She could've been a simple figment of Elizabeth's imagination. She remembered reading somewhere that victims of traumatic events could fill in mental blanks with memories of events and people who weren't really there. It was the brain's way of making sense of things. Maybe her brain was trying to convince her that Rita wasn't really dead.

She felt her hand tremble and her knees weaken. Elizabeth grabbed the handrail for balance. Forcing a look down the stairs and back into the living room, she was horrified to see the two boys, still dressed in their suits, standing together. They flickered for an instant, like an old television whose signal had been interrupted. They flashed between mere children to almost full grown adults and back again.

"They were my babies, you understand. I loved them more than anything on earth." Marylyn, now standing at the top of the stairs, looked down at Elizabeth. "I know what you're thinking. They would grow up to be like their murdering father. Probably true. But until that time they were my little angels. That bastard killed us all. That bastard Jack … I mean, Donald, killed my children."

Elizabeth felt a headache suddenly overtake her. She looked down at the kids again. Blood spurted forth from their chests as they smiled back at her. It looked black in the ambient light of the room as it bubbled out of them. A deep crimson color stained their shirts and formed pools on the floor under their feet.

"Jack, how could you do that? We loved our children," Elizabeth said. The idea that these weren't her children faded from her consciousness. She saw them as her own. Her memory provided her with images of a pregnancy and a labor that never happened. Her mind tried to reestablish a difference between the children in the living room and the kids she knew she didn't have. She loved them and was awash in maternal instinct. Willing to die for her own children.

Elizabeth thought of the horrible night her so-called boyfriend forced her into a bathroom and raped her. She felt his hand across her throat and his fists beating her into submission. He said he loved her and demonstrated that love by abusing her in the worst way someone could abuse another human being. It wasn't sex he sought it was control over her. Violent and ultimate control.

"That's right, honey, men need control and now you need to make this right. This will go on forever unless you do something about it. It's in your power and you know what you need to do, Elizabeth."

Elizabeth's foot rested on the second floor hallway. Her headache seemed to lift as quickly as it had taken root. Refreshed with a new sense of purpose, she thought about the boys and the man who had killed them. Looking to her right, she saw the bathroom door open and the light on. The floor was coated in thick layer of blood. The edges of the carpeting had begun to soak it in. The dismembered corpse of Rita lay piled up on the floor at the foot of the bathtub like a pile of chopped wood waiting for a campfire.

Marylyn stood in the doorway of the bedroom. "I have to admit, I had my doubts about you. Certainly, you were a stubborn pupil. But, you came along better than I could've ever imagined. I'm quite proud of you."

Elizabeth turned to face the specter, now standing in the bedroom doorway. Marylyn, like the boys, had a red streak in her chest where a wound formed. Blood now dribbled from her mouth as she spoke. Her impossibly tight bun had partially unraveled. Blood matted a streak of graying hair to her cheek.

"I have a really good teacher," Elizabeth said.

Marylyn reached out and grabbed Elizabeth's hand. "What a sweet thing to say. Come with me, it's time for your final exam." Marylyn led her into the bedroom, letting go of Elizabeth's hand when they reached the side of the bed.

Elizabeth felt a wave of panic overcome her. "Don't leave me. There is so much I don't understand and you can teach me. Please stay and help me."

"You're a sweet girl. I can't help you anymore, this is one of those things you're going to have to do by yourself. Time for me to go."

"I understand," Elizabeth said, wiping a tear from her eye.

"Oh, and, Elizabeth?"

"Yes?"

Marylyn smiled at her. "I did drop that picture on Jack. I wanted to kill him, to save you. It would have been the easiest way and I failed. You need to complete my mission." With that, she laid down on the bed. Her clothing had become so saturated with blood that it soaked through and onto the covers.

Elizabeth's foot touched something on the floor. The handle of the ax was just sticking out from under the bed. She retrieved it and felt its reassuring weight. The same ax as the one from downstairs, it was the home's chosen instrument of death. Linked by murderous intent to the house by one horrible deed, committed so long ago. A deed that was doomed to repeat itself unless someone ... unless *Elizabeth* did something about it.

Marylyn breathed her last as her eyes fixed into the deathly stare of someone no longer of this earth.

The door swung open behind her and Donald walked into the room. He was carrying a double-barreled shotgun. Elizabeth remembered the news article explaining that he had used the shotgun to kill himself.

Not waiting for him to get the upper hand, she swung the ax at him. With reflexes she would not have thought possible, he used the shotgun to parry the strike before it could find purchase. He swung the shotgun around to take aim at Elizabeth, and she countered with a parry of her own, using the ax handle. Letting the momentum of the tools weight carry her around, she sliced down with the ax head from left to right, catching his shoulder. She'd managed a slash across his chest. It sent him crashing to the floor and the shotgun skittered across the room in the opposite direction.

"You bitch, how could you?!" the man howled. He turned to face her, no longer Donald Anderson, but it was her own Jack.

She was tempted to bring up his murder of Rita, but thought better of it. "How could I do what? You killed our babies!" In reality, that husband seducing bitch got her poetic justice.

Jack lay sprawled out on the floor, bleeding heavily. The ax was sharp and had managed a significant cut.

"Rita was good. Hal had her trained well. It only took a little bit of convincing to get her out of those clothes and into the tub." Jack sneered back at Elizabeth.

"You killed her!" Elizabeth felt like it was someone else screaming at him.

He had a smug look on his face. "Of course, I did. And I'm going to do the same to you. Maybe I'll fuck your little dead cunt. You'd like that, wouldn't you? Then I'll carve you up into little pieces."

Elizabeth had heard enough. She raised the ax above her head. There would be no missing.

He sneered at her. "You don't have the guts. Nothing but a weak little woman. Always need your Jack by your side. Always need your big man Jack to solve all of your problems. Nothing but a weak, pathetic woman."

She swung the ax down as hard as she could. For a brief moment, she heard him scream in agony as the steel head found its mark and crushed its way through bone and sinew. The chest cavity gave under the intense force. It should have disgusted her, but it only made her feel empowered.

Something fell from her hand and hit the floor.

"Are you alright, sweetie?" Jack said. "You seemed to be off in your own little world for a minute."

Elizabeth's perceptions melted from the world of their bedroom where she had just killed Jack to the dining room she'd started this journey in. It took a moment for her to remember what they had been discussing. "Yeah, I suppose I'm alright. I don't know what got into me. Just got lost in my own thoughts and dropped the ax … I mean, table." She grasped her cup of coffee off of the table. It was still warm.

"So, as I was saying, there is a fair in Joliet next weekend. Maybe we could head up there and check it out. According to the website, they are going to have lots of books and handcrafts. What do you think?"

I think you aren't going to live that long, you murdering son-of-a-bitch. "That sounds like fun."

The sounds of a truck entering the driveway broke up their conversation. She remembered the people were coming for the table and the moving van were showing up today. So much to do. Arranging stuff in their new house, watching some more *Real Housewives,* killing her husband and hiding the body. Really, quite a bit to do.

Out with the Old

Jack came down early that morning. He didn't sleep well; the raccoon incident assured that. As he watched the coffee maker spring to life, he wondered why an animal, which had the great outdoors as its playground, would ever decide it needed to live in their cellar. That seemed like something which would happen in a southern state and not here in the heartland.

Maybe I'm just being a bit overly dramatic. I likely scared the critters away.

The coffee splashed into the bottom of the Pyrex coffee carafe, making a satisfying sizzling sound as it hit the bottom. The aroma was intoxicating. As the coffee machine continued to sputter away, Jack walked out the front door and down to the road where the newspaper dutifully waited. He liked the feel of the paper between his fingers every morning. He had a hard time reading the news on his laptop. Most days Jack only focused on the theater section, but would eventually read the entire paper if he had time. It took a few editions before he started to get the hang of the daily news from Chicago. It was definitely different than the papers out East.

As he extracted the folded paper from the plastic box at the end of the driveway, a truck drove down the county highway in front of the house. Waving at the motorists, they returned the friendly gesture. That was another big difference he noticed between living out East and here. Out East, people would probably ignore you if you waved to them on the street. In the Midwest, people actually slowed down and waved back.

At first, Jack had his reservations about moving out here. Life along the eastern seaboard was great; he had friends, the smell of the ocean, the beaches, and the summer which seemed to go on forever. It was really nice. The Midwest had a slower pace of life. It was relaxing. The people without exception, were gracious to a fault. Watching the truck disappear into the distance, he thought, *I could get used to this.*

Taking stock of their new house, the future of his construction obligations screamed out to him. He knew someone would have to be hired to repair the soffits and the siding, probably sooner rather than later. But it could keep for another season if they really wanted to put off those major projects to see how they liked the area. What bothered him most were the windows; those were looking pretty bad. Maybe he should just replace them.

There was a lot going on today. He received a text from Rita telling him they would be over soon to pick up the table and chairs. He didn't relish the idea of selling the big table; it had kind of grown on him, but their table would be here later today and they needed to make room. The moving company had sent an e-mail saying to expect them shortly before lunch.

As he poured himself a bowl of his favorite cereal, the sounds of Elizabeth moving around upstairs echoed off the hard wood floors. He suspected she had just as tough a time sleeping as he did. She didn't like anything furry and small, so the idea of something furry and a little bigger would really creep her out.

Jack could always go without coffee, but not her. In hotels, he would sneak out of their room early to make sure a cup was waiting for her when she woke. It was his way of keeping the peace.

She wordlessly stepped past him, and moments later he heard the sound of a ceramic cup filling with coffee.

Elizabeth declared, "Ahhhh. The elixir of the Gods."

Those were the magic words. It was safe to talk now. "Morning, honey."

"Good morning." She yawned.

He put down the paper. "Don't get too comfy. The people buying the table will be here in ten minutes."

"It'll be sad to see it go. I like it. There is something majestic about it."

Although it wasn't their style, it really was a nice table. It didn't match anything they owned and would have stood out like a sore thumb. There was something almost campy about the table. A table like this would fetch at least three thousand dollars back home, but here it was more common. The solid wood table truly was a beautiful piece of work.

In the corner of the room a folding table sat shoved behind a small curio cabinet they had resolved to keep. Elizabeth pulled it out. Based on the awful sound it made, it had likely been there for years.

Picking up his paper again, he glanced down at the small advertisement nestled into the farm report. "Hey, look here, there's a fair in Joliet—"

He was interrupted by a loud clunk on the floor. Looking up from his paper, he saw Elizabeth staring off at the wall in the living room.

She was mouthing something, but he couldn't tell what.

"Are you alright, sweetie? You seemed to have taken a little mental vacation from the house this morning."

She shook her head. "Yeah, I suppose I'm alright. I don't know what got into me. I just got lost in my own thoughts and dropped the ax ... I mean, table."

He frowned at her odd response. "So, as I was saying, there is a fair in Joliet next weekend. Maybe we could head up there and check it out. According to the website they are going to have lots of books and handcrafts. What do you think?"

Still evidently distracted, she said, "That sounds like fun." He could tell she was responding automatically to his question and not really understanding what he had said. Jack resolved to mention the fair again when she was more attentive.

His thoughts were interrupted by the sounds of a large truck backing into the driveway. Looking out the window, he saw a yellow rental truck large enough to get the beast of a table out of there.

"Wow, they are prompt, aren't they?" He put down his spoon. "I suppose, just like everyone else, they start early around here." Elizabeth still seemed to be off in her own little world. "Everything okay, honey?" He was still worried after her fainting spell the day before.

"Yeah, fine. Say, I have to run into town. Do you need anything?"

"Actually, there are a few things I need from the hardware store, but I can come with."

"No," she said, excitedly. "You need to be here for the movers. I'll go. Just write down what you need and I'll pick it up." Taking her cup of coffee, she went back upstairs to get dressed.

Rita came to the door with her normal smile. Dressed in a sports coat and wearing her realtor's name tag, she looked far more upscale than normal.

Jack faked surprise. "Wow Rita, all dressed up for us?"

"You know it, nothing but the best, darling." She gave him a hug. "Must look all official this morning, I have to work at the front desk in the office today. I have to take the desk a couple times a month when our regular receptionist is gone."

Rita reminded Jack of a great-aunt who would come over and sneak you candy when your mother wasn't looking. He had yet to meet Hal, but everything he'd heard led him to believe that he was just as charming.

"And these fine folks are the Williams'." Rita opened the door for a man and a woman.

"Hello there! I guess you're here for the table?" Jack said more for the sake of politeness. Everyone knew why they were here.

Two more large men entered the house and set to work on the massive piece of wood. They quickly removed the legs from the table, and the pieces were carefully wrapped in bedding and other materials the group brought with them to protect the wood from damage during transport.

During the commotion, Elizabeth came down and surveyed the work. Jack looked up at her. She looked a little sadder about the table than he thought she would be. But, they were getting good money for it, and their own table would be here soon enough.

Elizabeth waved at Rita, who was virtually pinned between the table, and the wall. Then she blew Jack a kiss and walked out the door to the car.

The men were done in quick order, and Jack had sixteen hundred dollars in his hand per the agreement with Rita. For a few moments, they sat in the quiet of the house, sipping coffee.

He turned to Rita. "I meant to ask you what you knew about the house before we bought it."

"Oh, you mean the stories? Yeah, I heard them too. Not sure I believe them, though."

"Did you do any digging?"

She shrugged her shoulders. "Not really. As an agent, you learn to be careful about how much digging into a home's past you do. I rely on the cold hard facts of a home before I sell it. The inspection report, any information the previous owner provided, things like that. If I dug into every single history of every home I sell, I'd never sell any houses. Every house around here has some sort of story, and every one of them has had someone die in it at some point."

"Fair enough. What exactly did you hear?"

Rita drew a heavy sigh. "Well, all I know are the rumors." Jack shot her a terse glance. "Seriously, I never saw anything in particular that led me to believe any of it was true."

He rolled his eyes. "Okay, now you're just stalling, get on with it," he said.

Rita threw her hands up in the air in surrender. "As you know, this place is called the Anderson farm. I'm not sure you'll ever live in this house long enough to live that name down. The farmland around it was sold off to the surrounding farms after the family died. Back in the eighties, farmland was going for cheap around here. Someone told me, at one point, these farms weren't worth the corn that grew on it. They were, literally, paying to farm. It was the same where I lived in Indiana, of course. Lots of farmers just let their fields go fallow for a season or two and depleted their savings. Many of them lost their farms to the banks.

"But, I'm getting off track here. I heard a rumor that old man Anderson went a little nuts and killed his wife and kids. After the extended family found out, no one ever went back in the house. A caretaker checked on it once in a while and the family maintained the place, but that was about it."

Jack took a sip of his coffee. "You don't sound like you believe the story."

She frowned at him. "Not really. You know all of the houses around here have stories to them. This one is haunted, that one has a body buried in it, that house was once a brothel. Those kinds of stories grow up on the prairie like wheat."

Jack reached into his pocket, pulled out the printed news story and handed it to Rita. He watched her as she read it. Her eyes went from the size of saucers to squinting as she re-read parts of the story. "Oh my God, Jack. I'm so sorry. I really didn't know any of this for sure, just rumors. Honestly, part of me didn't want to know. People around here don't talk about it and I really didn't want to ask."

"That's okay Rita, we didn't expect you would know."

Rita's eyes flew open wide. "Does Elizabeth know?"

"She does. Found out when she visited the library."

"How'd she take it?"

Jack let out a big sigh, folding his hands in front of him. "Well, I guess we decided to stick around here for a while longer. I told her we would move the second she no longer felt comfortable here. There's definitely something creepy about living in a house you suddenly find out was the scene of the most brutal murder the county had ever seen. Maybe it's explainable, maybe not. I don't know; Rita, this place just gives me the creeps."

"Are you sure you are not just reacting to finding out the house has a bad history?"

"That could be the case. But don't be shocked if a ghost shows up in the middle of the night and kills us all." Jack made a gesture across his neck suggesting his throat was being cut.

Rita chuckled. "Oh, wow. You know, you could open up a bed and breakfast here. Home of the famous Anderson murders! Just think about it, that could make you some extra—"

A loud crash came from upstairs. It sounded like something had fallen over. For a moment, both Rita and Jack sat there in silence.

"Maybe we should check that out?"

"Oh no!" Rita shook her head. "Your house ... your haunting. I'm staying right here," Rita said, clutching one of the couch pillows to her chest.

Jack went up the stairs, straining to listen over the sounds of his footfalls. Stopping about halfway up, he listened for a few seconds. It

238

could be one of three things, their furry visitors had returned, a ghost of the slain Anderson family wandering the halls, or a serial killer had intruded on their idyllic mid-western paradise. At least, for the moment, everything seemed quiet.

He advanced up the stairs and stopped at the top. In contrast to the downstairs which had the frequent whir of the refrigerator, the upstairs was silent.

Suddenly his mind flashed back to the funeral of a distant relative he'd attended as a child. The funeral home was a converted antebellum home. With little imagination, it would be easy to see Rhett Butler descending the grand staircase. To a child of eight, the entire scene seemed creepy. Wandering out of the viewing room where countless unknown relatives sobbed incoherently into handkerchiefs over a relative whom he never knew, Jack wandered into an empty viewing room. In contrast to the room he left, this one was simply furnished and at the front of the room a single coffin sat alone.

The lights of the room were purposely aimed shining down on the well-oiled casket as a display for families making arrangements. The room was separated from the rest of the building by a long hallway and thick walls, making it quiet. Approaching the casket, he could just see over the side to see the tip of the nose of a mannequin laid out in a suit, meant to represent the recently departed. His young imagination took over and in place of a stoic humanoid chunk of plastic, the chest of the mannequin rose and fall as if new life had been breathed into the previously non-living. In his terror Jack ran back to his mother and stayed by her side for the rest of the service.

Standing at the top of the stairs he wished he could run back to his mother once again. Jack was almost too scared to look into his own bedroom. He was convinced a casket would be standing open, some form of human laying inside waiting for him.

Rita yelled out. "Everything okay, Jack?"

He was started from his self-generated terror by her voice. "I haven't been hacked to death yet, if that's what you mean."

"Okay, but if you are, please let me know," she yelled back with a nervous laugh.

Jack was definitely unnerved by the sudden stillness. Maybe it was because he was all alone on the second floor. Or maybe it was his imagination playing tricks on him, but the air felt heavier. Like he was walking through water instead of air; pushing against some unseen force.

Jack was sure, one hundred percent, he had closed the closet door earlier that morning. Ever since the incident the night before, he would not leave that damn door open.

But, now the door stood wide open.

He moved down the hallway, toward the open closet. *Time to cowboy-up, Jackie,* he heard his father's voice ringing in his ears.

He paused for a moment, unsure if he was more afraid of the unknown or the possibility of finding some oversized rodent chewing on a burlap bag in the corner of the closet. Overcoming some of his fear, he willed his feet to propel him forward. Suddenly regretting not bringing his bat with him, he drew near to the open door. The light wasn't on, but this time of the day he could see inside the first third of the closet with little trouble.

Stepping forward, he almost had a heart attack as his foot landed on something soft. He drew his foot back in horror and his eyes grew huge. Convinced he had stepped on a severed limb or maybe the entrails of a murder victim, he reflexively put his hands up to protect his face. He looked down and realized what he had stepped on.

A mop.

The great Dr. Jack Milburn, educated man of philosophical thought, almost peed his pants because of a mop.

It must have fallen from its hook, and the door wasn't completely shut. A breeze blew through the house and then, boom. Mop hits the floor and the door bounces off the wall.

Turning on the light to check the closet, he was relieved to find nothing. He put the mop back on its hook and closed the door, pushing it hard and hearing the latch catch securely this time. Maybe he needed to talk Elizabeth into wanting to leave the house. Clearly, it was affecting him. It might be better to live somewhere he felt a little less … threatened.

Returning downstairs, he found Rita looking out the window at a moving van backing into the driveway. One man dressed in dark blue overalls, was guiding the vehicle as it backed in with a *beep beep* noise

.

Then again, I can stick this out for the time being. Our own stuff might make it a lot more like home.

The truck came to a sudden halt. Jack exited the house just as the man approached. "Hi'ya there," the man said with a heavy Minnesotan accent. "Name's Dan, I'm from the moving company. Are you Mr. and Mrs. Milburn?"

Rita laughed at Dan. "Oh gosh honey, thank you, but I'm old enough to be his mother."

"Mrs. Milburn is in town," Jack said with a laugh. "But we can get started. I know where we want everything."

"You betcha," Dan said in reply.

Another man jumped out of the driver's seat and opened the back of the truck. They moved with lightning-quick efficiency. Jack tried to make decisions based on where he thought things should go, knowing that Elizabeth would likely have him move them to somewhere else in the house anyway.

The unloading didn't take nearly as much time as the company had allotted. The moving men were fast and strong. They even helped Jack put together some of the furniture he had to disassemble for the move. It was really quite exhilarating to see his stuff again.

With the furniture set up and Jack and Rita sitting comfortably, he breathed a sigh of relief. It was a large step up from the furniture which had been there before, the remains of which sat out on the lawn.

Jack glanced at his watch. "Seems like Elizabeth should be home by now, wonder what's keeping her?"

Rita frowned in response to his question. "She told me she had a few errands to run today. Something about going to the hardware store and doing some grocery shopping."

Like fate had only been waiting for someone to ask the question, Elizabeth pulled into the driveway. Putting the car in park, Jack glanced over at her behind the steering wheel. She looked disappointed for some reason.

"Hey, Honey, welcome home. It looks a lot more like home now."

"Hey girl, you were gone a while," Rita added.

Elizabeth answered, "Yeah, I know, some things took longer than I thought they would. I stopped and had a burger for lunch. I was going to bring it home, but it was too good to wait. But I did get the rest of the stuff on your hardware store list. How'd the move-in go?"

Jack smiled. "Pretty well, the men worked fast. They had to get it done and over with. The truck has to be in Des Moines tonight. They have a long day ahead of them."

Rita asked. "I thought you were going to get groceries?"

"Oh I was, but I forgot my list. I have this migraine screaming in my head. Maybe I'll lie down for a bit. There are some things in the trunk which need to be brought in."

Without another word, Elizabeth marched past the two of them and into the house. Jack couldn't help but shake the feeling something was wrong with his wife. Something happened to her today while she was out shopping which unsettled her. Rita must have felt it too, as she shot him a quizzical glance.

Oh well, whatever it was, it'll surely pass.

Absence Makes the Heart Grow Fonder

Elizabeth listened to the thumping and bumping of the men in the driveway. For a moment she watched a three men and a woman jump out of the moving van. At the same time, Rita's car pulled into the driveway.

Turning from the window and stepping back toward the mirror, Elizabeth ran a brush through her blond hair. Marylyn stepped from the shadows as if she'd taken up residence in the closet. "Don't be too hard on yourself. Men are all the same. He betrayed you, didn't he? He was going to betray you no matter what."

Elizabeth's voice broke as she mumbled through a reply. "I don't understand it. I feel so—"

"Hurt, sweetie. The word you are searching for is 'hurt'. But you know, it isn't all bad."

Marylyn took the brush from Elizabeth and continued brushing her hair. The brush massaged the back of her scalp with every long stroke. Her hair made a satisfying crunch as it untangled the knots. Elizabeth couldn't help but feel a maternal connection to Marylyn. It reminded her of the times when her own mother had brushed her long hair in front of the mirror when she was a child.

Pools formed in Elizabeth's eyes. "What am I going to do?"

"Shhhh, Elizabeth honey. There's no reason to cry. You already know what you need to do."

"But I don't want to lose Jack."

Marylyn let out a sigh. "I know it's hard to hear, but he's already lost, dear. He deserves what all men deserve. You need to end him before he ends you. Maybe you should take out that little Rita of his as well. I'll bet there isn't even a real Hal."

Elizabeth said quietly, "You don't know that."

Marylyn replied skeptically. "Oh yeah? Have you ever met Hal? How about talk to him? Nope, I didn't think so." Marylyn turned Elizabeth around to face her. Look, honey, this here is a fool's circus and you're the clown. Do what you have to do, before it is too late. For any of us."

Elizabeth stood there, eyes locked with Marylyn for a moment. The thought of killing Jack had a strong appeal. It felt like the right thing to do. Blinking through the tears, she closed her eyes for a moment and when they opened, Marylyn was gone.

Descending the stairs, Elizabeth surveyed the packing materials the people had brought with them. Among the chaos of the men moving table and chairs, she saw Jack and Rita standing in the middle of it all, laughing about a joke she missed. Silently, she tried out the names Jack and Rita Milburn. Marylyn was right, she could see it in their eyes. It made her a little sad and angry as she walked through the door.

Reaching into her purse for her car keys. Behind her, the screen door slammed against the wood frame of the house. Elizabeth remembered the ax. There was no good way to sharpen it before she would need to use it, but maybe Mr. Gulliver would have an idea. She picked it up and for a brief moment, she was reminded of the heft and swing of killing her husband in that alternate reality. It was justice, it would make her whole. Maybe Marylyn would be so happy with her

246

they could stay in that house together. They were good, wholesome people.

Turning out of the driveway toward town, she passed a yellow moving truck coming up the opposite side of the road. It was probably their stuff being delivered. She briefly thought about turning around, but reasoned it would be better to let that cheating husband and his slut deal with it. Let them have their fun. It would be short lived.

Pulling into a parking space in front of the hardware store, she could see Mr. Gulliver inside, working at the cash register. As she opened the door, she thought about maybe bashing the old man's head in with the blunt end of the ax and then maybe doing in his wife as well. That didn't seem terribly neighborly since she needed his help. It also wouldn't be particularly sporting since the man was at least three times her age. Better to stick with the current plan.

He looked up. "Well, if it isn't Elizabeth. What can I do for you?"

"Good morning, Mr. Gulliver." She reached into her back pocket and retrieved the list of items Jack asked for. She figured it would be less suspicious if she just played along in her 'nice wife' role for now. Besides, she needed these things to fix up the house anyway.

"What do you have there?" the old shopkeeper pointed to the ax on her shoulder.

She held up the ax. "Oh yeah, really I am looking for advice more than anything else. Found this in the cellar. I was wondering if you could tell me how to sharpen it. We'd like to chop wood if need be."

Mr. Gulliver took the ax from her and considered it for a full minute. "This is a pretty old ax. Don't see them made like this anymore. I have new ones made of composite materials. The heads are basically the same though."

"You mean it's an antique?"

The old man chuckled. "Just like me, for sure."

"Can it be saved?"

Mr. Gulliver eyed it again for a few moments. "Why sure. There's nothing wrong with it, really. Granted, you'd be better off just buying a new one and finding some antique store to sell this on consignment. It'd fetch a pretty penny, as axes go. There are people that collect these kinds of things. Sort of a weird thing to collect, but people collect all kinds of things. I had this friend once who collected ex-wives."

Why can't you just shut-up, old man?

"So, if I wanted to remove the rust and give it a good sharpening, what would I need to do?" She flashed him her best innocent smile.

"If you're dead set on saving this old felling ax, I can help you out. You'll need a can of linseed oil, a small bucket, sandpaper, and a file. I can show you how to do it. But if you are just going to chop the occasional block of wood, I'd still recommend buying a new one." Mr. Gulliver pointed over his shoulder at the display of hand tools. He did have an appealing array of tools. Everything from canoe to large tree-felling axes.

Elisabeth smiled at his use of the term 'dead set'. "Just because something is old, doesn't mean it's necessarily bad."

He readily agreed, and for the next hour they discussed the process of sharpening her ax. Everything from soaking the head in linseed oil to working your way up with the sandpaper until the rust was completely removed.

The conversation was intolerable for Elizabeth. She was only interested in sharpening the thing, but he stymied any attempts she made at moving the discussion along. As soon as he was done, she put the things in her car and made her way back to the library. There was something that bothered her about the way her … or, Marylyn's boys were killed. Perhaps the newspapers would provide more information.

Cute-as-a-button Penny came from around the corner of the aisle. Still dressed in jeans and a tee shirt, and her hair was still pulled back in a ponytail. Elizabeth silently wondered if the girl ever thought about dressing in anything but the drab uniform of a modern day millennial.

"Good Morning, Elizabeth," Penny said, putting down the stack of books she was carrying.

Elizabeth glanced at her watch. "Hi, Penny. Good afternoon, actually. You know, it isn't really my place to say so, but have you ever considered maybe taking your hair out of that ponytail?"

Penny gave her a smile. "Yep, I have. Even tried it once. Don't like it. Between studies and work, I don't have the time to brush my hair like I should. Besides, if I looked pretty, then I'd have to deal with icky boys."

"Sure, I get that. No one wants to deal with icky boys."

From somewhere deep in her mind she heard the voice of Marylyn, *I'd bet that letch of a husband of yours would fuck her brains out, given the chance. Then he'd kill her, sure as shit. Get on with it, Elizabeth.*

Elizabeth tried to quiet the voice in her head. "So, I came back to look at the newspapers. I wanted to find out more about the house."

Marylyn's voice became more insistent in her head, but she shoved it aside for now. She seemed to take exception to Elizabeth's quest for more information.

"Sure thing, you know where the computers are. I'll be around if you need anything. I have a never-ending pile of work to do around here."

Elizabeth went back to the machines and continued her search on the house. What she found only confirmed what she already knew: Donald Anderson had killed his entire family with an ax. It was likely the same ax she now had in the back of her car. The investigation concluded that neither of the boys had a chance to even react before they were killed.

Defensive wounds were found on the hands and arms of his wife, Marylyn. The blade had sliced off some of the skin from her hands as it was brought down on her. While the newspaper had few images of the crime scene, Elizabeth didn't need to see them. She'd seen them first hand.

One of the boys was killed in the barn, and then the body had either fallen in or was shoved into the running engine of the truck they had been working on, post-mortem. The medical examiner said it was hard to tell because the time in between the two events was minimal. However, since the flesh and muscle of the hands and arms were essentially ground off the bones with little evidence the boy tried to resist, Dr. Gold concluded he was already dead when the boy was thrown into the engine block. This stood in sharp contrast to the pained attempts of the boy to escape the horrors Marylyn had shown her.

The floor of the barn was covered in blood when the police arrived on scene. The engine was still warm. The smell of burnt flesh was so bad they had to put on air tanks usually reserved for entering buildings on fire.

The second boy's head was found mostly severed. It lay at an odd angle to the body, which was on the floor. Elizabeth imagined the body likely came to rest exactly where the end of the dining table had been sitting that morning. It struck her how insensitive it was for her to be standing where the body of Marylyn's youngest child came to rest.

The murder of Marylyn had taken place upstairs, in the bedroom. One photo showed her body covered in a blanket, her left arm dangling off the side of the bed. Although they tried to cover her up, the bloody fingers were visible outside the blanket.

Just outside of the image she could see another blanket, likely the one used to cover up Donald Anderson.

Marylyn's voice played around in her head as she read the newspaper reports. *You're next, you know. Even if you leave my house, you can be sure that eventually, he'll do this to you as well. That's why men are no good for anything other than making babies.*

In the eighties, the newspapers were still careful not to print things which could be deemed tasteless. Standing in sharp contrast to what was routinely put out in the press today, which bordered on the insanely provocative. The newspaper clippings were careful not to print any pictures showing anything more than a finger or a part of a foot. They also kept the pictures with blood to a minimum.

One reporter dug deeper into the story. He seemed less interested in the event itself and focused on what caused it in the first place. What really caused Donald Anderson to lose his mind? According to the report, the crop prices that year were the worst the area had ever seen. One bank official admitted that the Anderson farm was going through foreclosure proceedings and would likely be repossessed.

Elizabeth fought back the voice of Marylyn in her head. She wondered why he didn't just move them all off the farm, maybe try his hand at another job. The world really wasn't that bad off at the time. It was just before the Reagan revival, and had he only held on for a few more years he might have been able to rebuild something of his life. Although she hadn't even been born when this tragedy took place, she knew times were hard back then, but the late eighties and the early nineties were considerably better.

Jack ... or Donald rather, must have been under a lot of stress, she thought. She seemed to remember a case where a guy had gone crazy because his wife had died and he ended up killing a bunch of people because he thought he could use their souls to bring her back to life. The modern world had no shortage of crazy to pick from.

Jack would never hurt her. Jack and Elizabeth had been in love from the moment they first laid eyes on each other. She remembered that morning seeing Rita standing in the living room. Jack hadn't killed anyone. Elizabeth felt she knew Rita well enough by now that she would never cheat on Hal. Granted, she'd never met him, but the way she talked about him always indicated a deep love.

It's that house, she thought. The house was making her think these crazy things. Maybe she needed to see someone. The idea of killing

Jack made her uneasy. Could she ever really go through with it? No, she was sure she wouldn't.

She'd also heard dust and mold can make people crazy and physically ill. Perhaps that explained why she had been feeling so strange. Maybe it's why her thoughts had been so clouded lately. Sure, all she really needed was some fresh air and maybe some more rest.

In the back of her mind, she could feel the voice of Marylyn trying to register protests with her sudden clear-headed thinking. But Elizabeth, in the air of the library and the fresh air from the drive, retained a grip on her own former perspective of the world. She knew Jack loved her, and his love was reliable and true. That love would see her through no matter what happened.

Maybe everything would be fine now. This moment of clarity brought her some peace. All she needed was to get out of the house for a bit and see the rest of town, to drive their hatchback around with the windows down, the fresh air of the farmland in her nostrils. A little joyride was therapeutic.

The news articles were surprisingly weak on details about Marylyn. She seemed to have no life outside her home. There were a few items which mentioned her at church and other places, but the majority of the articles only mentioned her in the context of being Donald's wife. She largely lived in the quiet shadow of her husband. One article gushed about her award-winning blueberry pie.

I can share that recipe with you. Marylyn's voice suddenly intruded into Elizabeth's thoughts. Elizabeth quickly waved her away.

Turning to leave the computers, she saw Penny standing off in the distance, staring at her. She had a curious look on her face. Elizabeth realized she was probably talking to herself while she was reading the newspaper clippings.

Elizabeth let out a smile and said, "You know, Penny, they say that talking to yourself is a sign of a healthy mind, answering your own questions is a sign of brilliance, but arguing with yourself is insanity."

Now it was Penny's turn to look embarrassed. "Sorry, I didn't mean to stare, but I just get so few people in here. Did you find what you were looking for?"

"I did. I guess I got a little peace of mind. Have you ever looked at the newspapers clippings about the Anderson farm?"

"Not really. I don't delve into that stuff too much. My life is books and data. This is my church, and we sing the praises of proper shelving. No time to dig up old ghost stories."

She smiled at the young librarian. "Penny, that's a great way to look at things. If you don't have time to dredge up old ghosts, then neither do I. I think I'll grab a burger and then drive around town a bit before heading home. I have some work to do. Our stuff showed up today."

"Oh, I know!"

Elizabeth shot her a quizzical look. "How on earth did you know that?"

She shrugged her shoulders. "Well, for two reasons. First, your local librarian knows everything. And second, your moving van is the first one to pull through town in like five years, and the last one that did was lost and needed directions back to the interstate. Are you excited to be getting your own stuff back?"

"You bet."

Elizabeth walked out the library door, secure that she was, once again, in charge of her own mental faculties.

Moments later, she stood inside Bacon Drug Store, watching them cook up the largest and juiciest bacon cheeseburger she'd ever set eyes on. She had intended to bring it home, but it was too much to resist. She sat down at the old lunch counter and ate her meal with gusto.

She hadn't realized it until that point, but even her appetite was off. Maybe she should make an appointment to see the doctor and have some blood work done.

A sign in the corner promised her the best shake in the county. She wasn't sure how accurate, or recent, that claim was. But it turned out to be one of the best shakes she'd had in a long time.

Elizabeth felt more relaxed than she had in days. Maybe it was just the house. If it was mold and mildew, it wasn't something she really needed to expose herself and her husband to. Someday, maybe soon, they wanted to start a little family and mold and mildew could affect a newborn.

A sudden decision pushed its way to the forefront of Elizabeth's mind, startling her. They needed to leave that house. Jack would take it hard, but she could soften the blow by insisting they stay in the same area. The little town worked its charms on her, and she loved the people she'd met, but she needed to get out of that house.

Elizabeth felt buoyant. Like a weight had been lifted off of her shoulders. Perhaps one more night in the house, and they could move into a nice hotel over by campus. They could find a new place to live and then have their stuff moved. Jack would do anything for her, and she would never ask him to give up teaching. Moving would be a small thing. And Rita certainly wouldn't mind finding them a new place to live.

Driving home, she turned the radio up and rolled the windows down. The weather was still grey and wet, but the rain had stopped and the wet fields smelled heavenly. Making the turn into the driveway, a headache erupted in her head like thunder rolling through the sky. The pain wiped the smile from her face. She knew, from past experience, this was the onset of a migraine. Sleep and a dark room would be the most effective treatment for a headache this severe.

She pulled into the driveway and headed inside. Leaving the things in the back of the car, she made her way upstairs. She needed to escape the light. Darkness was the only thing that seemed inviting to her.

Lightning in The Distance

Jack worried about Elizabeth. Although her migraines weren't unheard of, they could be debilitating. The quickness with which she ascended the stairs suggested this was going to be a bad one.

Rita left to take care of Hal and Jack suddenly felt alone in his own home. Surrounded by his own things was comforting, but with Elizabeth asleep, the quiet of the house was a little bothersome. He reflexively picked up the remote to turn on the television, but then put it down again, thinking Elizabeth might be woken by the noise.

He paced around the living room to the kitchen and back. Waiting a reasonable amount of time, Jack finally got up the courage to creep upstairs. A few of the stairs squeaked in protest as if they were designed to give a night stalker away-or to bother a wife with a migraine.

Reaching the top landing, he heard the sound of Elizabeth rustling the sheets. He pushed the door open a few inches, leaving the hallway light off. Peeking inside, he saw the dimly lit form of his wife, with her back to him. A blanket thrown over the window served as a temporary blackout curtain.

He turned from the door to make his way back downstairs when he heard her speak.

"Jack?"

She turned to face him, and they locked eyes. "Yeah, honey?"

"I need to ask you something. Promise you won't be mad at me?"

He let the thought sink in for a moment. There was no way in this life, or the next, he could possibly be mad at the beautiful woman laying in the darkness of their bedroom. In some ways the form in the bed was not that far removed from the girl he'd met in school. Elizabeth wore the look of vulnerability like a shroud. The need to protect her from the world was immense. "Sweetie, I'd never get mad at you. You know that."

"You remember when you told me that we could move out of this house anytime I wanted to?"

She now had his full attention. If she was starting out this conversation this way, Elizabeth had internalized something to the point it no longer took on the air of a discussion. She'd made up her mind on something and all that had to happen now was for her to verbalize it. "Yes, and I meant it. We're partners. Home is wherever you are."

"I know you said that. But it hurts me to ask you to do this." She let out a telling sigh, her eyes red from crying.

He took her hand in his. "What is it, honey? You know I love you more than anything on earth, right? Just name it, and it's yours."

"I want out of this house. I mean first thing tomorrow. Right now I want to sleep, but tomorrow we need to gather a few things and leave. I can't explain it, but I can't stay here."

Jack sat gingerly on the bed next to her. He knew buying a place without Elizabeth on the house-hunting trip was a potentially bad idea. They were fortunate though, walking away from this investment would be of little consequence. It was impractical, but in the end, this decision wasn't about money, it was about his wife.

He placed his hand on her shoulder. He knew not to touch her head or neck, where the pain was probably the worst. She put her hand on his in response.

"If you want, tomorrow we can burn this whole house down and never look back. I don't care one lick to be here a moment more than you want to be. My place is with you. If you asked me to give it all up and live on a beach somewhere as your boy-toy, I'd do it in a heartbeat."

She chuckled. "Don't make me laugh, Jack, my head hurts too much."

"Okay honey, you get some sleep and in the morning we'll go to a hotel and discuss what to do next. Anything you want, anywhere you want, anytime you want. I love you."

"I know. I love you too. No matter what happens, remember that I love you." With that, Elizabeth drifted off into a restless sleep.

Jack left the bedroom, closing the door as quietly as he could. He wondered what was bothering her so much. She wasn't a rash woman by any means. This was the woman who encouraged him to invest his own money; not because they really needed it, but because she was taught to save for a rainy day. Even with her family's resources, he watched his mother-in-law clip coupons every Sunday afternoon. It was a quality of frugality he saw in Elizabeth. For her to ask him to give this house up, she had to have some pretty strong feelings on the matter. But for him, he only needed one reason. She wanted out of the house.

It was too early to go to bed, so he took a beer from the fridge. It tasted good, as the night had suddenly become warm and humid. In the distance, he heard the sounds of thunder. He remembered reading somewhere that most lightning actually takes place inside the clouds, which is why they occasionally light up in the night sky. It was both frightening and beautiful.

Jack thrived on the chaos that came with uncertainty. Planning and execution of actions dealing with multiple variables remained one of his favorite situations. His mind raced with extensive lists of things they would have to do to get out of this house. The movers would have to be scheduled, the Internet person, whose contact information still lay on the kitchen counter, would have to be re-contacted. He started writing notes on a notepad.

He plugged in his headphones, connecting them to the television so he wouldn't disturb Elizabeth's sleep. Snapping on the television, the newscaster droned on about some rocket test North Korea had conducted.

A sudden cloud-to-ground lightning strike issued a frightening crack in the distance, which Jack jumped at despite the newscaster's voice in his ears. The world descended into sudden chaos as a squall opened up.

Meet Mr. and Mrs. Stimson

Although Hal and Rita had been together since high school, no one would ever describe their love as hot and passionate. It was always at a simmer, and had been that way since the day they met. Their parents accused them of settling for the first love they found. What most people didn't know was that behind the scenes, they would die for each other.

After helping Jack get the house in order, Rita went home, making a brief stop at their favorite Asian food place. She pushed her way through the door at home, joyfully announcing, "I've got egg rolls!"

No 'Hello honey', no 'I'm home', but a short and sweet announcement that made his heart flutter. He loved egg rolls and the woman who brought them home.

"How are the kids getting along?" Hal asked.

She gushed, "Oh, you should see those two, cute as a button."

"Better keep a close eye on them. Living in a cursed house could have consequences, you know."

She shot him a disbelieving glance. "Oh, Hal, you superstitious old cuss."

"I'm serious, love. I've been by that place a bunch of times. I even helped re-roof it a few years back. Something off about that place. Not sure how to describe it."

Hal spent some time on the Chicago Fire Department and then switched to selling farm implements in Indiana. After a few years, the company asked him to move to central Illinois and open their new store and he jumped at the chance. It was an opportunity to be his own boss.

Hal maintained he had a sixth sense about the world around him. He sensed things before they would happen. Rita thought he was nuts, but he'd learned to listen to his inner feelings and that house maintained a constancy of pain, loss, and trouble. The structure always gave him a sense of indescribable sorrow, like a prisoner rotting in prison for a crime they didn't commit.

He had feelings about the newcomers which started the day Rita told him about Jack and Elizabeth. It was hard for him to put his finger on, but he told her he was afraid for them. Passing on a couple of opportunities to go over and meet them, he promised he would soon.

Sitting in his recliner, staring at a point in between the tips of his white socks and the television, he tried to make sense of his present feelings. It was like he knew something was about to happen, but he had no way to put it into words.

"Is this one of your feelings again?" she asked.

He glared at her. "I'll thank you to not make fun of them. You know sometimes my feelings are dead on. I've learned not to ignore them. Time I meet to meet Jack and Elizabeth, I think. Not today, though, let's see if we can get them over tomorrow night for dinner."

Rita dropped one of the egg roll bags into the garbage. "Wait a minute. Are you recommending we actually be social for once?"

He frowned at her. "I'm not saying we do a wife-swap or anything. Just dinner. I'll throw stuff on the grill, and I think I saw some early corn yesterday. We can go get a dozen ears."

Rita came into the room carrying a cup of tea she made for herself. "Hal Stimson, you are a man of mystery. I'll give them a call in the morning and see if they'll be up for it. Lizzy has a migraine right now. Remember, darling—"

He sighed deeply. "Yeah, I know. No politics, religion, or football. Sheesh, woman, what would I ever do if my mother wasn't around to tell me these things?"

"Good boy. Not sure Jack is much of a football guy."

"Oh well, that kind of limits my topics of conversation," Hal said, barely hiding a smirk.

Rita sat down in the chair next to her husband, glaring at him. She picked up the newspaper and frowned at the article on the cover. "Did you see this article about this guy in Peotone who called 9-1-1 because he was having heart trouble? Police arrived to find a meth lab set up in his garage. What's the matter with these people?"

"Yep, crazy world we live in. Almost anything can happen, really." They sat in silence for a few moments. "I'm really worried about those kids, Rita. I have no earthly idea why, but I am. Maybe it's nothing, but I doubt it."

Possession is Nine-Tenths

For a moment, before sleep took her, Elizabeth savored the conversation with her husband. She knew how lucky she was to have a man who would agree to just drop everything and move. Not having too many serious relationships before Jack, she got the impression she was lucky he was such a wonderful man.

She surrendered to the sleep which promised respite from the throbbing in her head, feeling herself drifting through an ethereal realm where the world below her was but a distant memory.

In a sudden change to her dream scape, Elizabeth found herself standing in a space filled with roses. They sat in crystal vases on bases of varying heights. The only light came from twelve candelabras placed around the roses, giving everything a warm glow. Air swirled around the room in a gentle breeze, carrying with it the scent of baby powder and rose blooms. Past the candles and the roses, the space descended quickly into an impossible blackness giving no impression of any depth or width. Elizabeth felt that if she ran into it, the darkness would envelope her.

These feelings evaporated when the temperature suddenly dropped and an icy wind hit Elizabeth like the door of a freezer just opened somewhere in the darkness. The candles on the candelabras flickered only briefly in the rush of wind before resuming their steady glow.

From the depths of the darkness, she heard a voice. It was quiet at first, rising in volume as if trying to find the right pitch and tone for Elizabeth's ears. Erupting into laughter, it soon devolved into a low cackle. Elizabeth thought of the noise the Wicked Witch of the West made before she threatened Dorothy and Toto.

Elizabeth knew this was no fictitious witch. She instantly recognized the voice, and it made her tremble. A dream that started out so well had devolved quickly into something more terrifying. It was the voice of Marylyn. The intrusion enraged Elizabeth. Marylyn appeared before her in the red dress from the closet.

"You know, I changed my mind. You don't deserve the dress. Besides, looks better on me."

Elizabeth wanted to run, but she knew it would get her nowhere. "Marylyn, what do you want?"

"You know, I expected more out of you," Marylyn said. "I really didn't think we would have to have this conversation again. I feel betrayed, Lizzy."

"I am getting a little tired of this, Marylyn. Release me! I'll never do what you want me to do." Elizabeth wanted to put distance between her and the unearthly figure standing before her. But she had nowhere to run, nowhere to hide.

Marylyn's eyes drilled into her. "You knew what you had to do. I thought you understood how this would play out. I figured, in light of everything, you'd see reason. Reason is all it is. Men are harmful animals. Oh, don't get me wrong, I love my boys. For sure, I still love Donald." Marylyn suddenly looked off into the dark abyss with a contemplative look in her eye. "Funny really, even after all of this time, I still love my husband. Even though he murdered me in my own bed, I'd do anything to have him back."

Elizabeth pleaded, "But, that was Donald. You convinced me all men were like that. You hijacked my mind and talked me into attempting murder. Marylyn, think this through. What you want, it's insane. Jack isn't going to murder anyone. I know he isn't. Tomorrow, when I wake up, I'm going to pack a bag and move out of this house, you can have it. We're leaving, never to return. I don't want to live here anymore."

Marylyn still stared off into the darkness surrounding the small area lit by the candelabras.

"Do you hear me? I won't help you." Elizabeth begged for some sort of understanding.

Marylyn turned abruptly and pointed a menacing finger at her. "Oh yes, you will. You don't think I'm going to spend one more day in this hell, do you? No, I need to be free. I've earned that! There's only one way out. You needed to try and kill that wonderful Jack of yours. But you screwed it up. You're not completely to blame, of course. I shouldn't have let you leave the house. As soon as you leave I start losing my grip on you. A mistake, I can assure you, I won't make again."

Elizabeth's mind suddenly put all the puzzle pieces together. This wasn't about murder; it was about Marylyn's freedom. She'd been in this house for thirty years, unable to leave, and she'd stop at nothing to free herself of the torturous afterlife she'd designed for herself.

"You need me to take your place." Elizabeth's gaze shifted from Marylyn to one of the candles burning before her. "You need me to kill Jack and then myself so you can go free and I can be stuck here until someone else comes along. Is that it? Did I figure it out?"

Marylyn leaned into one of the candelabras and blew a candle out. It promptly re-lit itself in protest. "Well, sort of. Actually, I need him to kill you. But still, you have the basic logistics down. History, sweetie pie, really does repeat itself. And I need you to play a starring role in my theater. I want out of here, and you're my ticket. Oh, it's not so bad. The first few years are actually alright. Then it gets tedious. My relatives tried to live in the house after that husband of mine decided to bury the proverbial hatchet. I tried to contact them, but here's the funny thing about being a ghost; no one can see you. Sure, the old saying of seeing a ghost out of the corner of your eye and feeling their presence is true. But no one is ever willing to accept that you're there.

"So you and Jackie-poo show up, and I figured you could be my one-way ticket. So yes, I made you see things. An interesting side note, I tried to spook Jack, maybe convince him to go a little insane and kill you. Sort of a short cut. Bless his heart, he really doesn't have the right temperament."

Elizabeth covered her mouth in surprise. "But if I killed Jack and I didn't kill myself, you would be in this same situation."

"Silly little girl. There's no way I'd let you kill yourself. That's the beauty of the plan. You try to kill him and he kills you defending himself. He has to be overwrought with anger, and the only way to do that is to hit him with that ax. Not enough to kill him, of course, but bring him to a good boiling rage. It's sort of a poetic plan really. He kills you with the same ax Donald used to kill me."

Elizabeth shook her head and took a few steps backwards. "You don't know Jack."

Marylyn frowned. "What do I need to know? He's a man. A simple, stupid penis with arms and legs. It's in your vows, isn't it? Kill spiders, open jars, and making babies. I believe that's what you said. If not, it is still true enough."

Elizabeth silently prayed Jack would sit on the corner of the bed, in the waking world, and maybe drag her from this deep slumber. But the more immediate concern was to distance herself from this madwoman.

In a burst of energy, she shoved Marylyn to the floor. She took down one of the candelabras and a vase of flowers as she fell.

Elizabeth had no idea where she was going and in the piercing darkness there was no real sense of direction. Perhaps Marylyn's sense of direction would be just as bad in the seemingly eternal darkness. Behind her, she Marylyn shrieked in anger.

Her shriek was suddenly replaced by a loud laugh which sounded like it was broadcast through loudspeakers lurking nearby in the eternal darkness. "Oh run all you want, Lizzy. This is my world, and you're not done until I say you are."

Elizabeth ran as fast as she could. No walls, floor, or ceilings were visible. In front and behind her the world stretched out into nothingness. Without warning, Elisabeth's direction seemed to change under her and instead of running forward, she was suddenly falling. The fall either lasted an eternity or the briefest of moments. In this world it was hard to determine how much time had passed.

This must be how skydivers feel. But, then again, they have parachutes.

Without any warning, or even a sound, she landed on something soft. It was the couch in the living room. Not their newly-delivered couch, but the one that was in the house when they moved in.

For a moment she sat, completely stunned. The house seemed quiet. Elizabeth yelled out, "Jack, Jack are you there? Can anyone hear me?" There was no answer. The refrigerator made a dull humming noise as the fan turned on in the kitchen. "Jack, please! You have to hear me!"

At least she was away from Marylyn, if only for a moment. Attempting to calm her nerves as much as possible, Elizabeth took a deep breath and ran to the door and locked it. Maybe she would be lucky and Marylyn would stay outside. Then she ran to the outer door of the mud room and locked it as well. She quickly checked the windows, and felt satisfied there would be no way to get in on the first floor without breaking the glass, serving as an audible warning.

Glancing out the front windows, she watched the world Marylyn had created. This is the way things looked the day they all died. It was exactly what Marylyn remembered of her life before being trapped in this nightmare. She suddenly felt a slight pang of sympathy for her. It was easy to see how someone could go insane, being trapped in the house they died in for thirty years and being forced to relive the murder of her entire family over and over again.

The corn in the field stood still. The wind from the prairie apparently didn't touch this version of reality. The sky was a sickening rusty orange color. The tire swing hung from the tree limb like a pendulum which had lost its inertia.

She moved from window to window, checking for any sign of the enraged specter. For a moment there was nothing more than just the silently still stalks of corn and the dull orange sky. She felt momentarily relieved.

In the corner of the living room, a baseball bat leaned against the wall. She picked it up and put it over her shoulder. Not completely sure if she could defend herself with it, but she felt better having something in her hands. Approaching the stairs, she stood in silence for a few seconds to listen. She hadn't bothered to check upstairs after coming inside the house. It seemed unlikely Marylyn would be able to get inside the second floor, but in this twisted version of reality anything was possible. She forced herself upstairs to check the rest of the house, baseball bat in hand.

At the top of the stairs, she looked down the hallway in both directions. The door to their bedroom was open. She jumped into the room, ready to take a swing, but was relieved to find it empty. Checking the other rooms, she found nothing. The last room she checked, the one that scared her the most, was the bathroom. Pushing the door open, she couldn't help but feel sick thinking about the image of Rita bleeding out in the bathtub.

Just as she turned to leave, something caught her eye outside in the cornfield. Elizabeth tried to convince herself it might be an animal, but she knew better. Marylyn was making her way through the fields.

Bounding through the rows of corn, she delicately touched each stalk as she passed by. As she did, the green corn took on a sickening red color and started oozing crimson liquid. The delicate tassels of the corn stalks were bleeding simply by her touch. Each one looking like the end of a paint brush coated in a deep red hue.

At the edge of the cornfield, Marylyn stopped and stared at the house as if she were appreciating its classic style. Then she focused on the window Elizabeth was standing at. Their eyes locked. To Elizabeth, it felt like she had been stabbed in the heart with an icicle. The feeling was so potent she actually shivered. A smile broke out on Marylyn's face. The sickening smile of a murderer.

Marylyn took off like a shot toward the house, trampling corn stalks as she ran, leaving a trail of blood. For a moment, Elizabeth mentally went over her preparations, remembering locking each of the windows and doors.

She was so fearful of Marylyn, but why? She was a farmer's wife, not a mixed martial artist. She'd have a tough time breaking through the thick wooden doors, and the windows would slow her down enough to give Elizabeth the chance to deliver a few good whacks with the bat.

That's when she heard the noise and realized the fault in her plan.

It sounded like a block being moved over a piece of sheet metal. *Oh shit, the cellar door.* Someone put an old cinder block on top of the two aluminum doors to keep them from blowing open in the wind but the doors remained unlocked in case of a weather emergency. The interior door at the kitchen was lockable, but she forgot to check it. Marylyn Anderson was in the cellar.

Elizabeth hugged the bat closer as she listened for any telltale sounds. For the moment, everything was silent. Even the normal mechanical sounds of the house seemed to be absent. She tapped into a childhood wish that an inanimate object could give her magical powers. Right now she would settle for her husband stubbing his toe on the corner of the bed and letting out a scream to wake her up from this nightmare. But for now, Marylyn's dream world seemed to be holding perfectly intact.

With sudden resolve, Elizabeth pushed herself outside of her state of terrified inaction and threw herself down the stairs, taking them two at a time. Maybe she could reach the kitchen door and lock it before Marylyn could gain entry into the kitchen. A far cry from keeping her out of the house, but it was something. In her haste, she tripped over the corner of the couch and fell to the floor. In wild flailing of arms and legs, Elizabeth crashed onto the floor, sending the bat bouncing off various objects.

Marylyn's footfalls stopped at the top of the stairs just as Elizabeth regained her footing and, grabbing the bat, lunged toward the kitchen door. The tarnished brass of the doorknob turned clockwise, and the door inched open.

Elizabeth swung the bat through the now open door and heard a satisfying crack from the other side. She felt the fleshy report from the bat striking someone on the other side and a shriek from Marylyn. Her accomplishment left her momentarily speechless as she realized Marylyn could actually be hurt.

"You fucking little whore!" Marylyn screamed as she took two long strides into the kitchen.

Retreating for some distance between herself and the enraged woman, Elizabeth screamed back, "Stop this now! You can't keep me here!"

"You have no idea what I'm capable of. If you think for a second that I'm going to just let you go, then you're as stupid as you look."

Elizabeth took another swing at Marylyn, who jumped out of the way.

"You don't get it," she continued. "I control you. I control all of this. You're powerless to do anything here. This is my realm."

Marylyn raised her hands above her head, and the ax appeared. Blood dripped from its handle, covering her hands and forearms like the ax itself had suffered a major wound. She took a swing through the air, missing Elizabeth's face by inches and spattering her with blood.

Elizabeth yelled back. "This is my dream, and I can wake up anytime I want to."

"Oh? So sure of that, are you? Go ahead, try to wake yourself up then. Tell you what? If you can wake yourself, then you can leave my house. You're too much work for me anyway. There'll be another. Someone better suited to my needs. Go ahead and try."

Elizabeth knew she was right. Marylyn called her bluff. She had tried repeatedly to wake herself up, without success. If pure terror or the sense of falling couldn't wake her, then nothing inside this dream world likely would. A sullen look crossed her face.

A smile erupted across Marylyn's lips. "This is what we call checkmate, I believe. You know, as a matter of fact, I've been looking at this all wrong. I went to a lot of trouble, and I really should have approached this differently." The ax disappeared from her hands. At the same moment, the bat disappeared. "Why am I working so hard when I control you?"

"Marylyn, think about this," Elizabeth begged. "You're going to try and murder someone so they'll kill me. That doesn't make any sense. You need help."

"Sweetie, I'm a ghost trapped in a haunted house. Do you really think I can just march into the doctor's office and ask for counseling? Nope, I don't think so." Marylyn paced the kitchen like Elizabeth was no longer there, placing a finger on her lips as if deep in thought. "What to do with you? I can't keep you here, too much energy to keep you here. What to do?" After a few moments, she snapped her fingers. "Oh, I know!"

The house around Elizabeth vanished. The corn, the lawn, the tree with the tire swing, everything faded to an infinite black. Elizabeth reached out, trying to touch something in contrast to the blackness. Steel bars suddenly appeared in front of her. They moved toward her with alarming speed, pressing against her chest. Other bars appeared, holding her in place at her sides. They didn't squeeze her, as much as keep her from moving more than a few inches in either direction. Elizabeth realized suddenly, she was inside a tall, narrow cage.

Marylyn appeared out of the blackness, staring into Elizabeth's eyes. For a moment, neither one of them spoke. In desperation, Elizabeth grabbed the bars with her upturned hands and shook them. They wouldn't move, seemingly fused to one another by unseen welds. A prison made for one.

"Don't worry, love, you're not going to be there long. I just need to borrow your body for a while. It's actually pretty nice. Who knows, maybe I'll take that little Jack of yours for a ride first. You know, it's been a long time, and Jack looks like he could be tons of fun in bed."

Elizabeth sobbed openly. "You're sick, you know that! How can you justify murder with murder?"

"It's got nothing to do with murder. It has more to do with freedom. Oh, I forgot something." She snapped her fingers again, and Elizabeth felt a pillow form under her head. "I don't want you to be uncomfortable. Don't worry, this'll be all over very soon."

Marylyn vanished, leaving Elizabeth alone, in the impossible darkness, caged in a tiny prison cell.

A Day in the Life of Marylyn Anderson

Waking up for what seemed like the first time in thirty years, Marylyn blinked out the piercing rays of the sun. Borrowing some of Elizabeth's memories, a recent weather report indicated the day was supposed to be warm and sunny, in stark contrast to the day before.

Somewhere, deep inside of her, she knew stealing was wrong. But this was a whole other level of theft. Marylyn wondered what Pastor Stephen would have thought if he knew she'd stolen an entire body.

Whatever happened to him? Surely he was dead by now.

Marylyn knew possessing Elizabeth's body for more than a day would be difficult if not impossible. The better part of this day might be just long enough to pull off her plan; maybe with enough time left for her to take a quick drive into town and see what had become of it.

Soon enough, Elizabeth would figure out the great irony of her situation. It was her dream, and she was correct in insisting that she was really in control. Elizabeth could just as easily take back her own body as she could decide to make a fist or point at something she wanted. It was Elizabeth's own fear that allowed Marylyn to gain control of her. Fear is great at debilitating people. However, it could also be a great motivator as well. Marylyn would have to work quick to see this through.

Still, she did it. After thirty years, she was free of the hell she had created for herself. When her husband murdered them all, she was wracked with grief. She held onto the house for dear life, or afterlife as the case may be. Sure, when she died, other spirits came to visit her, to give her consolation and take her from the house, but she turned them away. Eventually they stopped coming.

Within the house, she felt closest to her children. She roamed from room to room. Occasionally she would clean, only to find that it was her version of the house she was cleaning. In the real world, the dust never moved, and the windows remained obstinately smudged.

Her despair turned to hate; her hate turned to anger. People tried to live in the house, but they either refused to see her, or they were terrified. Either way, they never stayed long. The last couple who tried to live here was her cousin Edith and her husband. She never liked Edith much and her husband was a lecherous drunk. Marylyn enjoyed manipulating Edith's dreams and toying with her mind, she came to the conclusion it might be possible to take control of her body if the resident consciousness could be convinced they were no longer in control.

Of course, Edith was too much of a prude to allow that to happen. Marylyn knew she needed someone young and impressionable. Older people are too set in their ways. Too young and it would be hard to instill the right level of terror. Then Jack Milburn came to look at the house. Young and handsome, he wandered the rooms and Marylyn followed Jack and that Realtor lady Rita. Then he spoke of his young wife Elizabeth, and Marylyn knew she was on the right track. She would have to work quickly.

The warmth of the sunlight hit her borrowed skin as it emerged from blankets. It was delightful. In her world, the world she left Elizabeth in, the sky was always the same color. There was no wind, noise, or movement, with the exception of her own rustling. Occasionally Marylyn would hit something as hard as she could to hear some sort of noise and feel some sort of sensation.

She heard the breeze rustling the leaves on the trees, a few cars or trucks making their way down the highway, and birds chirping. The sounds were intoxicating, and only vaguely familiar. It had been so long since her world had any sound.

Using her other hand, she reached down and scratched an itch on her thigh. The skin was soft. Feeling down to her knee, she was pleased that Elizabeth seemed to have taken good care of herself. She reached up her abdomen and to her breasts, still pert and perky. She'd have to take a closer look in the mirror.

There was another noise she couldn't immediately identify. It was a slight rasp behind her, but then she realized it must be Jack. She cautiously rolled over in the bed to look at her—no, *Elizabeth's* husband sleeping soundly. She felt a slight twinge of panic as he moved a little. Would Jack suspect anything? Maybe she would say or do something that would give it away? Thankfully, along with her body, she'd gotten access to her memories too and faking a proper response to any question should be fairly simple.

Standing up from the bed, she paused to look at Elizabeth's reflection in the mirror. The visual was even more ravishing than the version she felt below the covers. It reminded her of a girl from high school. Stephanie Chambers, that was her name. So amazingly beautiful. That was the girl all the other girls caught a surreptitious glance at when they were in the shower after gym class. She got everything she ever wanted and more, all because she was pretty. Marylyn hated Stephanie, that pretty little bitch.

She wondered if Elizabeth was the same way at that age, someone everyone wanted to either be with, be like, or be far away from. It made sense that Jack was like a lost puppy around her. Her body had not yet been ravaged by childbirth, age, or processed fast food.

She glanced over at Jack, whose back was exposed to her. She could just catch a peek of his left buttock. He was way better looking than Donald. Less hairy too.

Maybe I could just wake him up for some morning sex?

Of course, that would be a risk. If Elizabeth had any sense of the physicality, she could feel the sex and it would help draw her back to her own world. This whole expedition could be over before it had a chance to get started. Also, she remembered that Elizabeth was not a morning person, so waking Jack up that way might be a little too far out of character. But it would be nice to take a shower. After all, it had been thirty years since her last one.

She climbed out of bed and made her way to the bathroom. It was completely different from when she was alive. Some fool cousin renovated the bathroom and then ran out of money to continue with the rest of the house. She liked the renovations.

Stepping into the shower, the hot water just washed over her. She always loved a morning shower, to rinse away the night. In spite of herself, she started singing a hymn she loved as a child. The risks involved in this short vacation from her own cold, motionless world was worth it. And now it was time to make this all permanent.

Behind her, a noise interrupted her that she hadn't heard in years. It was the sound of a man peeing in a toilet. She froze in terror. Perhaps Jack would be angry to find her in the shower. Donald would never have cared because he always showered at night, after working on the farm all day. Then he was up and out before the rest of the family, except on Sundays.

"Hey babe, how is your head this morning?" Jack asked.

She instantly froze in place. In a sense it was show time in her own little play. Digging through Elisabeth's memories to figure out how to answer left her more confused than ever. A peculiar thought entered Marylyn's mind: *I wonder if I actually sound like Elizabeth?* By now she knew the sound of Elizabeth's voice, but she really wasn't sure how her words would sound coming from Elizabeth's mouth.

The door to the shower opened and Jack stepped in behind her. "A shower before your morning coffee? This is a new one."

"Thanks for asking," Marylyn said, handing him the bar of soap. "My head is feeling better. I just needed some sleep." Thankfully the words sounded exactly like Elizabeth. Maybe not exactly her choice of words, but it would work well enough to get her through the day.

She glanced down at Jack. He was certainly far better looking than the image she saw from her world. The warm water rolled off his skin and down the drain. She watched him soap up his hands and found herself wanting him to rub it all over her. Something about it felt so wrong, but felt so right. Parts of Marylyn's borrowed body suddenly heated up in ways she hadn't felt in so long. She'd forgotten what it felt like to want that kind of touch.

He turned her around and started lathering up her back. As he did, she suddenly felt the warmth of his erect penis brushed up against her. There was no mistaking what he was interested in.

Men are so predictable.

He lathered her up and touched her in places she desperately wanted to be touched in. Soon he'd pulled her up and inserted himself into her, sending a wave of lust through Marylyn. It had been so very long. Although she was still worried about Elizabeth feeling these things, having sex with Jack was really not the worst side effect of her operation. She grabbed the back of his head and pulled him into her, enjoying the ride.

She reasoned that technically, it wasn't cheating on her husband since he had murdered her and had been dead and buried for thirty years. Something about it still felt wrong, but it was too late for second-guessing now.

Jack, as it turned out, was a very physical lover. At first, Marylyn was resistant, but then let it just happen. *Screw the consequences, I may only have this one day to be alive again, but I'm sure as hell going to enjoy it.*

Marylyn knew she had to move this along as quickly as possible. When he was done having his way with her, he washed her hair. She thought that was a nice touch. Donald would never do anything like that. He was always either working or too tired to have sex. One day she tried to surprise him and, to his credit, he did seem interested, but fell fast asleep before they even started.

Getting dressed, he playfully tugged and caressed her. It made her feel good to be wanted, even if it wasn't her own body. Marylyn always considered herself to be fairly attractive, but Elizabeth was on a different level. In a perfect world, she could just keep this body and have another try at life. *It would be different this time*, she thought.

"So, where do you think we should go? That is, assuming you haven't changed your mind," Jack said.

She smiled at him. "Well, Jack, you still have your job, so maybe we move more toward the University?"

"I seem to remember a nice hotel near there we can go to for a while. Can you call Rita? I have to run to work for a few hours this morning and do a couple of things. Maybe I'll check us into that hotel and get back as fast as I can so we can be on our way."

"Okay, take your time. I have a few things I need to do before we leave. Thank you, Jack, I mean, really, thank you for doing this."

He looked into her eyes. "I said it before, and I'll say it again, I'd do anything for you." He gave her a kiss. "I need to get going, I'll be home in the early afternoon, after lunch."

She certainly hoped he meant what he said.

It took her a while to find Elizabeth's clothes in the drawers. Soon she was admiring her image in the mirror again. She never was a fan of the jeans-and-tee-shirt look, but it suited Elizabeth well. She mused that there was no perfect ensemble for attempted murder, but most of that day would be spent preparing the ax for the work that had to be done. There would be no time to do a proper job sharpening it; this would have to be done on the quick.

Before leaving the room, something vibrated on the dresser. It was

Elizabeth's cell phone. She hit the answer button which featured Rita's face.

"Hello?" she said, somewhat timidly.

"Elizabeth, good morning girl. How are you feeling? I know you had a big headache last night."

"Oh, I'm feeling right as rain." Trying to sound as much like Elizabeth as she could. "All I needed was a little sleep."

"Glad to hear it. Say, I was wondering if you and Jack were available tonight for dinner. I want you two to come over and meet Hal."

"That would be splendid," Marylyn said. Granted, she had no intention of keeping the appointment. By the time dinner was supposed to be served, she hoped Elizabeth would be safely ensconced as the new spirit of the Anderson farm.

Rita sounded genuinely thrilled at the idea. "Great, I know Hal is excited, well as excited as Hal ever gets, to meet Jack."

"Can I bring anything?" She found herself instinctively thinking about the dozens of wonderful pies she could make for dessert.

"Tell you what? You can bring some wine. Other than that, I think we have everything we need. Nothing too elaborate. Just some meat on the grill, early corn on the cob, and good company. I also have a recipe for the best peach cobbler you have ever tasted. It was from my grandmother in Georgia."

Marylyn didn't want to sound overly enthusiastic; better to get this phone call over and done with quickly. "Looking forward to it. Well, I have to run. I have some things to do around the house before Jack comes home."

And then I'm going to attack him with an ax.

Ending the call, she marveled at the idea of cell phones. This was the first time she'd used one, and it seemed surprisingly intuitive. She vaguely remembered reading about someone who had a large phone in a bag that he could use while driving.

Rita's timing couldn't have been better. They would certainly come over shortly after Elizabeth and Jack failed to show up for dinner. If all went according to plan, they'd find a very confused Jack standing over the body of his dead wife.

She did mean it when she thanked Jack. She was just thanking him for something he was blissfully unaware of. He was sacrificing his own welfare to make her life whole again. If there was anyone in the equation she felt bad for, it was Elizabeth. That girl was too stupid for her own good. Marylyn saw the way she looked at Jack. Those big expressive eyes adoring her husband was enough to make someone sick. She was stupid with love. It'd wear off soon enough, much to her dismay. Then it would be a life of bake sales, pumping out kids, and making sure dinner was on the table for her man.

It was no life. She just wished she'd realized it sooner rather than later. Donald was a good husband most of the time. He never yelled, never hit her, and was a great father. She just wished someone would have told her it would become so tedious. Once in a while, he would come home drunk and a little amorous. Those were typically the nights when she'd been home with the boys, who were sick all day. Thankfully he didn't drink a lot and his friends were farmers too so they didn't make it too late of a night.

None of that mattered now. Her past was well behind her. As she watched Jack's truck disappear out of the driveway, she thought of her boys. Really, they were the most innocent victims in this whole sordid horror story. One that started with their deaths and would only now come to an end.

Opening the door to the cellar and descending the stairs was like a trip back in time. Many of the tools had belonged to Donald. The rakes, garden implements, hand tools, and garbage cans were familiar to her, but not in their present locations. Jack and Elizabeth moved things around. She knew it really wasn't her legal property anymore, but their attempt to change her world annoyed her more than she was willing to let on.

Then there was the ax. That hateful, murderous weapon. The last time she saw the tool it was swooping down toward her chest. Defending herself was a useless gesture, as the momentum of the ax cut through her skin and bone. Only a mere second passed through her mind to process what her husband had done to her, before everything went dark. There was surprisingly little pain as she succumbed to death.

Then she found herself standing next to her own body, watching Donald lay down next to her, placing a shotgun under his chin. She tried to yell out to him, to get him to stop what he was about to do, but it was no use. She watched her husband in deepening horror as he blew his brains out. Then she moved downstairs and discovered what he had done to her boys.

Elizabeth hadn't done any of the work to prepare the ax. "Oh well, no time now." She'd just have to make do with what she had. Shuffling through the items left in the bag from Gullivers Hardware, she took out the can of linseed oil and set it off to one side. Then Marylyn pulled out the metal hand file and, clamping the head of the ax to the tool bench, she went to work sharpening the blade.

An Ax to Grind

With every pass of the metal file, the edge of the ax gained more and more of an edge. Marylyn watched its colors change from the dull rust to a more lustrous silver. The old ax screamed, or maybe begged for a second chance. She thought about how ironic it was that the one giving it a second chance was its last victim.

Marylyn understood why Donald loved to spend hours in that stupid barn of his, working on his tools and their farm machinery. The therapeutic effect of watching every long stroke of the metal file against the ax blade had a hypnotic, mildly erotic effect.

Elizabeth's cell phone struck Marylyn as a modern wonder. It not only worked as a phone anywhere in the house but it also gave the time, date, and something called e-mail which seemed to be very busy doing whatever it was doing. Glancing at the time, she realized there was only a short while longer to prepare. The process had to be hurried along if she was going to be ready.

As the file made a satisfying scrape against the blade, Marylyn wondered about Elizabeth. How was she doing in that little prison cell she'd built? It could probably be viewed as a little cruel to imprison Elizabeth like she had. After all, Elizabeth was doing her a favor, albeit reluctantly.

She thought about Jack and how wonderful he was in the shower. It was a shame it had to end like this, but she knew there was really no other way. The shiny surface of the ax was coming along nicely. She put down the metal file and picked up the sandpaper to hone the edge to something sharper.

In the nightmare of her existence, Marylyn suffered the daily pain of being murdered. Every time, the blow of the ax was just as painful as the time before. It wasn't fair that it never got easier. At some point, the pain should have become routine, just a part of doing business. But, then again, it wasn't necessarily the pain she was reacting to. It was the betrayal.

Marylyn stopped for a moment. Her face flushed at the thought. Truly, the pain in her heart came less from the violent end of her existence, and more from the betrayal. Why did Donald think that was the way out? Marylyn tried to be an exemplary wife in all respects. What supreme sin had she committed to warrant their execution? She stared into the shine of the ax head as it lay there, a tear escaping from Elizabeth's tear ducts, making its way down her cheek and then off the chin, landing on the wooden handle of the ax. It trickled off its edge and hit the floor.

There were happier times, before it all went so terribly wrong. The Anderson family rarely took vacations; maybe once a year Donald would take a weekend off and they would go up to Chicago. On one occasion, they decided to take a real family vacation. Donald's brother looked after the farm while the family spent ten days touring the countryside.

She vividly remembered the morning they loaded up the car. The boys had their coloring books, puzzles, and action figures. She had everything packed into the trunk they would need for the long vacation. Donald borrowed a Lincoln Continental from a friend, as the pick-up would likely never make the journey.

They traveled up north into Michigan. She remembered standing along the lake shore, marveling at how something so long, wide, and deep could simply be called a lake. It seemed more like an ocean to her.

They stopped at the Mackinaw Bridge, which connects the main part of Michigan to the upper peninsula. It was something to behold. Certainly, the longest bridge she'd ever seen, or would ever see again. Afterward, they traveled west to Minneapolis. To her, it looked like Chicago, but Donald marveled at everything he saw.

They drove the Lincoln into the Black Hills of South Dakota. It was there, marveling at Mount Rushmore, that Donald first told Marylyn he was worried about the future of their little farm. At dinner, they talked about consequences and possible ways to keep it functioning. He let her know how much he appreciated everything she'd done to keep them going as long as they had, but it could be time to call it quits.

Thinking about it now, she realized Donald was pleading for help. Marylyn refused to listen, encouraging him to go on and that they'd find a way to all stay together, no matter what. She talked to him as though he was a simple child, overreacting to a scoop of ice cream that had fallen off its cone and onto the ground. He wanted to sell off part of the farm, maybe get some more working capital to help meet their bills and then reassess. He wanted her permission to prepare for what he saw coming and she did everything she could to talk him out of it.

Now, standing in the cellar, she questioned her decision that day. The farm was in trouble, but it was all they had. Perhaps he was right, but she knew it was what defined him as a person. If the farm fell apart, he would fall apart with it, and that worried her. Perhaps she just needed to try harder. He tried to tell her it wasn't an indictment against her, but against the changing reality of the farm culture in America.

To Marylyn, it was about keeping them together as a family and she hated change. She would do anything to keep her world from crashing down on her. This was the end of their lives. And in her mind, it was the end of her family. Giving up the farm meant giving up on them.

Maybe she should have listened to him. "No, that's not right, we needed to stay together." She said to no one, while wiping away a tear from her eye.

A man's voice called out from the shadows of the basement. "Why didn't you listen to me, Marylyn?"

"Because you loved the farm. You loved farming. I never wanted to see you give that up."

Donald's form materialized from the shadows. "But, honey, it drove me to my end. You left me no way out, no way to keep it all going. This farm didn't define us as a family. It was just a thing. All that really mattered was that we were together. We could have been together anywhere. It was your own stubbornness that worked against us. I could've saved us all, but you wouldn't let me and it drove me insane."

"He's right, Mom," another voice said.

She turned to face her son who stepped forward into the light of a naked light bulb hanging from a time worn wire. Marylyn peered into the innocent depths of Matthew's face. His eyes, just as they were in 1984, shined back at her. She never noticed how much he resembled Donald. "Matthew, my dear sweet Matthew."

"We didn't have to die, Mom." Robbie's voice called out from the shadows. Moving forward, a young man, six inches shorter than Matthew joined them. We could have given up the farm and done something else. You were still young enough, and my brother and I could have helped."

"No!" Marylyn screamed as she turned toward the work bench. She threw the metal file across the room and it buried itself deep into the pegboard against the wall. For a full thirty seconds she leaned silently, palms down on the workbench, trying to regain her composure.

She began to sob. "I'm sorry children. There's no excuse for my outburst." Turning back to her deceased family, she said, "It ain't right to ask your father to give up the farm, children. You know that. This farm has been in his family for many generations. You remember that story, don't you, boys?"

As Matthew stepped back into the shadows, Robbie walked forward, stopping just under the overhead lights. "Dad always told us how his great-grandpa rode across in a horse-drawn wagon to this area. He bought it for a dollar."

"That's right, kids. And I had no right to ask your daddy to move from here."

Donald spoke, stepping toward her. "But now we're trapped. It's not just you. All of us are prisoners here. We live out the same day, a day I regret, for eternity."

293

"I'm sorry," Marylyn sobbed. "Deeply and truly sorry for the major sin I've committed. I just didn't want things to change. We love this house. This is where we were supposed to die, Donald."

Robbie and Matthew spoke in unison. "And we did that."

"But I'm still here!" she screamed. Turning away, she grabbed the ax handle on the table. She let out a sigh.

"So, what are you going to do, my love?" Donald said, putting his hand on her shoulder.

She turned her attention back to the ax. "You know what I have to do, Donald." Marylyn ran her hand over the handle of the ax. "You and the boys can go now. I need to get out of this, and there's only one way to do that."

Donald motioned to the boys, still waiting in the shadows of the cellar. "C'mon boys, your mother said we should go on. I think it's best."

Marylyn didn't want to take her eyes off the ax. The sharpened tip of the blade glinted in sharp contrast to the weathered look of the rusty ax head. It wasn't perfect but it would have to do. She sensed her future was growing impatient with her. She was ready for release, and it seemed that release was ready for her.

"Marylyn, look at me," Donald said.

She forced herself to face her husband. "Yes, Donald?"

"For what it's worth, I forgive you. All I ask is that you forgive me for what I've done. If I could, I'd take it all back. You have to believe that's true."

She reached up to hold the sides of his face. One last tender kiss from the man who ended her life. But her hands vanished into his visage as he began to fade.

"You can't hold me, Marylyn. I need to go now. Boys, tell your mother you love her. We'll be leaving, and we're not coming back. This is the end."

"Goodbye, Momma," they both said. "We love you."

Tears streamed down her face. She regretted telling them they could go. "Oh sweet boys, I love you too. I'll see you soon and we'll all be together again."

Donald turned to leave. Heading into one of the dark corners of the cellar, he said, "I love you, Marylyn. Hurry home."

"I love you too, Donald. I'll hurry, I promise." She held out her hand toward her long dead husband as his shape folded silently into the shadows of the cellar. For the moment Marylyn stood cherishing the short time she had with her boys. It had been a long time since she'd seen them as they were the day they died, without the event being distorted by time and her unclear recollections.

Taking a deep breath, she scanned the cellar. With its gravel floor and musty smell, it still looked mostly as she remembered it. Turning again to the ax, she released the clamps holding it in place. It was as sharp as it was ever going to be.

Marylyn's attention was suddenly focused on something outside. A sound she knew too well from her own memory. It was the sound of truck tires making their way across the driveway. An oddly soothing sound, she thought.

Touching the ax handle, she ran her hands over its rough exterior.

In a proper world, she would have time to shave the burs off and smooth the handle down, rubbing it with the linseed oil. She sighed at the aluminum container. The time for preparation had ended.

Jack was home from his errands.

A Final Homecoming

Jack pulled into the driveway. Next to him, on the seat, were a bunch of files his grad students had handed to him, along with one of the university laptops. Working from home would be a huge plus. There were still a ton of textbook revisions, and he needed to get his class files set up for the semester. He was going to run out of time quicker than he'd wanted and if they were going to undertake another move, that would mean some long afternoons and evenings.

The house looked different somehow, something he couldn't put his finger on. As if someone had snuck up to it earlier in the day and whispered in its ear that they were planning on leaving. He wondered, not for the first time, if something of wood, brick, and glass had a soul.

Perhaps it would be better to say it looked angry. Not necessarily at him, but just angry in general. He imagined how he might feel if everyone in his life left right after meeting him. He would feel betrayed. Maybe that's how the house felt, less angry and more betrayed. The realization left Jack with a twinge of guilt.

How odd, to feel sad for an inanimate object.

It wasn't the house's fault it was the site of some unfortunate incidents, any more than it was the house's fault that people were never comfortable living in it again. In stark contrast, he loved living there. It had character.

Now that was coming to an end. "I'm sorry," he said out loud as he climbed out of the truck.

* * * *

From inside the house, Marylyn watched Jack. Trying to stay out of the windows as much as possible, she thought over her plan. She needed a place to hide. A place to strike; not trying to kill Jack, merely wound him enough to tap into the primal rage she knew every man had inside the dark places of their souls.

She briefly thought about hiding in the bedroom closet, but that would make it too hard to take a swing at him. Maybe the kitchen offered the perfect place. Then when he entered, she would attack. But the kitchen made it impossible to track his movements and the timing would be key.

She had to be careful. Starting a fight like this treaded a thin line. It was important that she only take a swipe at him, a non-lethal shot to his shoulder. Marylyn needed him to strike back, and hard. The top of the stairs would offer the best opportunity. She could hide in the bathroom which afforded a commanding view of the stairs.

Tense with anticipation, sweat trickled down her back. Her heart … or rather Elizabeth's heart, raced.

* * * *

Elizabeth, felt sweat dripping down her back as she pulled and tugged at the metal bars. They refused to budge. The pillow Marylyn put under her head was soaked with tears.

How could Marylyn do this? For that matter, how could anyone do something like this?

It would seem logical that years of being forced to witness the destruction of her own family should have made her far less likely to commit murder. Even if it meant her own freedom.

298

Her mind raced back to the farm, not the version she saw today, but *her* version. Something about the entire scene was wrong.

What Marylyn showed her was flawed. It was far different than the reality Elizabeth knew existed. The difference was the key. She felt like she was on the verge of discovering an important detail. It all had to do with the house.

Matthew, if she remembered his name correctly, was killed in the garage. But in the vision Marylyn showed her, he was lying in a casket. It was likely he was not inside a casket when he was killed.

And Robbie, from what the newspaper said, was almost decapitated. But in the vision Marylyn showed her, he was completely beheaded. That didn't fit the published narrative.

No, it's not right.

What she showed Elizabeth simply didn't fit. The couch, the sky, even the corn fit a narrative but not reality. Maybe time, anger, and repeatedly being forced to relive that horrible day did something to the house? The floors and chairs felt like the ones she remembered in her doll house she had as kid. The orange of the sky looked familiar somehow. It looked very much like the sky in a painting her mother had hanging in her bedroom as a child. It used to give her terrible nightmares she had to shake herself out of.

"That's it," she yelled to no one. "I'm trapped in my own dream."

That little bit of knowledge lifted her spirits, and immediately the cell felt larger and she moved with more ease. She understood now; the only thing holding her prisoner was her own mind. Marylyn convinced Elizabeth she was trapped inside her world. Marylyn still controlled the dream and now her body, but she could fight to get back control of both. There could still be time to save Jack.

Elizabeth pushed on the bars and they stressed under the pressure. She willed them to be gone, to obey her commands. At that precise moment, the bar in her hand burst free of the cage and vanished.

* * * *

A cool breeze swept across the threshold as Jack stepped into the house which stood in sharp contrast to the devastating heat of the Illinois summer. He let the screen door close behind him with a dull wooden thud. "Elizabeth, honey? I'm home. Are you ready?"

The house was eerily quiet; the kind of quiet immediately preceding a surprise party. He half-expected a bunch of people to jump out from behind doors and yell "Surprise!"

After putting his books down on the chair, he walked toward the kitchen. Not a dish out of place, not a soiled cup on the counter, which was odd. If Elizabeth had eaten lunch today, there would've been dishes in the sink. "Elizabeth, sweetie, are you here?"

"Yes, Jack, up here," her voice called from upstairs. He felt a sudden sense of relief.

He moved into the living room. "Are you about ready to go? I have a hotel room for us. Maybe some poolside time and a couple of daiquiris would make you feel better."

"Just a minute, Jack. Can you please come up here?"

His brow furrowed in puzzlement. Something was wrong. From how she acted the night before, he figured she'd be ready to leave the second he got home. But her voice sounded hesitant.

Ascending the stairs, he thought he could hear her in the bedroom, rooting around for something. Maybe she wanted him to help her with their bags. Either way, he was eager to get underway. A little room service and poolside relaxation would do them both good.

As his trailing foot came to rest on the top stair, his arm suddenly screamed out in pain. Losing his balance, he fell backwards and tumbled down the stairs. He felt his skull hit the wall, and the world around him went fuzzy, then gray, and then he completely blacked out.

* * * *

Marylyn felt a satisfying connection as the ax caught some fleshy part of Jack. It put a nice gash in his upper arm. Blood sprayed everywhere, turning the off-white walls to a sickening liquid crimson pattern. A sweeping, wave-like pattern of blood painted a mural along the wall as he tumbled down the stairs.

She let out a prolonged sigh. Jack wasn't supposed to fall down the stairs. He was supposed to get mad and snatch the ax from her. Then it would be a sweet release for Marylyn. This, too, had gone terribly wrong.

Stupid Jack. Can't even get his wife's murder right.

The ax glanced off of his shoulder, probably doing less damage than she thought. Jack lay at the bottom of the stairs, apparently unconscious. The ax unceremoniously dug itself into the plaster wall. She would need to wrest it free if she was going to make this work.

Pulling on the handle, little bits of plaster fell onto the floor and clung to the blood painting the walls. Deeper than Marylyn thought, entangled as it was in a web of wires she gingerly reached in and pulled the wires free by their insulation, being careful not to electrocute herself. She worked the ax free and turned back to Jack, expecting to see him lying in a pool of blood, hopefully still alive.

Jack was gone. "Great."

Something bothered her though; her strike should've sliced through part of his shoulder. She'd obviously missed the mark and lost control of the ax completely. The strike should have been controlled; just enough to cause damage, but not enough to kill him. There was only one explanation. That twit of a girl, Elizabeth, figured out the genius of her prison.

I have to find Jack and speed this up.

Dusting off the plaster from the handle of the ax, Marylyn crept down the stairs. She didn't want to be surprised by Jack. If he were smart, he'd wait somewhere and subdue her. If he calmed down before carrying through with the retaliatory murder, the plan would fail. Nothing short of her own murder would do. "Oh Jack, where are you? I have something for you."

Through the house, starting at the bottom of the stairs, she followed a thin line of blood marking Jack's path. Occasional hand prints marked where he had touched the banister to help himself up and the dining room table where he put a hand down to steady himself.

The crash of the back door slamming shut startled her. Rushing to the kitchen window, she scanned the back yard for any movement.

The grass, in desperate need of mowing, was matted down in a narrow trail, disappearing into the corn stalks. There was no question in which direction Jack had fled. He was using the corn to hide.

Opening the door and cautiously stepping out onto the back porch, Marylyn yelled out, "Oh, Jack darling. Come here, sweetie!"

"Elizabeth, have you lost your mind?" Jack yelled back from the depths of the field.

A part of Marylyn wanted to keep up the charade that she was still Elizabeth, but it didn't seem sporting. If she could convince Jack she'd killed Elizabeth and taken over her body, then he'd be more likely to kill for revenge. "Oh Jack, you silly, stupid man. You can't even see what is happening in front of your own eyes, can you? Elizabeth is dead, honey. And now I'm going to kill you. The question is, are you really going to let me do that?"

Marylyn made her way into the corn, cautiously following Jack's path. She spotted occasional blood on the corn stalks where Jack entered the field. Another one, further in, had even more blood on it. Jack was bleeding, but so far she hadn't seen enough blood to think he was in danger of bleeding to death.

If Jack moved fast enough, he might get behind her. In the seemingly endless rows of corn becoming disoriented was a distinct possibility. Since he hadn't struck out in immediate rage, it was possible he might try to simply disarm her. If that were the case, Elizabeth would find herself in a mental hospital, and Marylyn would be no better off than she was before.

"Jack, sweetie, don't make me come in there to get you. Since your dear, sweet, Elizabeth is dead. Why don't you come out to get me? Wouldn't that be easier."

"I don't believe you," he said.

She let out a cruel laugh which definitely didn't belong to Elizabeth. "Oh sweetie, come on now. I took care of that little whore yesterday morning and now it is only me left in this hot little body of hers. By the way, thank you so much for the shower this morning. It's been a long time since any man has touched me that way. You're not as good as Donald, but it has been thirty years so I'm not going to be picky."

Without warning, Marylyn was hit by a wave of weakness. As she struggled to regain her composure, she felt the ax drop from her hand as it flexed uncontrollably. She moved her foot out of the way before the ax smashed the bones in her toes. Or was it actually Elizabeth that moved the foot? It was hard to tell.

She had a nagging feeling that it was the latter.

* * * *

Elizabeth pried another bar of her prison cell loose. The more she worked at it, the easier it became. With each moment she more fully embraced the idea of being trapped inside her own dream, the more empowered she felt. This gave her inner strength she didn't even know lurked inside.

Pulling and bending the bars, Elizabeth experimented with the idea of controlling things outside of her cell. With a thought, a light source appeared from nowhere. She controlled its brightness with another thought. Not entirely sure how she did it, the fact remained that she had established some control.

Beyond the darkness, voices rang out. Like voices one hears when they are under the water in a swimming pool, she could tell people were talking, but not really what they were saying. Marylyn, using Elizabeth's own voice, yelled to Jack, followed by Jack yelling something back. While the words were unclear, it sounded like he was demanding to talk with Elizabeth. He understood he was dealing with Marylyn and not her. Hearing Jack speak caused a moment of panic as she realized Marylyn had caught up with him. The bars stopped moving in protest.

She closed her eyes, calming herself, and after a few deep breaths Elizabeth swore she felt her own hands in the real world again. She flexed them to see if they would respond and was rewarded with the sense of her own hands responding in the real world. It also felt like her leg moved as well, but it was more of a reflex action than a conscious decision.

A thought, telegraphed to Elizabeth, drilled through the consciousness they shared. *You little whore, back in your cage! You've lost, don't you see that? Jack's better off without you anyway!*

Elizabeth felt Marylyn shove her out of her own body, but this time it was different. She seemed weaker, much weaker, than before. Elizabeth shoved back, managing to retain the foot hold she'd made back into her own body. The strength Marylyn had to maintain control of Elizabeth's body was waning.

* * * *

How could his wife be dead? Hot tears stung his eyes. This woman, whoever she was, certainly looked like Elizabeth. She'd thanked him for that morning, indicating it was the very same woman he was sure was his wife. What did she mean it had been thirty years? He remembered reading stories about houses possessing people, but had always assumed such stories were pure fiction.

Could it be possible?

"Marylyn?"

"Oh sweetie, you aren't as dumb as you look. Congratulations. If we were at the county fair, I'd have to give you a big ol' blue ribbon. Yes, darling, it's Marylyn."

It all fit. Elizabeth's strange behavior, the headaches she'd been having recently, her sudden insistence that they move. It all fit in an odd sort of way. The only question remaining was, how any of this could be possible?

He remembered Mr. Gulliver's odd warning to Jack upon learning they were moving into the house. The old man seemed convinced some evil dwelt there; worried enough to advise caution. It could be the blood loss, and Jack was certainly no expert in the paranormal, but he wondered if it was truly possible.

However, he had seen enough movies to know that if Marylyn possessed Elizabeth, then it was possible that Elizabeth was still inside there. And if he knew his wife, she would be scraping and clawing her way back with every ounce of energy she had left to give.

This meant Elizabeth needed him to buy her time to do what she could to loosen Marylyn's grip. The bleeding continued and time was in short supply. Maybe, if he could circle around in the corn, he could get back into the house, and call for help.

Patting his pockets, the sudden realization sunk in that his cell phone was still in the truck. And, the truck keys were on the dining room table. Jack would have to move as stealthily as possible to get those keys.

But what about Marylyn? He had to think of a way to control Elizabeth while Marylyn was still in control of the body. That meant he either had to tie her down or drive her away from the house. Anything to get her away from this house might help.

Either way, he needed to do something quick, before the bleeding caused him to lose consciousness.

He ran a little farther until he was in line with the far side of the house. Taking a few hurried steps forward, a branch, laying in the dirt, seemed to reach up and grab his ankle, sending him crashing to the ground. The slip sent him crashing through corn stalks as he fell. The racket could probably be heard all the way to Iowa.

Crap.

"Oh Jack, there you are!" Marylyn called out from somewhere behind him.

No longer laboring under the illusion he could keep his location a secret, Jack scrambled to his feet and ran toward the house as fast as his legs could carry him.

* * * *

Marylyn moved cautiously through the corn, slightly paranoid that something was about to go wrong. Success was so close, she could feel it. Almost taste it. The thought of her plan slipping through her fingers was terrifying.

What she also felt was Elizabeth's impending escape from her prison. There was no denying it, Marylyn's brief day off from her own hellish nightmare was just that, brief.

Moving toward the noise Jack made, a clearing was formed where he'd pushed a bunch of stalks to the ground. Listening for a moment, only the sound of the wind blowing across the prairie punctuated the calm of the cornfields.

Jack fell. It wasn't clear if it was due to his own clumsiness or loss of blood. One of the stalks had fallen over another one, causing the top one-third to stick up at an odd angle. On top of the plant, the first few tassels of the season, soft and brown had connected to Jack's shoulder during his fall and the tassels remained coated in blood, like the tip of a painters brush. Jack's blood shined in the sunlight. Marylyn could smell its heavy metallic scent. Reaching down, she squeezed the tassel in her fingers, causing the blood to squeeze out onto her fingertips. The smell was intoxicating.

Licking the blood, she tasted its copper-like flavors. It only accentuated the smell of the blood in her nostrils. There was something slightly erotic about it all.

A few more blood-swiped corn stalks gave her a bearing to follow. Coming to where the cornfield ended and the back yard began. Marylyn's, or rather Elizabeth's, body froze in protest.

Elizabeth pushed her way through Marylyn's control and used their shared mouth. "I'm not going to let you do this. Leave my husband the hell alone, you psychotic bitch!"

Marylyn growled in frustration. "Temper, temper, Lizzy. This play is already in its final act. Blasphemous words will get you nowhere. Beside, I've already cut him pretty bad. Even if you get rid of me, he's still going to die. Why not let me make him kill you, and then we all get what we want. All of us, together in the afterlife. The four of us, You, Jack, me and Donald can have lunch together. We'll all have a big laugh. You can meet my boys. How about it?"

"Fuck you! Stop this now. Think it through; can you even hear yourself? You've lost your fucking mind. Stop now and I promise I'll do everything to release you from this house."

"Elizabeth," Marylyn said. "You're sweet, but naive. People love to say they'll try to help. They love to make themselves feel better by saying they're on your side. But they never are. If you want something done, you have to do it yourself. Why would I trade a sure thing for your empty promise?"

Marylyn wrested back control of the body, continuing her quest to find Jack. It took so much effort that she wasn't sure she'd be able to do it a second time. The next time Elizabeth regained control, it would be the last. The time to end this game was now.

* * * *

Jack rounded the corner of the house, stopping briefly to catch his breath. The blood, now drying on his hands, made them sticky and brown. The coating made them appear brown in the sunshine.

The cut on his arm, thankfully, wasn't as bad as he'd thought. It would need a few stitches, but for now his shirt, soaked with blood, temporarily squelched the bulk of the bleeding. It was still ugly and seeping, but he'd survive.

Jack's immediate concern was orchestrating a showdown with Elizabeth, or Marylyn, to be more precise. She still had the ax which meant she had a weapon. Even if he had a weapon, using it against Marylyn also meant using it against Elizabeth so he would have to either disarm her or knock her out.

Trying to open the screen door as quietly as possible, it let out an indicting squeak. While not overly loud, it was certainly something that could be heard in the back yard. Closing the door behind him with far less noise, he saw his keys silhouetted on the tile surface of their dining room table.

Just as he retrieved the keys, he heard another tell-tale squeak as the door opened behind him.

He turned in time to see Marylyn run at him with ax held high. He rolled out of the way, falling to the floor and toward the door to the kitchen. The head of the ax connected with a section of their wood table and sent splinters flying everywhere.

"Dammit Jack, can't you stand still?"

He crawled backwards to get away from Marylyn's next swing. "Why are you doing this?"

She smiled at him. "Isn't it clear by now? I want you dead."

Jack wasn't sure why he didn't notice it before, but he realized that her voice, while it was Elizabeth's, was not really hers at all. It sounded different. The tone, timbre, even word choices were not those of his wife. This was definitely not Elizabeth.

"Why do you want me dead?"

"Because, you should know—" Marylyn abruptly stopped talking.

The voice changed. "Jack, don't believe her, she wants you to kill me." This time the voice was clearly Elizabeth's. Marylyn lied,

Elizabeth was still alive.

"Elizabeth, fight her! You have to hang on!" Jack yelled.

Marylyn growled, "Shut up, you little bitch."

"Let me talk to Elizabeth. I need to talk to her!"

"I'm sorry you had to hear that little outburst," Marylyn said. "It doesn't matter. Who knows, maybe you two can share this cozy home of mine. I don't want it anymore. Let's just set the sale price at … say … two souls? Mine and Elizabeth's. One freed, and one encumbered."

Marylyn started toward Jack, she had the ax slung over her shoulder. Jack jumped to his feet and ran through the kitchen. Losing his footing on the stairs, he rolled down the stairwell into the basement. The rocks ground into his wounded shoulder and the side of his head as he slid to a stop.

Getting up from the cellar floor, he ran to the stairs and gave the exterior doors a shove. They refused to move. He pushed them even harder. Even in his injured state he should have had enough strength to open them with little resistance.

Marylyn laughed at him from the top of the stairs. "Oh, Jack, did I forget to mention? I locked that drafty old cellar door. Always bothered me, leaving it open like that. That's right, honey. You're trapped. The only escape is through me. To get through me, you have to kill her."

Marylyn's footfalls down the stairs stung his ears as she closed the distance.

"You have no idea what it was like, Jack," she said in a singsong voice. "Stuck here in this house for the last thirty years. I showed Elizabeth what I went through every single day. That's what hell looks

311

like, Jack."

Elizabeth broke through again, her voice desperate. "Jack, I can't control her yet. You have to find a way out."

Marylyn raised the ax toward Jack. "Take this ax from me now and kill me, or you die. Defend yourself, Jack, or by God, I'll strike you down where you stand and then make your little Elizabeth eat the end of a revolver. I know where the handgun is and I'll end us all right now. And then I won't be alone in this house anymore. Just think of it, the three of us for eternity. Maybe we can all relive this day over and over again. What a lovely change of pace."

She swung the ax at Jack, but as she did, her arms fell downward and the ax head was forced to the right, missing Jack completely. She let out a shrieking howl and prepared to take another swing. The next swing was even clumsier, and the ax flew from her hands, sending it crashing into the table and smashing open the can of linseed oil.

Jack and Marylyn both stood in silence for a moment. The oil gushed from the gash in the can, forming a pool of oil on the table and then it began to move like a snake looking for somewhere to hide. A line of oil dripped from the table top, onto a wooden leg where an electrical socket had been shoddily installed to provide a plug for power tools. A few sparks shot out as the oil suddenly burst into flames, quickly igniting the rest of the oil soaked wood and the can.

Marylyn screamed, "This is your fault. You ruined this for me!" She grabbed a piece of lumber from the base of the stairs and swung hard at Jack's head, but missed him completely. As she fell over, Jack tried to grab her. He missed and she spun away from him and hit block pillar in the center of the cellar. Her body fell limp on the floor as the flames began consuming the rafters above them.

Blessed be the Ties that Bind

Jack carried Elizabeth to the top of the stairs just as the basement became completely engulfed in flames. The old wood of the house made ready tinder for the fire. Elizabeth was light as a feather to him normally, but between his injury and sheer exhaustion, carrying her was excruciating. The smoke had already begun to fill the lower level of the house as he crossed the living room. He tripped on the steps and fell through the screen door and onto the porch, sending them both tumbling. The blood loss made it increasingly hard to keep moving, and his vision was becoming blurrier by the minute.

They were out of the house, but they weren't out of danger. He looked up to see the eaves erupt into flames. He remembered reading somewhere that fire spread quickly in old houses like this. He knew they were too close to the structure to be safe. They would both die in the blaze when the walls collapsed if he couldn't muster the strength to save them.

He tried to get up again, but his legs buckled under him. He reached out for Elizabeth's hand. Maybe he could wake her, but she seemed to be in a deep sleep. And then everything went black.

A hand gripped his shoulders...

He had a feeling of weightlessness, like someone carried him. Trying to speak, he wanted to tell whomever it was to save Elizabeth, but the words wouldn't come no matter how hard he tried. The world around him chilled as undefined sounds around him rang out. Jack felt something soft under his head. Sight, which had left him, started to fight its way back. Blurry at first, the edges of his vision filled with brilliant light.

"There now, I think we're coming back around." There was an unidentifiable voice sitting next to him, a voice Jack didn't recognize. It belonged to an older man sitting on the seat next to him, his hand on Jack's shoulder. "Relax, Jack, you gave us quite a scare. You and that wife of yours."

Jack looked toward his arm, which bore a thick bandage. His clothes were torn and bloody.

White fluorescent lights filled the space. If it were not for the plethora of medical equipment lining the walls, he'd guess this might be heaven. An IV bag hung above him, attached to his arm. An oxygen mask covered his face. An ambulance, Jack realized.

He pulled off the mask and threw it aside. Jack tried to speak, but his mouth felt like someone had shoved an entire bag of sawdust into it. Panic over what happened to Elizabeth set in.

The man, seeing his sudden agitation said, "Just relax. The medics said I could keep an eye on you for a bit while they tend to Elizabeth. Quite an ordeal you went through today. Not sure why, but I knew there'd be trouble at the old Anderson farm today."

Out of the window of the ambulance, Jack looked at the house, completely engulfed in flames. The man must have seen the look of shock on his face. "Fire Chief says there's nothing they can do about it. When they got here, it was already too late. The best thing they can do now is let it burn to the ground. Since it's the only house out here, nothing else is in danger. Your truck is going to need a new paint job, though."

Jack tried to speak. After a considerable effort, he squeaked, "Elizabeth." He remembered his failed attempt to get her clear of the house before the fire took over. If the paramedics couldn't save her, there was no way he could go on. Life without her was simply not worth living.

"Relax, Elizabeth is fine. We got here just in time. Rita pulled Elizabeth away from the house, and I drew the short straw and had to carry you. She fared better than you did and they are checking her out now. I suppose we haven't been introduced, although I feel like I know you pretty well already. Name's Hal and I think you already met my wife, Rita. Certainly not the circumstances I wanted to meet under. I guess this is as good a time as any."

Jack settled back. They watched the flames take the house. Through the door, he could make out the large staircase on fire. The house almost looked like an old photo negative of itself. Everything dark was white and everything light had turned black.

His eyes shifted to their bedroom window. For a brief instant, he thought he saw a woman looking out at him. Her piercing eyes met Jack's gaze. He would forever insist it was Marylyn Anderson staring down at him. In that moment he thought she looked almost relieved, as if a terrible weight had been lifted from her shoulders.

Hal handed Jack a bottle of water. "What happened in there, Jack?"

The way he said it seemed more like a police officer questioning a suspect than a kindly neighbor.

What did happen in there? Did his wife truly attack him with an ax? He knew, in his heart, that couldn't possibly be true. She loved him and he loved her. Somehow, defying explanation, the lost soul of Marylyn commandeered his wife's body and tried to do the unthinkable. For reasons he couldn't fathom, they had been the targets in an otherworldly plot.

Jack took a long drink of the water. "An accident, it was an accident. Fire in the cellar, and I got hurt rescuing Elizabeth."

"I see. You know, I was once in the army. I had this sergeant, Staff Sergeant Cook was his name. Good guy. He told me there are times in life that things become so strange that they defy logic or explanation. At those times, it's permissible to tell a little white lie to make some sense of it all. I believe that's true." He shook his head. "An accident, huh?"

Jack breathed a deep sigh and sipped some more water from the bottle. "Yes ... an accident."

Just then, the doors to the back of the rig opened and Rita and a paramedic helped Elizabeth inside. For a moment, Jack and Elizabeth just looked into each other's eyes. Their wordless exchange communicated everything they needed to say. Elizabeth fell into Jack's arms, crying into his shoulder.

"Did you see her Jack? She was up in the window, only for a moment. Did you see her?"

"Yes, my love, I sure did."

Redemption and Release at the Anderson Farm

Elizabeth looked to her left. Through the metal handrails of the hospital bed, she could make out the form of Jack, already sleeping soundly. Initially, the hospital staff refused to put them both in the same room. Elizabeth had a severe panic attack at the idea of being separated from him.

She clearly recalled everything Marylyn did to them. The way she was able to convince Elizabeth that Jack had to die was frightening. And then there was her battle to regain control of her own body. It was all there, fresh in her mind.

The sound of his breathing was reassuring. To come that close to losing someone you love had proven an inestimable weight for her to carry. Every time she thought about it, she wanted to reach out and touch him. She needed to make sure he was still there, still real.

They were both treated for mild smoke inhalation from the fire, which burned quick and complete. Any evidence of what took place in that house burned up along with their belongings. Rita told Elizabeth that they knew something was wrong when they saw smoke coming from the direction of the house. They found Jack and Elizabeth passed out at the foot of the deck. They pulled them both out of harm's way minutes before the front porch joined the rest of the inferno. Had they not acted when they did, Jack and Elizabeth would have surely burned to death.

Elizabeth settled down into the blankets. Last night she spent coughing up the inhaled smoke and waking up at odd hours for another urine or blood test. Tonight she needed some sleep. Tomorrow stood with the promise of them being released.

She pressed the button to shut off the overhead light. The sudden darkness was a little unsettling, but there was still the glow of the hallway light filtering through the modesty drapes shielding Jack's bed from the open door. Jacks chest gently rose and fell with each breath.

Allowing her need for sleep to overtake her, she was whisked away into a world where she flew effortlessly through the air. Below her, she saw cornfield after cornfield. The stalks moved like waves on an endless green ocean. She felt like an airplane, or maybe a bird. She saw the occasional house and roadway. Soon she was flying over their little town. She came in low to see the library, the drugstore, and Gullivers Hardware.

She recognized their own home, the Anderson farm, in the distance. She swept down toward the corn, settling gently on the ground in front of the house. It looked completely whole and undamaged, no more singed than the day they first met Rita there.

While it didn't look different, it certainly felt that way. Less threatening than before.

"Beautiful isn't it?" A voice suddenly said.

Ice shot up Elizabeth's spine as she turned to see Marylyn standing slightly behind her and off to the side. "What do you want from me? Haven't you already done enough!"

Marylyn turned toward the house, lost in thought. "Relax, Elizabeth, I just want to talk." She sighed, wistfully. "It's beautiful. The house, that is. There's something special about a house like this, you know. A place where you raise your children, where you work with your husband to build a life. Then something happens, something awful, to take it all away."

Elizabeth pleaded with her. "Marylyn, you know that I had to do what I did. I couldn't let you kill him."

She smiled at Elizabeth. Not the sadistic smile she'd seen before, but a genuine one. Elizabeth thought there was something different about her, a peacefulness in her eyes. "Jack's a good man, Elizabeth. I only had the chance to know him for a little while, but now I see where I was wrong. I only ask that you don't judge us too harshly. My Donald is a good man too. We just let things get away from us. He lost his mind, and I suppose I did too. The blame lays squarely on my shoulders."

Out of the field, next to them, Jack came stumbling out of the corn. "Elizabeth, get away from her!"

Jack grabbed Elizabeth by the hand and pulled her away from Marylyn. "What the hell do you want?" He spit the words out of his mouth.

"Relax Jack, I only want a moment of your time, that's all. I need to tell you both something, that's why I brought you here."

"I'm pretty sure you don't have anything to say to us," Elizabeth said, clinging to Jack.

"I understand why you wouldn't want to talk to me. Then let's just say that I have something I need to say for my own benefit. Jack and Elizabeth, I'm sorry about all of this. There is nothing I can do to fix what I've done. But you gave me something I was never going to achieve on my own." Marylyn's eyes filled with tears. Elizabeth couldn't help but feel these tears were genuine.

The front door of the house opened. Three men came out onto the porch that Elizabeth recognized as Donald, Matthew, and Robbie. Her eyes flew wide as the three of them joined Marylyn. "You did it, Elizabeth; you gave me release. You said you would do anything to help me, and I didn't believe you. Had my plan worked, I'm not sure what would have happened. I just hope someday you can forgive me. Maybe, someday, we'll meet again."

Jack and Elizabeth watched the four vanish from in front of them as a fog blanketed the dreamscape that was the Anderson farm.

For the rest of the night, Elizabeth slept a dreamless sleep.

THE END

ACKNOWLEDGMENTS

I say it often, but I can't possibly say it enough, thank you dear reader for choosing to read *Crimson Tassels*.

Of course, *Crimson Tassels* couldn't even exist without my wife who supports my obsession of writing; although, I know my wife would love nothing more than to have me stay off the computer for at least a few of the nights. Her love and understanding is a huge part of everything I do. I also have to thank my children for putting up with all of this!

There's a funny thing about this book. It took years to finish. Why? You might ask. Well, I originally wrote it with the idea of a house being possessed by a farmer who died in the house and cursed anyone who moved in. The farm grew canola and not corn. I had to do some major restructuring.

Some of you will notice that this story is actually placed in a non-specific location somewhere south west of Joliet Illinois. This is a nod to my upbringing in northern Illinois and my time in Indiana.

I want to dedicate this book to anyone who has ever loved a dog so much their heart ached when they thought of how they had to say goodbye. This book is for Hannah the Wonder-Lab who had

to leave this world when the first edit of this novel was being undertaken. Dogs teach us how to be better humans.

Check out my other books!

The Dramatic Dead (Bentley Mystery Series Book 1)

The Reverent Dead (Bentley Mystery Series Book 2)

Riapoke

Code Name: Formula-12

The Diamond Studded Legs Matter

The Fallen Oath Matter

The Bagorian Chronicles

Usurper's Throne (Bagorian Chronicles Book 2)

www.bryannowak.com

e-mail: bryanthewriter@bryannowak.com

https://www.facebook.com/Bryanthewriter

Twitter: @Bryan_TheWriter

Bryan the Writer